DOG GONE

A MIAMI JONES PRIVATE INVESTIGATOR MYSTERY
BOOK 19

A.J. STEWART

For Simon.
And Heather.

Jacaranda Drive Publishing

Los Angeles, California

www.jacarandadrive.com

Cover artwork by Streetlight Graphics

ISBN-13: 978-1-945741-81-4

CHAPTER ONE

AUTUMN WAS THAT ONE TIME IN FLORIDA WHEN THE STATE STRUGGLED to find its identity. Not like New England, when the leaves turned spectacular, and everyone suddenly realized why they put up with shoveling snow that turned black on the roadside and summers in saltboxes that weren't built for central air. For Floridians, fall was a crap shoot. Summer might hold on and deliver ninety degrees and humidity off the charts, or it might plummet into an early winter that the snowbirds thought was glorious, but those of us who endured the place full-time found reason to pull out the long pants.

Right now it was the former, and the locals were turning into savages, the way we did when the humidity lingered too long. Things weren't made better by the fact I was in a gym that had no air conditioning whatsoever.

I hadn't spent much time in gyms after I retired from the minor leagues, but the scent of sweat and leather was again becoming part of my DNA. It enveloped me as I leaned against the heavy bag, catching my breath. Stone's Gym buzzed with activity, a mix of seasoned boxers and young kids training side by side. The rhythmic thud of gloves hitting bags and the sharp snap of jump ropes slapping the floor filled the air.

I wiped my forehead with the back of my hand, surveying the

scene. My gaze landed on the faded lettering above the ring, now reading *Stone's Gym* once again. How I'd ended up a part-owner in a smelly, sweaty, boxing gym was a story that I seemed to relive whenever I came to work out here.

I blamed Mick. I was fairly sure the grunts I got in return suggested he blamed me, but we were both okay with that. The fact was, we now had a place to work out that didn't have mirrors on every wall, and so did the folks who without Stone's, would have had nowhere else to go.

The clientele was a little rougher than the average thirty-minute workout place, but their faces were etched with determination, the sweat glistening on their brows a trophy of its own. I watched a lanky kid, maybe fifteen, working the speed bag. His hands moved with a natural rhythm, the bag singing under his touch.

"Keep that elbow in, Jake!" Harv, the head trainer, called out as he passed by. The kid adjusted his form without missing a beat.

Harv's attention shifted to the ring, where a pair of boxers danced around each other. "Watch your footwork, Tommy boy. Remember, it's ballet."

The older of the two fighters, a guy I recognized from the amateur circuit when I had been helping Mick's friend, nodded at his younger opponent. "You're telegraphing your jabs. Try to keep your shoulders relaxed until the last second."

I was waiting for a bench to open up but was happy for the break as I stood in front of the big fan moving warm moist air around the space. The place was old and rundown when we had taken it over, and we really hadn't changed much—Danielle had insisted we refresh the ladies' bathroom—but one of the few changes was the photo I had hung just outside the office, and I glanced at it and smiled. It was a shot of three men—me, Lucas, and Lenny. I figured Lenny needed to see this place, what we were doing here, even if he couldn't walk in through the front door.

That door was also new. The old glass door had kind of been destroyed, but the replacement creaked in the exact same way, and it was that which caught my attention. I turned to see a familiar silver mane entering the gym. Ron's cheeks were flushed, but that was nothing new; years of Florida sun and who knew how many cocktails had left their mark.

He spotted me and made his way over, slightly out of breath, eyes darting around. I knew the look. Ron had something on his mind, and that usually ended in work for me. Some days that was a good thing—a man had to eat—but other days, not so much.

"MJ," he said, leaning in close. "Got a minute?"

I raised an eyebrow. "You wanna spar in the ring?"

"Maybe in the next lifetime. I might have a job."

"You leaving us? Lizzy will be heartbroken."

"I'm talking about a case." Ron glanced around the room before continuing. "A dog's gone missing from a Palm Beach estate."

I worked hard to keep a straight face. I failed. "You interrupted my workout for a lost Pomeranian?"

He held up a hand, his expression serious. "First of all, you were standing in the middle of the room watching other people work out, and second, this isn't just any client. We're talking serious Palm Beach society here."

"What's the other sort of Palm Beach society?"

Ron investigated those boring insurance cases that paid well but made my eyes glaze over, and I was about to put the missing dog in the same bucket, but his earnest look gave me pause. We moved towards a quieter corner of the gym, passing a young girl practicing her footwork.

Ron leaned against a wall plastered with old fight posters. "Look, I know it sounds trivial, but you know how things work in Palm Beach. It's all about connections, favors owed and returned. You help find Muffy or Buffy or whatever the hell this dog's name is, and doors continue opening."

I listened, my furrowed brow furrowing further as I considered his words. Ron loved Florida more than anyone I'd ever known. The only place he enjoyed more than the Sunshine State as a whole was Palm Beach. The Venn diagram of his love for those two things might have looked like a single circle.

"You know what they're like. These people, they've got their fingers in everything. Real estate, local politics, charity boards—you name it. You do right by them, and suddenly we're getting calls for the interesting cases. The ones that'll really put us on the map."

I wasn't sure I wanted to be on the map. I had worked for Palm Beach elite before, and they were among my worst clients—they paid slow and complained a lot. My eyes drifted back to the young boxers, a reminder of the financial responsibilities we'd taken on with the gym. The monthly bills weren't going to pay themselves. Neither, it seemed, were the monthly dues.

Ron read my mind, a rather annoying habit. "Plus, think about the gym. These are the kind of folks who write big checks to youth programs without blinking an eye. We play our cards right, and we could set this place up for years to come."

I sighed, watching a guy wipe down a bench and offer it to me. "Alright, alright. I'll take a look. But if I end up chasing some yappy little fur ball through hedgerows, you will forever remain in my bad books."

Ron's face split into a wide grin, his ruddy cheeks somehow getting even redder. He clapped me on the shoulder. "Forever?"

CHAPTER TWO

WE PULLED UP TO THE KAZARIAN ESTATE IN MY SUV FEELING distinctly out of place among the gleaming luxury cars lining the circular driveway. We had dropped Ron's beat up old Corolla at the office, and I might drive a Cadillac, but it wasn't your grandfather's classic Caddy. It was a soccer mom car, through and through, which rendered it invisible in most situations and thus perfect for PI work. Just not in a driveway filled with Mercedes and Bentleys.

Ron climbed out, straightening his jacket and running a hand through his hair. I didn't bother. My hair lived a life of its own and made me look like a surf bum. I had taken a surfing lesson once, but I preferred to leave the sharks to their business if they left me to mine.

He eyed me up and down. He must have approved of my choice to wear long pants because he didn't mention my attire. "Try not to touch anything," he muttered. "Or break anything. Or say anything… You know what? Just let me do the talking."

I rolled my eyes. "Relax, Ron. I've been to fancy places before."

"The Outback Steakhouse doesn't count, MJ."

I didn't care for the suggestion that I considered anywhere but

Longboard Kelly's to be fine dining. If Mick got an inkling of that untruth, there would be hell to pay.

But before I could retort, the massive front doors swung open. A butler—an honest-to-goodness butler—emerged, a stoic-looking man with graying temples, his posture so straight I wondered if he'd swallowed a broomstick.

"Mr. Bennett and Mr. Jones, I presume?" His voice was as crisp as his pressed uniform, but his accent wasn't English. Perhaps those butlers cost more. "Please, follow me."

He didn't go back inside. We trailed after him, marching around the side of the house. I started to get a *service entrance* feeling in my guts. The grounds were immaculate, a sea of green punctuated by splashes of colorful flowers. The requisite number of queen palms. Fountains gurgled softly, their mist catching the morning sun.

As we rounded a corner, I nearly walked into a life-sized marble statue of a woman pouring water from a jug. "Geez," I muttered, sidestepping it. "Is there an audio tour available?"

Ron shot me a warning glance, but I caught the corner of his mouth twitching.

The butler led us past more sculptures, each probably worth more than my car, and I wondered if our new client was Medusa. We climbed a set of wide stone steps, passing between towering columns that made me feel like I was entering some ancient Greek temple.

"Mrs. Kazarian will receive you in the solarium," the butler informed us, pushing open a set of ornate glass doors.

The solarium was a sight to behold. Sunlight streamed through windows that were more floor-*and*-ceiling than floor-to-ceiling, illuminating a room that looked like it had been plucked straight from a magazine spread. Exotic plants in ornate pots dotted the space, their leaves reaching towards the sky. I wondered how it wasn't a thousand degrees inside.

My attention was drawn to the woman rising from a plush white sofa. Pixie Kazarian was a force of nature, even in her distress. Her platinum-blonde hair was coiffed to perfection, not a strand out of place. She wore a flowing sundress in a bold floral pattern. Oversized sunglasses perched on her nose, but they couldn't hide the worry lines creasing her forehead.

"Ron," she said, her voice carrying a hint of a tremor despite her composed demeanor. "Thank you for coming so quickly."

She gave Ron an air kiss on either side, and then he gestured to me. "This is Miami Jones."

She extended a hand adorned with enough diamonds to fund an America's Cup campaign, and I shook it gently, afraid I might break something.

"I've heard such good things," she said to me. "I know you can help me."

"Mrs. Kazarian," I said. "That's why we're here. Please, why don't you tell us what happened?"

Pixie gestured for us to sit, sinking back onto the sofa with a grace that belied her age. I perched awkwardly on the edge of an armchair that looked like it belonged in a museum, half-expecting an alarm to go off the moment I touched it.

"It's Layla," Pixie began, her voice catching. She took a deep breath, visibly pulling herself together. "My precious Layla. She's been taken right from under our noses."

"And Layla is your dog?" I asked.

"Oh, Mr. Jones, she's so much more than that. A companion. A confidante."

I figured a dog would make a good confidante. They rarely ended up in the witness box.

"What kind of dog is she?" I asked.

"She's an Afghan Hound. Pedigree, of course. One of the most magnificent dogs I've ever shown."

"Shown?"

"Oh, she's a show dog, Mr. Jones."

I had a vague memory of watching a movie about dog shows, and I recalled all the owners being lunatics. "And when was she taken, Mrs. Kazarian?"

"Call me Pixie, please. Consuela discovered her missing this morning."

"Consuela?"

"Yes, my home assistant."

I nodded, but I really wasn't sure if she was referencing a person or one of those speakers that told you your packages had arrived or if you hadn't gotten your quota of steps in yet. I didn't have one of either. Lizzy accepted my packages at the office, and at home Danielle told me if I needed to go for a run on City Beach. But I had heard people gave them names, so I tried to frame a question to ask if Consuela took human form when I saw a familiar face enter the solarium.

I smiled. "Detective Ronzoni."

"Jones," he said through lips that looked like he'd just eaten an anchovy. "What are you doing here?"

"Oh, Detective," said Pixie. "You know Mr. Jones?"

"Yes, ma'am."

Ronzoni was big on deference to the Palm Beach elite he served. The detective stood there in his perpetually wrinkled suit, looking about as out of place as a penguin in a chicken coop. "Mrs. Kazarian, I assure you that the police are more than capable of handling this. There's no need for you to hire a gumshoe."

I enjoyed being called a gumshoe. Not because I identified with it, but I knew it meant I was under Ronzoni's skin. The detective and I had worked together before, and we had developed an understanding. I could work on his turf as long as he got all the credit. It was mutually beneficial most of the time, but that didn't mean he wouldn't try to edge me out of a case now and then. Especially when my presence was a direct comment by the client on his ability to do his job.

Pixie Kazarian, however, wasn't having any of it. She waved a bejeweled hand dismissively at Ronzoni, her eyes never leaving mine. "Detective, I appreciate your efforts, but I intend to use every resource at my disposal to find Layla. Ron lives here on the island and he and Mr. Jones come highly recommended."

Ronzoni's face flushed, and I wondered if he needed a glass of water. It was a thing with him. He didn't have sweat glands or something, so he was prone to overheating, which was a real cross to bear in South Florida.

"Now," Pixie said, "let me show you where Layla was taken from. You might find something the police missed."

She stood, gesturing for us to follow. As we trailed after her through the mansion, I caught Ronzoni's eye. He shrugged, a silent admission that he couldn't stop me from being here. I gave him a small nod in return.

We headed out of the solarium and through a living space that appeared to have never actually been lived in. I listened intently as Pixie explained the situation. The façade of the composed socialite started to crack as she spoke about her beloved dog.

"Layla, my darling Layla." Pixie's voice quivered. "She's not just any show dog, you understand. She's Champion Layla of the Silk Road, the most exquisite Afghan Hound you'll ever lay eyes on."

I nodded. I had no idea what an Afghan Hound looked like. I was picturing something tall, with long hair, like a Great Dane with dreadlocks. Beside me, Ron offered his concerned face as if Pixie was talking about a lost child.

"She was here yesterday evening. She had her bath, and then she was brushed out until her coat shone like spun gold." Pixie's eyes misted over. "This morning, well…she was gone. Just…gone."

Her composure slipped further, a tear escaping down her cheek. She dabbed at it with a monogrammed handkerchief. "You don't understand," she continued, her voice barely above a whisper. "Layla isn't just a show dog. She's family. We've been through so much together."

I felt a twinge of sympathy. Rich as she was, Pixie's pain was genuine. I couldn't relate to the connection with an animal—I'd never had a pet as a kid, and certainly didn't have time for one now, but I understood losing a friend.

"Can you tell us about yesterday?" I asked. "Did you notice anything unusual? Any strangers hanging around?"

Pixie shook her head, her platinum-blonde hair barely moving. "Nothing out of the ordinary. We had our usual routine. Aram was working late in his study. I said goodnight to Layla, and she went home around nine, then I retired myself."

"She went home?"

"Oh yes." Pixie nodded, pushing open French doors to a yard that looked like a botanical garden. "Layla has her own little palace in the backyard. I'll show you."

I exchanged a glance with Ron. A dog with its own house—welcome to Palm Beach.

Pixie led us out through the French doors onto a sprawling patio. The backyard stretched out before us, a manicured paradise of lush green grass and meticulously trimmed hedges. But what caught my eye wasn't the resort-style pool or the tennis court in the distance. It was the structure that stood about fifty yards from the main house.

"This is Layla's home," Pixie announced, a hint of pride creeping back into her voice.

I blinked, not quite believing what I was seeing. Calling it a doghouse would be like calling the Taj Mahal a vacation cabin. This was a miniature mansion, complete with a wraparound porch and tiny Corinthian columns. The exterior was painted a soft cream that matched the main house perfectly.

As we approached, Pixie produced a small golden key from her pocket and unlocked the front door. She ushered us inside, and I had to duck to avoid hitting my head on the doorframe.

The interior left me speechless. Climate-controlled air hit my face as I stepped in, a welcome relief from the clammy heat in the garden. The floors were covered in plush carpeting, and as I was wondering if I should remove my shoes, I saw Ronzoni do just that. Custom-built furniture, scaled down to dog size, or maybe a hobbit. The ceilings were only a couple of inches over six feet high. I knew this because when I stood straight, I could feel the plaster ruffle my hair. There was even a tiny chandelier hanging from the ceiling, its crystals catching the light and sending rainbows dancing across the walls.

It would have been impressive as a separate home that could later be repurposed into an ADU or let out on a house-sharing website, but that was never going to happen.

Pixie moved through the space, touching various items with a trembling hand. "This is where Layla slept," she said, gesturing to a small four-poster bed with silk sheets. "And here's where she was groomed before shows."

She pointed to a state-of-the-art grooming station complete with a custom-built bathtub and what looked like professional-grade hair dryers.

As I surveyed the room, I heard Ronzoni say, "Hello."

I turned to see a small woman in a black button-up shirt and matching skirt standing in the doorway. Fortunately for her, she was not far north of five feet tall. For a moment I wondered if we were in her house, then I recalled the dog.

"And you are?" asked Detective Ronzoni.

The woman glanced at Pixie, who did the speaking for her. "This is Consuela, my home assistant."

That was a mystery solved.

"Consuela," said Ronzoni. "You found the dog missing?"

I wasn't sure if you could find something missing. It felt wrong somehow, but I had spent my college years on a baseball diamond, not wading through the reeds of English Lit.

"Yes," she said. Her voice was as small as she was, and she had an accent that suggested she originated thousands of miles to the south.

"Can you tell me what happened?" asked Ronzoni.

She shrugged her tiny shoulders and looked like a starling in a bird bath. "I came to give her breakfast, and to prepare her for her walk."

"And she was gone?"

"Yes."

"Do you lock this door?" he said, gesturing at the tiny hobbit door behind her.

"Yes. It was locked."

"Is there another way out?" I asked Pixie. "An open window, maybe?"

"No," said Pixie. "The windows remain locked until winter. The house is climate controlled."

"Is that right?" Ronzoni asked Consuela.

"Yes."

"Okay. Will you be here all day? I may have more questions."

Consuela looked at the lady of the house.

"She'll be here," assured Pixie. "Thank you, Consuela."

The home assistant left, and I took a look at the windows. Everything was locked up tight and to code. This place would be standing after the next hurricane. As I moved back toward Pixie, I noticed a framed photograph on the wall. I had seen a similar sort of thing at the home of a guy who owned racehorses. It was a picture of a very large dog—Layla. I had been close with my Great Dane thought, but not the dreadlocks. This pup was tall but had a long, straight haircut that had been pulled from the television show, *Friends*. It was an aristocratic-looking thing and seemed to suit Pixie well.

The dog was side on in the photo, head held high. Behind her were four people. Two men in suits who looked like judges or organizers, Pixie, and an athletic woman with auburn hair. The redhead held a lead that was attached to the dog's collar, while Pixie held a winner's trophy. The caption underneath the photo was written in cursive scrawl:

GCHS Layla of the Silk Road, Best in Show

Owner: Mrs. Pixie Kazarian

Handler: Ms. Evelyn Moreau

Pixie stepped in beside me. "That was Orlando, last year. Best in Show."

"What's all that GCHS and Silk Road business?" I asked.

"That is her pedigree name, Layla of the Silk Road. The GCHS is her champion status, Grand Champion Silver."

I cocked my head. "Silver? So she didn't win?"

"Of course she won. The silver means she has amassed two hundred points in AKC events." She glanced around and then said, "Shall we return to the house?"

I figured she meant her place, unless she had a terrapin with an SUV-sized terrarium, so we followed Ron and the detective out, and Pixie locked the door.

"Anyone else have a key?" asked Ronzoni.

"Yes. We keep one in a hidden place in the kitchen. Consuela uses that, and Eve has one."

"Who is Eve?"

"Evelyn Moreau, Layla's handler."

Ronzoni looked around the yard. "And where is she?"

"She has a facility here on the island."

"So, why does she have a key?"

"So one of her staff can walk and groom Layla twice a day."

"You don't walk her?" I asked.

Pixie glanced at Ron as if the question needed translation, then she lowered her eyebrows at me. "Goodness, no. She's a very large, very powerful animal. I leave that to the professionals."

I nodded. I had figured that walking your pooch was part of the deal of owning a pet. I might reconsider, now that I knew I could outsource all the work.

We made our way back to the main house, my mind still processing the opulence of Layla's mini-mansion. Pixie led us into what could only be described as a trophy room. The walls were lined with shelves, each one crammed with gleaming cups, plaques, and ribbons.

"This is my legacy," Pixie said, her voice swelling with pride. "All my show dogs over the years." Suddenly, she lost the verve, and her body seemed to deflate. "None better than Layla." She gestured to a large silver trophy in the center of the display that was the size of the Stanley Cup. "This is from Crufts."

Even I knew about Crufts. It was like the FA Cup of dog shows, held annually in the UK.

"Layla won Best in Show at Crufts?" I asked, impressed despite myself.

Pixie nodded, her eyes misting over. "She was magnificent. The judges couldn't take their eyes off her. And now..." Her voice trailed off, and she dabbed at her eyes again.

Ron stepped in, his voice gentle. "That's quite an achievement, Pixie."

Pixie sighed and lifted her chin, composing herself. "Yes. The only pinnacle left to conquer was Westminster. We received an invitation just last week."

"That's the big one in New York?" I asked.

"Indeed."

"And that was Layla's next event?"

"Ah, no," Pixie said. "We were planning to compete in the Grand Canine Classic next week. It's not as prestigious, of course, but it's excellent practice. Keeps Layla in top form for the big competitions." She moved to a side table and picked up a framed photograph. It showed Layla in all her glory, standing proud in a show ring, her silky coat gleaming under the lights. "This is what they've taken from me," Pixie said, her voice barely above a whisper. "Not just a dog, but a champion. A once-in-a-lifetime companion."

As I was about to ask Pixie another question, the room's atmosphere shifted. A tall, distinguished man in his early seventies strode in, his presence commanding attention.

"Pixie, my dear," he said, his voice smooth as Cognac, with a hint of something European about both it and his eyes. He was impeccably dressed in a suit with a silk pocket square. The whole look made me reconsider my palm tree print shirt and chinos.

But despite his polished exterior, I caught a flicker of something in his eyes. Tension? Worry? It was gone in an instant, replaced by an easy smile.

"Aram, darling," Pixie said, her voice brightening. "These detectives are here about Layla."

Aram nodded at us. "Of course, of course. Terrible business, this. But I thought the police were here."

"We are, Mr. Kazarian," said Ronzoni.

Aram looked at the detective with sad eyes, perhaps for the missing dog, but just as likely for Ronzoni's wrinkled JC Penney suit.

The detective smoothed one of his lapels. "I was telling your wife that these private eyes really weren't necessary."

"I had to cover all the bases, darling," Pixie said to her husband.

He offered a troubled nod and turned to me.

"Mr. Kazarian," I said, shaking his hand. "Miami Jones. You've been home all morning?"

"No, I just came from my office," he replied, his tone clipped. "I leave for work early. Fashion never sleeps, you know."

I nodded, choosing not to engage the metaphor. I had attended *some* English Lit classes in college. "And you don't visit Layla's... quarters often?"

"I'm afraid not. That's Pixie's domain. I'm more focused on business. That is my diversion."

"Mr. Kazarian, can you tell us anything about last night? Even the smallest detail might help."

Aram's eyes narrowed slightly. He ran a hand through his salt-and-pepper hair, a gesture that seemed less than suave. "I'm afraid I don't have much to offer. I was at a business meeting last evening. When I returned home, I worked in my office for some time, and then I went to bed."

"And you didn't notice anything out of the ordinary when you got back? No strange cars or unfamiliar faces around the property?"

"Nothing of the sort," he replied.

Pixie chimed in, her voice tinged with frustration. "Aram

hardly ever goes near Layla's house. He's always so busy with his empire."

I caught a flicker of something—annoyance or maybe even guilt —cross Aram's face before he smoothed it away. I wasn't sure if the empire reference was literal or a barb. These Palm Beach types did tend to work long hours until they made their billions, at which point they either doubled the workload for fear of losing it all, or they took up golf.

"That's true," he said. "I'm afraid I'm not much of a dog person. My work keeps me occupied most of the time."

"And what kind of work is that, exactly?" I asked.

Aram tugged at his cuffs, a hint of pride creeping into his voice. "I'm a fashion designer. My brand is very prominent."

"Would I know it?" asked Ronzoni. It was important for police to ask questions, but it must have made it easier for the detective that he was so oblivious.

Aram pursed his lips and looked Ronzoni up and down. "Perhaps not. We are a high-end luxury brand. In fact, we have a very big new launch coming soon. Very exciting."

I nodded, filing his words away. In my experience, prominence was kind of like intelligence. If someone had to tell you that they were, then they probably weren't.

"Well, Mr. Kazarian, I appreciate your time," I said, deciding to change tack. "Is there anything else you think might be relevant to Layla's disappearance? Any enemies, competitors in the dog show world, anything like that?"

Aram shook his head. "Nothing comes to mind. But then again, as I said, I'm not very involved in that world. Pixie would know more about that side of things."

"Do you have a security system, Mr. Kazarian?" asked Ronzoni.

"Of course. Our security is top-notch. Well, usually," he added with a grimace.

"Usually, sir?"

"Jenkins just checked it. There seems to have been an outage."

"An outage?"

"An interruption."

"An interruption?"

"Yes."

I stepped in before Ronzoni could repeat the word. "Who's Jenkins?"

Aram blinked as if two people firing questions was too much. "He's our butler."

I nodded. "And what kind of interruption did you have?"

"The video feed cut out."

"Does that happen a lot?"

"I've never seen it before, but we don't trawl through the video very often. The walls keep most trouble at bay."

Ronzoni stepped forward. "Could we see the video you have?"

CHAPTER THREE

Aram led me, Ron and the detective into his study, a room that reeked of old money and power. Leather-bound books lined the walls, and a massive mahogany desk dominated the space. But my attention was drawn to the large flat-screen mounted on one wall. I didn't own a television, but this swimming-pool-sized thing might make me change my mind on that.

Aram Kazarian sat and used his desk phone to call Jenkins. It was such a butler moniker I wondered if it was a stage name. He came promptly and stood at the door.

"Jenkins, if you would," Aram said, gesturing to the television. "Can you show these men the video feed?"

Jenkins nodded forcefully and then stepped to a walnut bureau, where he slid open a thin drawer to reveal a wireless keyboard. His posture remained ramrod straight and he tapped the keys with the finesse of a pianist. The massive television on the wall flickered to life, showing a high-definition view of Layla's luxurious doghouse. *Two* high-definition views, in fact. One outside the front door, the second a voyeur's view of Layla's bed. The screen was split in half, like a first base replay.

"This is from last night," Jenkins explained. "You can see the time stamp, bottom right."

I watched intently as the timestamp in the corner of each image ticked away. In one we saw Consuela deliver Layla to the doghouse, then lock the door and leave. In the second, Layla wandered around the room, her silky coat gleaming even in the low light. She looked like she was preparing for sleep, because once she had done a few laps of the space, she lumbered over to the impressive bed and lay down.

For a long time, nothing happened. The dog napped, and nothing moved outside. Jenkins suggested he fast-forward, and Ronzoni agreed. The images didn't leave the screen, and they didn't change much, but for the dog's occasional movements.

Then, without warning, the feed cut to static.

"What happened there?" I asked, leaning forward.

Aram gestured at the screen. "That's the malfunction. For some reason, it went down at this exact moment."

Jenkins fast-forwarded through about ten minutes of static before the image returned. The doghouse looked exactly the same, except for one glaring detail—Layla was gone.

"And you have no idea what caused this convenient outage?" I couldn't keep the skepticism out of my voice.

Aram shook his head, appearing genuinely perplexed. "None whatsoever. We have experts coming to look at it, so I don't have an answer yet. It's as if someone just turned off our cameras for those crucial minutes."

"How did it go down?" asked Ron. "The system, I mean. Did someone cut the lines?"

"If they cut lines, how did it come back?" asked Ronzoni.

Ron shrugged.

"Where are the tapes stored?" I asked.

"What tapes?" asked Jenkins.

"Of the videos? Or is it on a hard drive?"

"There's a box in the armoire over there," said Aram.

Jenkins opened the armoire and showed me the box. It was, as claimed, a box. A plastic cube with technology inside. I couldn't say more than that, so I took a photo of it, then I lifted it to get a shot of the labeling underneath. Like Palm Beach royalty, I too had people, and my people knew about things like this so I didn't have to.

"Mr. Kazarian," I said slowly, "does anyone besides your immediate household have access to your security setup?"

Aram's eyes narrowed. "What are you implying, Mr. Jones?"

I held up my hands. "At the moment I'm just asking questions."

"You don't think one of our staff was involved?"

"Let's not jump to conclusions," Ron interjected smoothly. "We're just exploring all possibilities."

I nodded, grateful for Ron's diplomacy as Pixie appeared at the door.

I turned my attention back to her, trying to move away from the cloud that the suggestion of an inside job had put over the room. She was twisting a diamond-encrusted ring on her finger.

"Pixie, can you tell me more about your involvement in dog shows?" I moved back across the room to her. "How does that whole process work?"

Pixie's face lit up, momentarily forgetting her distress. "Oh, it's quite the affair, Mr. Jones. I've been in the show circuit for years now. Layla is my pride and joy, the culmination of all my efforts."

"So, you mentioned you don't show her yourself, in the—what is it called? The floor, the ring?" I asked, picturing Pixie trotting alongside the elegant Afghan Hound.

She let out a tinkling laugh. "Oh, heavens, no! It's called the ring, but I'm afraid I'm not as spry as I once was. No, I employ a professional handler."

"And that's the woman in the photos?"

"Yes." Pixie nodded. "Evelyn Moreau. She's absolutely marvelous with Layla. They have such a special bond in the ring. Eve's been handling champions for years, and she's the best in the business. In fact, she handles all Layla's health and grooming needs."

I pulled out my phone. "I'd like to speak with Ms. Moreau if possible. Do you have her contact information?"

Pixie bustled over to an antique writing desk in the corner of the room. She pulled out a leather-bound address book and flipped through it with manicured fingers. "Here we are," she said, scribbling down the details on a message pad. "That's Evelyn's number and address. Her facility is not far from here, actually."

I glanced at the information. The address was down the island, not far from Southern Boulevard. Clearly, being a professional dog handler paid better than I thought.

"I'd like that address, too," said Detective Ronzoni.

"I'm sure Mr. Jones will be happy to share," said Pixie with a dismissive smile.

Ronzoni's shoulder's sagged as they often did when he got treated like he was the help.

"Thank you, Pixie," I said, handing the paper to Ronzoni. "How often does Evelyn interact with Layla outside of shows?"

Pixie thought for a moment. "Oh, they have regular training sessions, usually twice a week. And of course, more frequently in the lead-up to big shows. But her staff come twice daily to walk and groom. They were here just before she disappeared." Her voice caught on the last words.

I turned to Ronzoni, who was scribbling down Evelyn Moreau's address in a tiny, dog-eared notebook. He caught my eye and cleared his throat.

"Mrs. Kazarian, Mr. Kazarian," Ronzoni began, his voice gruff. "In your opinion, who might have a motive to steal Layla? Any enemies, rivals in the dog show world?"

Pixie's hand flew to her throat. "Oh, Detective, I can't imagine anyone wanting to harm our precious Layla!"

Aram shifted in his seat. "Well, there are always unsavory characters out there," he said, his tone measured. "I recall seeing a television exposé recently about black market traffickers and puppy mills. Despicable business, really."

I leaned forward, intrigued. "Black market traffickers?"

Aram's eyes darted to his wife, then back to me. "It was just a general report, you understand. About how these operations target purebred dogs, especially champions like our Layla. They either sell them for breeding or ..." He trailed off, leaving the grimmer possibilities unspoken.

"But you don't know of any specific threats?" said Ronzoni.

"No one has demanded a ransom or anything like that?" I pressed.

Aram shook his head. "A ransom? Goodness, no." He raised his eyebrows like he was considering the possibility for the first time. "No. We've never received any threats. It's just, well, when something like this happens, you start to wonder, don't you?"

I nodded, making a mental note to look into these black market operations. It seemed like a long shot, to steal a dog to sell, but this was Palm Beach.

Ronzoni cleared his throat again. "We'll certainly look into all possibilities, Mr. and Mrs. Kazarian. Rest assured, the Palm Beach PD is on the case."

I watched as Pixie sat at the rolltop desk and reached for her checkbook. She scribbled on a check, tore it out, and handed it to me with a smile that was anything but happy.

"Mr. Jones, I trust you'll do everything in your power to bring our Layla home," she said, her voice quavering slightly.

I nodded, pocketing the check. "I'll do my best, Pixie."

Pixie then turned to Ronzoni, producing a crisp twenty-dollar bill from thin air like a magician. "And for you, Detective, for your time and effort."

Ronzoni's face flushed a deep shade of red. He held up his hands, backing away slightly. "That's, uh, not necessary, ma'am. Just doing my job."

The awkward moment hung in the air until Pixie finally lowered her hand, looking slightly bewildered.

I cleared my throat, eager to not be in the stuffy room any longer. "Well, I'll go and chat with your handler, and I'll let you know how we get on from there."

Aram stayed at his desk, and Pixie walked us to the office door. Jenkins showed us the rest of the way to our car. Then he retreated inside without a word. Ron slipped into the passenger seat as if we were making a getaway from a bank heist.

Ronzoni's eyes narrowed in the hot sun. "Now, listen, Jones. You may have been hired here, but this is still an active police investigation."

I smiled as I rounded the front of my SUV. "I'll keep you in the loop, Rigatoni. Don't worry."

"Ronzoni. And this is my investigation. Are we clear?"

"If you mean, do I know you'll want the credit, then yeah, we're clear."

"Good," he said. He really was an irony-free zone.

I opened my door, fired up the engine so Ron didn't melt, then leaned on the frame and nodded at Ronzoni. "You wanna come visit the handler?"

He huffed, gesturing at the check in my pocket. "I'll get to it in time. You're the one with the fat check. You can update me."

"As you wish, Detective."

"Just…keep me informed, all right?"

I nodded, suppressing a smirk. "Sure thing. I'll let you know if I turn up anything useful."

I was about to get in when I realized something was missing. "Where's your car, Ronzoni?"

He looked at his shoes. "It's around at the service entrance."

I smiled. "You want a ride?"

"No, Jones. I can walk."

CHAPTER FOUR

THE ADDRESS PIXIE HAD GIVEN ME WAS TUCKED AWAY IN A LUSH, secluded area just down island from Southern Boulevard. As we approached, I couldn't shake the feeling we were entering some kind of exclusive resort rather than a dog facility. The sign, on a stuccoed gate post, read *The Pawlace: Elite Canine Resort & Concierge.*

"Pawlace?" I asked, eyeing the sprawling Mediterranean-style building with its terracotta roof and cream-colored stucco walls.

Ron nodded, looking equally impressed. "Evelyn Moreau doesn't do things by halves."

"Are we sure the GPS didn't take us to The Breakers?"

We stepped out of the car, and I took in the meticulously landscaped grounds. Palm trees swayed in the breeze, and vibrant tropical flowers surrounded the immaculate lawns. It looked more like a fancy liberal arts college campus than a place for pooches.

As we walked towards the entrance, I noticed several fenced areas that could only be described as canine playgrounds. There was even a bone-shaped swimming pool.

I shook my head, bemused. "You know, Ron, I'm starting to think these Palm Beach dogs live better than I do."

Ron chuckled, but he didn't disagree.

We entered a lobby fit for a five-star hotel. Marble floors gleamed beneath our feet, and plush bench seats lined the walls. The reception desk looked like it belonged in a spa, not a kennel.

As we waited for someone to greet us, I couldn't help but compare this place and the Kazarians' home. While the Kazarian estate was undoubtedly luxurious, it felt sterile and museum-like. This place, though—with the bustling energy of so many dogs— was opulence with a whole different level of energy.

A well-groomed woman in a cream dress that seemed to be a disaster in waiting with dogs everywhere offered us a welcoming smile. I was a connoisseur of smiles. I saw a lot of them in Florida. Beach vacations did that to people. Of course, I saw the opposite, too, mostly driving on the A1A. But this one was as genuine as they came, the expression of someone who actually liked what they were doing for a living.

I asked for Evelyn Moreau.

"Do you have an appointment? Or can I help in some way?"

"Pixie Kazarian sent me. It's about her dog."

"Layla?"

"That's the one. Pixie asked us to speak with Evelyn as a matter of urgency."

The receptionist made a call and then told us to wait on one of the bench seats. They were velvet or some kind of synthetic fabric made to look like it, and they didn't have a single dog hair on them.

Ron and I sat in the lobby for a few moments and watched another dog—if asked to name the breed, I would have said puff-ball—dribble all over the marble floor, before a striking woman in her mid-thirties approached us. Her auburn hair was pulled back in a practical ponytail, and she moved with the grace of an athlete.

"Gentlemen, I'm Evelyn Moreau. Welcome to the Pawlace," she said, extending her hand. Her grip was firm, her blue eyes sharp and assessing. "How can I help you?"

I introduced myself and Ron, then got straight to the point. "We're here about Layla."

Evelyn's professional demeanor softened at the mention of the Afghan Hound. "Layla, yes. One of our star pupils. What about her?"

I hesitated, realizing Evelyn might not know about the dog's disappearance. "Ms. Moreau, I'm afraid I have some bad news. Layla's been stolen."

The color drained from Evelyn's face, and she was pretty pale to begin with. "Stolen? That's not possible. When? How?"

I gave her a brief rundown of what we knew so far. Evelyn listened intently, her brow furrowing with concern.

"I can't believe it," she said, shaking her head. "Layla's such a special dog. Who would do something like this?"

"That's what we're trying to figure out," I replied. "We were hoping you might be able to help us. I understand she came here?"

"Often, yes. She trained here. I handle her in competition."

"Yes, Pixie mentioned that. It's quite the facility."

Evelyn nodded, visibly pulling herself together. "Of course. Let me give you a quick tour."

Evelyn stopped by the reception to grab us two visitor's tags— not the scribbled name in a plastic pouch or even a sticker with *hello my name is*. These were white keycards on lanyards adorned with the Pawlace branding.

As we walked through the campus, Evelyn explained the layout. "We have five acres here, all dedicated to providing the best care for our canine clients. There's the main building with luxury suites for boarding, a full-service grooming spa, indoor and outdoor training areas, and even a veterinary clinic on-site."

She pointed out various features as we passed them—the bone-shaped pool I'd noticed earlier, agility courses, and what looked like a small show ring for practice.

"And your security?" I asked, trying to keep my tone casual. "I imagine with such high-profile clients, you must have quite a system in place."

Evelyn held up the keycard hanging around her own neck. "Absolutely. We have state-of-the-art security throughout the property. Cameras, motion sensors, the works. Plus, we have staff on-site twenty-four-seven."

I made a mental note of this. "So, Pixie mentioned that you walked her dog as well?"

"Yes. One of my team walked and groomed her twice a day. Afghans have impressive coats that must be maintained. If not, well, it's a nightmare."

"Is it the same staff member every time?"

"Are you suggesting that one of my people had something to do with her disappearance?" Her eyes pinched, and she focused on me like I was a bad dog.

"Not suggesting anything. They might have seen something. That's all."

"Like what?"

"I honestly have no idea. Where did they walk the dog?"

"For Pixie? We just walked her on the estate. Even for a big dog, there's room. Plus, no traffic. And, like I say, twice a week she was here, so she got a good run then."

"Could we speak to the dog walker?"

"He's a canine concierge, and his name is Nunzio." She took out her phone and made a call to have Nunzio meet us at reception.

We headed back toward the main building, around a manicured field fit for a football scrimmage.

Ron dropped in beside Evelyn. "So, I'm curious about the financial side of all this. These shows must have considerable prize money, am I right? I mean, with all the effort and expense that goes into them."

Evelyn let out a small laugh. "You'd think so, wouldn't you? But actually, there's very little prize money in dog shows."

"Really?" I said. "Even for something as big as Crufts?"

"Even Crufts," Eve confirmed. "When Layla won Best in Show there earlier this year, Pixie only received about two hundred pounds. That's less than three hundred US dollars."

"That's it? For the biggest dog show in the world?"

Eve nodded. "I'm not sure I'd call Crufts the biggest in the world, but yes. The real value comes from the recognition and the potential breeding fees. A champion dog can command thousands for stud services or puppies."

"What's the biggest show, then?" asked Ron.

"Most people would say Westminster."

"In New York?"

"That's right."

"What's the prize money there?" I asked.

Evelyn smiled. "In the breed judging, none. That's pretty standard for AKC events. There's a nice trophy, though."

" AKC? What exactly is that?"

"AKC stands for the American Kennel Club," Evelyn explained. "It's the primary registry for purebred dogs in the United States. They set the standards for each breed, oversee dog shows, and maintain pedigree records."

"So they're like the big dogs of the dog world?"

Evelyn sighed. There might have been an eye roll. "That's one way to put it. The AKC is responsible for recognizing and registering purebred dogs. They also sanction events like conformation shows, obedience trials, and agility competitions."

"So let me get this straight. People spend thousands, maybe even hundreds of thousands of dollars on these dogs, their care, and showing them, and there's no real prize money? How does anyone afford this?"

Evelyn smiled, a knowing look in her eyes. "It's not about the money, Mr. Jones. It's about the prestige, the recognition. You boys do any sailing?"

I looked at Ron. That was his bag. He perked up with an emphatic nod.

"Think of it like yacht racing. Those boat owners spend even more."

"Maybe millions," said Ron.

"Right, and for what?"

"A trophy. Maybe a pennant. I won a fleece once."

"Exactly." Evelyn nodded. "It's a similar principle. The reward is in the accomplishment, the status it brings."

"All right, so break it down for me," I said. "What kind of costs are we talking about here?"

Evelyn began ticking off items on her fingers. "Well, there's the initial cost of the dog, which for a show-quality pup can be anywhere from five thousand to fifty thousand dollars or more. Then you've got ongoing expenses like premium food, grooming, veterinary care, training. Not to mention travel costs for shows, entry fees, handler fees if you're not showing the dog yourself."

"That's quite the list," I said.

"Oh, we're just getting started," Evelyn said with a laugh. "For top-level competitors, you might be looking at custom-built facilities like this one, specialized exercise equipment, even things like acupuncture or massage therapy for the dogs."

I stopped in place. "Acupuncture? Seriously? Next, you're going to tell me they do yoga."

"Some do."

I couldn't escape the feeling that some people just had too much money. I was all for free enterprise and everything, but dog acupuncture seemed a little ridiculous. "And you're saying there's no payback for this other than prestige?"

Evelyn nodded. "Not necessarily. While there isn't much direct prize money, top show dogs can land endorsement deals. Pet food companies, grooming product lines, even luxury brands sometimes partner with champion dogs and their owners."

I started walking, still struggling to make sense of it all. "If there's no real money to be had, why would anyone bother stealing a dog like Layla?"

Evelyn's expression turned serious. "You're conflating revenue with profit. There is some revenue; it just doesn't usually cover the costs. However…" She paused, her eyes narrowing. "If you didn't pay those costs, if you just stole the dog, you might make something."

"How so?" I asked.

"Breeding," Evelyn explained. "Take Layla, for instance. She's had one litter of six pups. Each of those puppies was worth about ten thousand dollars. In fact, I have one of them here at the facility, training to enter shows."

"That's not nothing," said Ron.

Evelyn nodded. "But on the black market, you can't show the dog because everyone will know it's stolen. However, an unscrupulous buyer might just want a particular breed, like an Afghan, or even a specific dog like Layla."

"So it's like art theft?" I mused. "People steal paintings they can never display publicly."

"Sure," Evelyn agreed. "After her Crufts win, Layla might be worth twenty thousand dollars or more on the black market."

I frowned, doing the math in my head. It wasn't chump change, but it didn't seem like enough to risk a felony over. Then I recalled how little it took for some people to lean toward their lesser angels.

We got back to the reception and found a young man in a polo and chinos waiting for us. He nodded with a toothy smile at Evelyn.

"Gentlemen," she said. "This is Nunzio. One of our lead concierges."

I shook his hand. He had a hell of a grip, and his forearms, although thin, were nothing but muscle. He was a fit-looking package, only about five-nine but strong, like he spent a lot of time in the gym or yanking on dog leashes.

"Eve said something happened to Layla?" His concern showed in his eyes. Unlike mine, his forehead was smooth and wrinkle free.

"She was stolen from the Kazarians' home early this morning."

His jaw dropped and he looked from me to Ron and back again. "Are you kidding me?"

"I wouldn't be standing here otherwise. When was the last time you saw her?"

He shook his head as he thought. "Last night. I walked her in the yard and then groomed her."

"You didn't go this morning?"

"I was about to head over there when I got the call to come to reception."

"Do you lock up the doghouse when you leave?"

"No, not usually. The maid feeds her, and I think she takes care of that."

"Consuela?" asked Ron.

"That's right."

"You ever see anyone hanging around?" I said. "Maybe casing the joint."

"No, nothing like that. Like I say, we generally stay in the yard. It's pretty big."

"I know."

"And for her bigger runs, I bring her here. She works with Eve."

Evelyn nodded, and so did I. The story all fit with what we had seen on the security video, at least the part that worked.

"So, should I get over there?" asked Nunzio. "To see Pixie, maybe?"

"I'd leave it for now," I said. "She's in a bit of a state."

Ron gave Nunzio a card, and I asked him to call us if he thought of anything that might help us. Ron handed Evelyn a card, and Nunzio held his up.

"Will do," he said, then he strode over to a golf cart and headed onto a grass field where another staffer stood waiting with a pack of dogs on a leash that looked like a spiderweb.

I thanked Evelyn and repeated the request to call if she remembered anything useful. People rarely did, but it happened often enough to make the effort worthwhile. As I was about to leave, a thought struck me. I turned back to Evelyn, who was still standing in the reception doorway.

"One more thing, Evelyn. Is there anyone who might have something against Pixie? Someone who'd take Layla just to cause her grief?"

Evelyn's brow furrowed. She shook her head slowly. "Hurt

Pixie? I can't imagine why anyone would want to do that. Everyone loves Pixie."

"Everyone?"

"Well, you know how it is in Palm Beach," she said with a shrug. "There's always some kind of drama or another. But Pixie? She's different. She's genuinely kind, generous. She's been a patron of so many charities, helped so many people in the community. I've never heard anyone say a bad word about her."

I nodded, taking in Evelyn's words. It was hard to imagine someone being universally loved in a place like Palm Beach, but stranger things had happened. Still, something about it didn't sit right with me. In my experience, even the nicest people had enemies. Even if they didn't know it. I made a note to get Ron to ask Cassandra about it.

"All right," I said, shaking her hand. "Thanks for your time, Evelyn. I appreciate the insight."

She nodded to Ron and walked inside. As we headed for the parking lot, I glanced toward the field and changed tack. Ron didn't see my move and kept walking toward the car, so he had to jog to catch up.

"What's up?" he asked.

"Just curious," I said, making a beeline for Nunzio. He was throwing tennis balls with a ball launcher, sending canines rushing all over the field. He nodded as we approached.

"Something more I can help you with?" he asked.

"I'm sure there is," I said as he heaved the ball and a collie took off like a shot. "You worked here long?"

"Few years."

"You a dog guy?"

"Funny job to have if I wasn't."

"Plenty of people do jobs they don't love."

"Not here."

"So you know the dog show scene?"

"I guess. Not like Eve or anything, but I follow it. Why?"

"Because someone stole a dog, which seems pretty strange to me. So I'm wondering who might do that?"

"I have no idea."

"Evelyn says Pixie doesn't have any enemies."

"I wouldn't really know about that." The collie returned and dropped the ball at Nunzio's feet, looking like he was having the time of his life. "I work there, you know? We're hardly besties."

"Yeah, I get that. But what about in the show world? Layla's a winner, right? Winners always attract haters."

"Yeah, I suppose they do." Nunzio threw the ball again.

"Anyone you know who might be jealous or want the next trophy for themselves?"

"Plenty want the next trophy, but to steal a dog? I can't think of many who'd do that."

"I don't need many. I just need one."

"I don't want to get anyone in trouble."

"You're not. It stays between us. And whoever's name you have, they might not be the one. They might just be the first link in the chain that gets us the answer we need."

The collie ran back and dropped the ball, ready to go again. The little dog was like the Energizer bunny.

"You might look into Graham Albright."

"Graham?" said Ron, a flash of recognition in his eyes.

"What's his angle?" I asked.

Nunzio shrugged. "He likes to win."

I looked around the campus. "I imagine there are plenty of people here who like to win."

"There are, but Mr. Albright *really* likes to win."

"One of those guys," I said.

Nunzio nodded, then threw the ball again. That dog was going to sleep well.

I watched the collie charge away. "So, you think he might elimi-nate the competition?"

Nunzio let out a whistle like he was the Queen Mary and a curly-haired dog stopped smelling the backside of a pug and looked at him with a *who, me?* face. "I'm not saying that. But Layla's disappearance might make us look bad."

"And how does that help this Albright guy?"

"Word is he's looking to open his own canine resort."

"So, competition with this place?"

"Maybe."

"Maybe it's competition, or maybe he's opening it?"

"Both." He shifted his feet in the grass.

"And you know this how?"

"There's talk."

"Among who?"

"Staff."

I watched the collie retrieve the ball, then ran back toward us. "Is this guy poaching staff?"

Nunzio nodded. "A couple have left."

"What about you?"

"I'm happy here."

"But you were approached?"

He shrugged. It was as good as a yes.

"Were you asked to disappear Layla?"

His head snapped to me. "I had nothing to do with that. I'm helping you out here. I wouldn't be telling you anything if I did it, would I?"

It was my turn to shrug. People incriminated themselves all the time, but I didn't tell him that. "Where's this other doggie resort?"

"Don't know."

"You were approached about a job, but you don't know where."

"Nope. Apparently, it's in development. The people who left had to sign NDAs." The collie came back and dropped the ball, but this time Nunzio attached a leash to him. The collie looked dejected.

"I gotta get these guys into the bath," he said.

"Sure. Thanks for your help." I watched him and the other staffer gather up the dogs and lead them away.

We were most of the way to the perimeter of the property, so I decided to do a boundary walk and see what security was really like.

"So you know this Albright guy," I said to Ron as we wandered along a tall wall covered by hedgerow.

"What makes you say that?"

"Your excellent poker face."

"I know of him. Cassandra knows him." His wife knew everybody in Palm Beach society.

"You think you could find out about this other resort?"

"I can sniff around."

I wasn't sure if it was a pun, but he wasn't smiling, so I left it. We walked off the fields and across a service road, and around the back of some buildings to a parking lot. It looked like the staff lot because the cars were a whole lower class of vehicle than what parked outside reception.

"What do you think?" Ron asked.

"I think the dog went missing for a reason, and crimes are usually committed for one of two reasons."

"Money or love."

"Or the absence of either."

"So, which is it?"

I didn't know. Not yet. I scanned the lot and saw the rear gate. Employees had to scan a keycard to get in or out. I wandered over and waved my card over the small black box and got nothing. The gate didn't budge. So there were permission levels, which meant the security was pretty good.

I caught a flash of color out of the corner of my eye as we turned back toward reception. A woman stepped out from behind one of the buildings, and I stopped in my tracks. She wore blue scrubs and a head wrap adorned with playful patterns, each shade bursting with energy—like she had a little sunshine trapped in her outfit. Her dark skin glowed against the vivid colors, and her athletic build suggested she was no stranger to movement.

She paused, looking around as if she were in some sort of spy flick. I squinted to get a better view. The woman clutched a black plastic storage tub. She glanced over her shoulder like she expected someone—or something—to pop out from behind the hedges. After what felt like an eternity, she strode purposefully toward a Lexus SUV parked at the end of the row closest to the building.

The rear hatch opened before she reached the car, and she set the tub down inside. Then, she once again scanned her surroundings with a little too much effort. She turned back toward the building and walked away from the car. She was halfway back to the door when the hatch decided to close, as if the decision was of its own making. The woman stepped inside, and I heard both the building door and hatch click closed on electronic locks.

I stood for a moment until Ron called me from a good ten yards ahead.

"What?" he asked.

"Just thinking," I said.

He didn't ask me what I was thinking about as we wandered back across the campus. We dropped off our visitors' tags at reception and then headed to my car.

As we got in, Ron said, "What do you think?"

I turned the engine on but sat and looked across a field where a dog was running through an agility course. The little mutt was having a good old time. The trainer seemed pretty happy, too.

"I don't know. But if they think they're getting one over old Miami Jones, they're *barking* up the wrong tree."

"That's terrible," said Ron.

"Quit *hounding* me."

"Just stop."

"It's been a *ruff* morning."

"No, seriously, stop it."

"So let's get some lunch at Longboards."

"Finally, some sense from you."

CHAPTER FIVE

The midday sun beat down on the asphalt in the parking lot at Longboard Kelly's, creating shimmering mirages across the parking lot. The familiar sight of the weathered palapa came into view, its fronds rustling gently in the breeze.

We made our way toward our usual spots at the outdoor bar, where the worn wooden stools were molded to our backsides. Muriel spotted us and started pouring our usual before we got halfway across the courtyard.

"Two fish sandwiches coming right up," she called out, disappearing into the kitchen.

I leaned back, feeling the tension from the morning's investigation ebb away. It was a universal truth in our business that someone was always lying, and being lied to dragged on the soul. Nothing refreshed that soul like a cold beer at Longboards.

"Cheers," Ron said, taking a long drink. "So, where's your head?"

I mulled over the question as I sipped my beer, letting the condensation dribble down onto my fingers. "We have a dog stolen from a high-security estate, but no video, which feels all kinds of *inside job* to me. But it's Palm Beach, so there's money involved here somewhere. The dog's worth a decent bundle, so we gotta look at the staff. But it wouldn't be the first time one of these rich and infamous jerks just stole something to take someone else down a peg or two. But if you believe Evelyn Moreau, Pixie Kazarian's some kind of saint."

Ron nodded, his beer half gone. "I hear you. It's not often you find someone universally loved in that crowd."

"Exactly," I said, drumming my fingers on the bar top. "And then there's the husband, Aram. He's no dog lover."

"But he does care about his wife."

"How do you know?"

"That's hard to fake."

I shrugged. I wasn't so sure. I couldn't do it, but then I didn't have to.

Muriel returned with our sandwiches, the smell of freshly grilled fish making my stomach growl. I took a bite, savoring the tender flesh inside.

"What about the dog handler?" Ron asked between bites. "This Evelyn Moreau?"

"She knows the scene, that's for sure."

"And she had a guy at the Kazarians'."

"But the video was pretty clear. Consuela put the dog in her box and locked up. Nunzio wasn't there." I took another bite and pointed my sandwich at Ron. "And what would Evelyn have to gain? She handles Layla. They just won a show together. That's got to be good for her business."

We ate in silence for a while, then Ron wiped his mouth and suggested checking local vet clinics.

"Worth a shot," I said. "We should probably start with the high-end places. Anyone stealing a show dog isn't likely to take her to some back-alley joint."

"Or maybe they are," said Ron. "If the dog is stolen."

"That's a good question. How would they know?"

"Don't dogs get tagged or something?"

"That's elephants."

"No, I think there's something with dogs. I'll get Lizzy to check it."

Ron pulled out his phone, tapping away as he added to his growing to-do list. He took a long swig of his beer, then set the glass down with a soft *thunk*.

"You know," I mused, picking at the coleslaw beside my fish sandwich, "we might want to look into any recent dog shows in the area too."

"You thinking a competitor might have done this?"

I shrugged. "Anything's possible. A guy got shot at a cornhole tournament in Hialeah last spring. Maybe someone got tired of losing to Layla and decided to even the odds."

"Could be. Pixie was pretty eager to show off Layla's trophy room. Might have rubbed some folks the wrong way."

"Exactly," I said, warming to the theory. "We should get a list of recent shows, see who Layla beat out. Maybe there's a pattern there, someone who always came in second."

Ron nodded, adding it to his list.

I took another bite of my fish sandwich. As I chewed, my mind wandered back to the security footage we'd seen at the Kazarian estate. "And there's the security video," I said, swallowing. "The way it cut in and out. It's just too convenient, you know? Like someone knew exactly when to disrupt the feed."

Ron nodded slowly. "It certainly felt like it was tampered with."

"Could be. But like you said, if wires were cut, they would stay cut, wouldn't they?"

"Maybe someone just turned it off."

"Maybe. But the time stamp kept going, like it was just, I don't know, off."

"Pulled the plug from the camera?"

"Wouldn't you see someone do that in the video?" I took a swig of my beer, then set it down. "I think I need to talk to Sally about that."

"Sally?" Ron raised an eyebrow. "You think?"

"Not Sal himself. But he knows people. People who know about security systems and how to mess with them, I'm betting."

"All right," Ron agreed. "You do Sal."

I finished my last bite and tapped my lips with a napkin, then I did my happy spin on the stool to take in the sunny courtyard. I stopped halfway through. Danielle was making her way through the parking lot entrance, rocking a brown pinstripe suit that hugged her in all the right places. As she approached the bar, I noticed a slight tension in her posture.

"Hey, you," I greeted her. "Vodka tonic or just the tonic?"

She shook her head, remaining standing between Ron and I. "Can't stay long. I just got a call from Orna Tetweiler."

I felt my eyebrows creep up. Orna worked for the Department of Children and Families and had become a fixture in my life since we applied to become foster parents.

"Oh?" I tried to keep my voice neutral, but I could feel a knot forming in my stomach.

Danielle nodded, her expression a mix of concern and determination. "She's got a short-term placement for us. A thirteen-year-old girl needs a place to stay while her mother's in rehab for some alcohol-related issues."

My eyes widened, and I could feel a wave of nerves wash over me. We had only ever housed one kid before and that had been a toddler, even before we were formally checked out to foster. That was a hell of a learning curve. But a teenager? That felt well outside our skill set for our first real time out.

"Thirteen?" I said, my voice sounding strained even to my own ears.

Ron looked between us, clearly sensing the tension. "Teenager. Fun."

Danielle nodded, her gaze fixed on me. "I know it's scary, but Orna says she's a good kid. Just needs a stable environment for a week, maybe two, while her mom gets help."

I took a deep breath. Danielle wanted this. We wanted this. But now that it was happening, I felt like I was taking the mound in the World Series without ever having played a real game.

Then a thought hit my guts like one of the punches at Stone's Gym. "What about the pool fence? It's not up. Is that going to be a problem?"

Danielle's expression softened. "I'll check with Orna, but you got it up in no time before. I'm sure it won't matter for when she arrives. We'll get it done. The important thing is that you're home on time. We need to be there when she arrives."

I nodded, trying to process everything. A teenager. A girl. In our house. For possibly two weeks. I really wanted to order another beer.

Ron, ever helpful, let out a chuckle. "At least you've been practicing your dad jokes."

I shot him a look that was equal parts amusement and panic. "No practice required. I'll just use your material."

"You got any more dog puns?"

"I'm just trying to stay *paws*-itive."

Danielle rolled her eyes. "You guys are hilarious. But seriously, we need to make sure we're prepared."

I could see the tension in her face. She was as panicked as I was. "You're right. What do we need to do? Should we set up the spare room? Buy anything specific?"

"Orna said she'd give us more details later, but for now, just make sure you're home by six. We can figure out the rest together."

I nodded, my mind already racing with all the things we'd need to consider. What did thirteen-year-old girls eat? What time did they go to bed? What did they do for fun? We didn't own a television, and that was the center of the universe for a lot of kids when I was thirteen. Not me. I was on a sports field of some description.

Ron, still grinning, raised his beer in a mock toast. "To Miami Jones, soon-to-be father of the year."

I couldn't help but laugh, despite the knot of anxiety in my stomach.

Danielle gave me one last look, a mix of excitement and apprehension that probably mirrored my own expression. She kissed me, then headed out.

I turned back to Ron. "So, where were we?"

"The dog case," Ron reminded me, but I could see he was enjoying my discomfort a little too much.

"Right, right." I tried to focus, but my mind kept wandering to the spare room at home. Did we have clean sheets? What about towels? Did thirteen-year-olds need special towels?

Ron was saying something about the security footage, but I found myself glancing at my watch. It was just past one. Five hours. I had five hours to get home and...do what exactly?

"Miami? You still with me?"

I looked up, realizing Ron had asked me a question. "Sorry, what was that?"

Ron chuckled. "I said, I'm going to head back to the office. You coming?"

"Yeah, I guess." I nodded, my eyes drifting back to my watch. Four hours and fifty-nine minutes now.

"You know, the clock's not going to move any faster just because you keep staring at it."

I slipped off my stool. "Actually, you know what? I'm gonna go see Sal. Find out what he knows. I should be able to fit that in. What time do kids finish school?"

Ron shrugged. "Beats me. My experience with kids ended when I stopped being one."

CHAPTER SIX

I drove along Okeechobee Boulevard until I got to the wrong side of the turnpike, where I saw the sign for Sally's Pawn and Check Cashing. The strip mall lot was bursting with the lunch rush at the Chinese restaurant next door, so I left the SUV in the far corner where it might get towed if not for the fact that Sal knew every tow truck driver in the area, and for the hundredth time since leaving Longboards, I had cause to look at my watch.

I stepped inside, and the bell above the door jangled. The girl behind the Plexiglass didn't look up from her phone, but I didn't stop. I didn't need a check cashed. I passed the old microwaves and musical instruments and then stood there until Sally Mondavi looked up from behind the counter, his nicotine-stained smile spreading across his face.

"I'm telling ya, no Belichick, no Patriots."

I approached the counter, leaning in. "You want me to start in on the Jets?"

"Nope. Jacksonville won a game, so the whole world's gone crazy." He put a camera lens in the display cabinet. What can I do you for, kid?"

"I've got a question about security systems. Wondering if you might know someone who's good with that sort of thing."

Sal's eyes narrowed. "What kind of *good* are we talking about here?"

I shrugged. "The kind that might know how to mess with them. Hypothetically speaking, of course."

Sal nodded, his wrinkled face thoughtful. "I might know a guy. Let me make a call."

As Sal picked up the phone, I found myself thinking about his network of kids—all those at-risk youngsters he'd helped over the years. Many of them were no longer kids, not by a long shot, which made it a useful and extensive network.

Sal's eyes lit up as he spoke into the phone, his gravelly voice warm with affection. "Hey, kiddo. How's tricks?" He listened for a moment, then chuckled. "Listen, I've got a friend here with some questions in your particular field. You got time for lunch?"

When he hung up, that crusty face of his split into a wide grin. "We're in luck. He'll meet us there."

The smile on Sal's face told me exactly where we'd be heading. I couldn't help but grin back.

As we pulled out of the strip mall, I cranked up the AC, fighting a losing battle against the unseasonal heat. The dashboard thermometer read ninety-five, but it felt like a hundred and ten. Sal shifted in his seat, his face already flushed from the short walk to the car. This was what being braised felt like.

"So, Sal," I said, navigating through the West Palm Beach traffic, "Cracker Barrel, right?"

Sal's eyes lit up at the mention of his favorite restaurant. "You're not a PI for naught, huh? What can I say, kid? Those biscuits are a slice of heaven. Crispy on the outside, soft on the inside, and when you smother 'em in that gravy ..." He closed his eyes, savoring the imaginary taste.

I shook my head and suppressed a laugh. "The only other time I see you this happy is when we're at a ball game and you've got a hot dog in your hand."

"Ah, now that's living," Sal agreed, his voice wistful.

As we inched forward in the congested traffic, I couldn't help but smile at Sal's simple pleasures. Here was a man who'd seen it all, done it all, some of it pretty ugly, and yet he found joy in the most basic things—mass-produced biscuits and processed meat inside ultra-processed bread at the game.

The car's AC struggled, barely keeping up with the sweltering heat outside. The west side of West Palm was a good ten or fifteen degrees hotter than Palm Beach, where the cooling ocean breeze made life bearable. Sweat beaded on my forehead as I leaned forward, trying to catch some of the cool air. Sal didn't seem to notice, lost in his culinary daydreams.

"You know," he mused, "I've been thinking about asking the guys at Cracker Barrel if they'd consider adding hot dogs to the menu. Imagine it—their biscuits, but as hot dog buns."

I laughed, picturing Sal's ideal meal. "I'm not sure that's going to fly with their whole Southern country kitchen theme, Sal."

"Add pimentos, I don't know." He shrugged, undeterred. "A man can dream, can't he?"

We finally reached the restaurant off the freeway, and I dropped Sal at the door, then went and found a spot. As we crossed the porch lined with rocking chairs and walked through the county store, the smell of homestyle cooking hit me. I spotted a young man waving us over to a table. He stood as we approached.

He was tall and lean, with an athletic build that spoke of regular gym visits. His dark skin contrasted sharply with a crisp white dress shirt, and he wore a pair of stylish glasses that made him look like a college professor. His smile was warm and genuine as he extended his hand.

"Miami, this is Treyvon Ellis," Sal said, his gruff voice tinged with pride. "Trey, meet Miami Jones." We shook hands, and Sally watched liked a proud father. "Trey owns his own security consultancy."

As we settled into our seats, I found myself wondering about Trey's journey. How many others like him had Sal guided over the years? The old man's gruff exterior hid a heart of gold, and his impact on the community was far greater than most people realized. Here was another success story, one of many. From brushes with the law to a successful consultant—it was impressive.

The waitress approached, notepad in hand. "What can I get for you, gentlemen?"

"I'll just have an iced tea," I said, patting my stomach. "Already ate."

Sal frowned and swept sweat and the solitary hair across his head. "Sweet tea with biscuits and gravy for me, sweetheart. And keep 'em coming."

Trey glanced at the menu before deciding. "I'll have the chopped salad with grilled chicken, please. I'll do an iced tea, too. Unsweetened."

As we waited for our food to arrive, I leaned in and explained that I was an investigator. "So, I've got this case I'm working on. Over in Palm Beach, at the Kazarian estate."

Sal's eyebrows shot up. "The fashion mogul?"

I nodded, surprised Sal knew the name, but then not surprised at the same time. "That's him. Someone stole their prized Afghan Hound from its doghouse in their backyard."

Trey's eyebrow flattened. "A dog? Serious? People hire investigators for stuff like that?"

"You don't know the half of it," I said. "But the security system they have in place? It just cut out. Right when the dog was taken."

Trey leaned forward with a focused expression. "Cut out how?"

I described what I'd seen in the security footage. "It was working fine, then suddenly, nothing. When it came back on, the dog was gone."

Trey's brow furrowed. "That's not normal behavior for a security system. What kind of setup do they have?"

I pulled out my phone, scrolling through my photos. "I managed to snap a picture of their security hub. Maybe you can make something of it."

I found the image and slid the phone across the table to Trey.

He picked it up, studying it intently. His eyes widened as he zoomed in on certain parts of the image.

"This is a Wi-Fi-based system," he said, looking up at me. "Pretty high-end, but still vulnerable."

"Vulnerable, how?" I prompted.

Trey pushed his glasses up on his nose. "These systems, they're convenient, plug and play, but they have a major flaw. They rely on a constant connection to the cloud to send camera data and to store footage. If that connection is interrupted, then you get nothing."

"The footage disappears," I finished, starting to see where this was going.

"Does footage that isn't actually recorded need to disappear?" Trey said.

"That's too deep for me."

The server dropped off our drinks. "So, how do you interrupt this connection? Just turn off the internet router?"

Trey shook his head. "They could, but that's amateur hour. The logs would show the router went down. There's a much sneakier way. Even with a Wi-Fi system, the hub and the router are often connected with an ethernet cable. It's between the camera and the hub where the real vulnerability lies." He held up his hands, palms facing each other. "Imagine this is the signal between the camera and the hub." He wiggled his fingers. "It's constantly communicating, sending data back and forth."

Then he stood the menu up between his hands, like a wall. "Now, introduce a jammer." He tapped his hands back and forth into the menu, mimicking interference. "It floods the area with noise on the same frequency the system uses. The camera can't talk to the hub anymore."

I frowned. "And that's it? The system's down?"

"Not down, just blind." Trey nodded. "The camera works, but it just can't send the images anywhere. When the jammer's turned off, the system comes back online like nothing happened."

"And what did you say does this? A jammer?"

"That's right."

"How much would something like that cost?" I asked.

Trey sipped his tea. "That's the kicker. You can pick up a decent jammer for about twenty bucks online. It's not exactly high-tech stuff."

I sat back, processing this. A twenty-dollar device could take down a so-called high-end security system. It seemed almost too easy.

"So anyone with basic tech knowledge and a few bucks could pull this off?" I mused.

Trey nodded. "Pretty much."

As our food arrived, Trey continued his tech talk, his words almost drowned out by the clatter of plates and the chatter of diners.

"Hardwired systems are the gold standard," Trey explained, pausing to take a bite of his salad. "They're not susceptible to jammers like Wi-Fi setups. Plus, with local recording and cloud backup, you've got redundancy."

I nodded, sipping my iced tea. "Sounds foolproof."

Trey shrugged. "Nothing's foolproof, but it's as close as you can get. But here's the rub: they cost more. Sometimes, way more. And folks, even rich ones, can be surprisingly cheap when it comes to security."

As Sal dug into his biscuits and gravy with gusto, I mulled over what Trey was telling me. It was an early piece of the puzzle, and I wasn't sure where it fit yet.

When the check came, I snatched it up before either of them could protest. "My treat, gentlemen. Consider it payment for the education."

Sal grumbled something that sounded like thanks through a mouthful of biscuit, while Trey nodded appreciatively.

We made our way to the parking lot and stood sweating as we said our goodbyes. Trey headed off to his car with a wave while I helped Sal into mine.

As we drove back to his shop, Sal contentedly patted his stomach. "Won't need to eat for a week," he said, a rare smile creasing his weathered face.

I nodded absently, my mind still churning over what Trey had told me. The ease with which someone could disable a Wi-Fi security system was troubling. And it didn't answer the one nagging question: How did you get a huge dog out of a gated Palm Beach compound without being seen by anyone?

CHAPTER SEVEN

I PULLED INTO THE PARKING LOT NEAR MY OFFICE BUILDING, THE midafternoon sun glinting off the windshield. My preferred lot had become another building, so I walked along Banyan and into the small foyer. A group that worked at some marketing firm with a name so ridiculous it could only have been developed by a committee waited for the elevator. I took the stairs. It was those little bursts of energy use that kept Danielle from implementing a lettuce and water diet.

Lizzy looked up from her computer, her black hair framing her face like a curtain. She'd toned down the goth look over the years, but the vermilion lipstick remained her signature. Her eyes lit up as I entered, a sure sign she'd found something interesting.

"You've got to see this," she said, waving me over. "I've been digging around online and found a news report in the *Palm Beach Post*. It's about a young girl whose dog was stolen."

I leaned over her shoulder, scanning the article on her screen. "Are you kidding me? Another one?"

Lizzy pulled up the article. "It says that the girl has shown her French Bulldog, Gaston, at local dog shows."

I straightened up, surprised. "Dog shows? Huh. What the hell—"

"Miami!"

"What the *heck* is going on? A serial dog napper? Is that even a thing?"

"Dog napper? I think so."

"Sounds like someone sleeping against a Labrador's belly."

"It's a word."

"If you say so. Where does this girl live?"

"Riviera Beach," Lizzy replied, a hint of triumph in her voice. "Just down the road. And get this—I used the mother's name from the article to search our databases. I've got you an address."

I glanced at my watch, remembering my commitment to Danielle and our soon-to-arrive foster kid. "Nice work, Lizzy."

"Don't forget you need to be home by six."

"You know about that?"

"Danielle asked me to make sure you remembered."

"Oh, ye of little faith."

"Hardly, *Mr. Jones*. She's just nervous, is all. She wants this, you know that. Maybe it's more than that. Maybe she needs it. But she wants it to go well. That's all."

"I know."

"Do you?"

I nodded. "It's Riviera Beach. I can swing by there on my way home."

Lizzy nodded, already printing out the address for me. As she handed me the paper, I offered my silent thanks. Without her, this office would fall apart in a week. If that.

I took the long way around the lake, cruising past the Cracker Barrel where I'd just had lunch with Sal and Trey. I ignored my homing beacon that beckoned me onto Blue Heron Boulevard and headed onto North Military Trail.

The trailer park appeared on my right, a far cry from the opulent estates of Palm Beach. Despite its modest nature, the place was well-maintained, dotted with a mix of RV spaces for snow-birds and semi-permanent manufactured homes.

As I drove through the park, I took in the surroundings. A

community center stood near the entrance, its faded sign advertising bingo nights and potlucks. Kids milled around in a playground, the equipment too hot to touch.

Near the center of the park, a kidney-shaped pool sparkled in the afternoon sun. A few retirees lounged on plastic chairs, sipping iced tea and more. Further back, I spotted a man-made lagoon, a faux waterfront that probably looked better in the brochure than in person.

I followed the winding road to the back of the park, where I found the Marshall residence. It was a single-wide unit, blue paint washed out by years of sun and rain. A tiny porch jutted out from the side, barely big enough for a chair or two, and a concrete pad stretched out under an aluminum carport, probably the coolest spot in the whole setup. Away from the lagoon and the pool area, it was quiet, only the distant hum of traffic from Military Trail breaking the silence.

As I parked and stepped out of my car, I paused for a moment. This place was only a fifteen-minute drive from my home on Singer Island, but it might as well have been on another planet. My basic rancher was hardly palatial, but the contrast was still stark.

I knocked on the door, the hollow sound echoing through the thin walls of the trailer. After a moment, it swung open, revealing a young girl with long, wavy chestnut hair and bright hazel eyes. She looked about fourteen, dressed in a floral top and jeans, her expression a mix of curiosity and caution.

"Hi there," I said, flashing my most reassuring smile. "Is your mom home?"

The girl shook her head. "She's at work."

"What about your dad?"

"No," she replied, her voice firm.

I frowned, concern creeping into my voice. "Should you be answering the door if you're alone?"

She cocked an eyebrow, a hint of sass in her tone. "You'd rather stand on the porch all day?"

I smiled. The kid had spunk. "Fair point. I'm Miami Jones," I paused before asking, "Are you Sophie?"

"Yes," she said, her eyes narrowing again.

"Did you lose your dog?"

Her face brightened immediately. "You found Gaston?"

I shook my head. "No, I'm afraid not."

Her soft features dropped once more. She was a rollercoaster of expression.

"Can I ask you about Gaston?"

Her face clouded with suspicion. "Why?"

"I'm an investigator. I'm looking into a missing dog case," I explained. "I heard about yours and thought there might be a connection."

She hesitated for a moment, then pointed to the carport. "We can sit here."

We settled into plastic chairs on the small concrete slab, the aluminum awning providing welcome shade.

"You want to tell me about what happened to Gaston?"

"He went missing while I was at school. He was here when I left and gone when I got home."

"Is there a chance he could have run away?" I asked.

Sophie shot me a look that could wither plants. "He's a Frenchie, not Curious George. Gassy doesn't *run away*."

"Okay," I said. "The paper said you show him?"

Sophie's eyes lit up. "He's loves it. He's a total show pony."

"Do you have a handler?"

Once again, the expression fell toward the ground. "Of course not. I show him myself."

"You do? That's awesome."

"Wait here," she said, jumping up from her chair. She disappeared into the trailer, returning moments later with a framed photograph. She handed it to me carefully, as if passing over a priceless artifact.

The photo showed Sophie, beaming with pride, on one knee next to a stocky French Bulldog. Gaston's coat was a striking brindle pattern, his bat-like ears perked up attentively. He wore a red ribbon around his neck.

"This was from our first podium. Second place," Sophie explained. "In Wellington."

I nodded, impressed, but my eyes were drawn to the text beneath the photo. It listed Gaston's full pedigree name: *Gaston de la Côte d'Azur.*

"That's quite a mouthful," I said. "Where do they come up with these names?"

Sophie shrugged. "All pedigrees have these funny names. Henry named him. Something about French elegance and the Riviera."

"Who's Henry?"

"He's a breeder and a show handler, like me. He gave me Gassy when one of his dogs had a litter."

I handed the photo back to her. "Did people in the park here know about Gaston?"

"Of course," Sophie replied, as if it were the most obvious thing in the world. "I walk him every day. Well, I used to." Her face fell.

I leaned forward, resting my elbows on my knees. "Sophie, have you noticed anyone who might want to take Gaston? Maybe someone watching you walk him around here?"

She shook her head. "Not really."

"What about at dog shows? Anyone pay particular attention to him?"

She shook her again, then paused. "Well, there was Vicki."

"Vicki?"

"Victoria," Sophie clarified. "She was yelling some crazy stuff at a dog show, but that was ages ago." She waved her hand dismissively. "And she wouldn't take Gassy. She doesn't even like dogs."

I glanced at my watch and got a cold shiver. I was sitting out here chatting with one teenage girl and needed to be at home to receive a different one.

"Where does your mom work, Sophie?"

She tilted her head like she didn't understand. "When?"

"What do you mean, *when*?"

"Mom has a bunch of jobs," Sophie explained.

"Okay, where does she work most of the time?"

"Mostly, Smokes and Things. But there's a bunch."

Sophie rattled off a list of her mother's various employments. I jotted them down in my notebook, impressed by Amanda Marshall's work ethic.

After a moment, Sophie's curiosity got the better of her. "Whose dog are you looking for, anyway?"

I hesitated, then decided honesty might be the best policy. "It's an Afghan Hound named Layla. She belongs to the Kazarians."

Sophie's eyes widened. "Oh, I know her! Pixie's dog. She's beautiful."

I nodded, reaching into my pocket for a business card. "Listen, Sophie, if you hear anything about Gaston or Layla, give me a call, okay?" I handed her the card. "Any information could be helpful."

She took the card, examining it closely before tucking it into her pocket. "I will, Mr. Jones. Thanks for listening about Gaston."

"No. Thank you."

"I'm sorry for Pixie. I hope you find Layla. It sucks when you lose someone you love."

I walked out to my car and glanced back. Sophie had gone back inside. I climbed in my SUV thinking how it did indeed suck when you lost someone you loved, and how that feeling shouldn't be going through a fourteen-year-old's mind.

CHAPTER EIGHT

I got home in time—I thought—but a gray Camry was already parked in the driveway. Orna's car. My stomach did a little flip at the thought I might be late. I stopped on the street, took a deep breath in through my nose and out through the mouth, and went in.

As I walked up to the front door, it swung open. Orna stood there, her large frame filling the doorway, clipboard clutched to her chest as always.

"I'm sorry I'm late," I blurted out before she could say anything.

Orna's eyebrows rose. "You're not late, Mr. Jones. We're early."

"Oh, good. I mean, welcome."

I followed Orna inside, where a young girl stood waiting. "This is Bella," Orna said.

I took in the sight of our temporary foster child. Bella had curly blonde hair that fell to her shoulders. Her bright blue eyes darted around, taking in everything. She wore paint-splattered jeans and an oversized sweater with a unique pattern that looked like graffiti. A worn-out notebook was clutched tightly in her hands.

What struck me most was her expression. Bella's face was set like concrete, as if she'd rather be anywhere else but here. I got that. I was uncomfortable, and I was in my own home.

"Hi, Bella," I said, trying to sound welcoming. "I'm Miami."

She nodded slightly but didn't say anything. The silence stretched between us, growing more awkward by the second. I searched for something to say, anything we might have in common, but came up blank.

"So, uh, do you like sports?" I asked lamely, immediately regretting the question.

Bella shook her head, her eyes dropping to her notebook.

"Right, okay," I mumbled, looking to Orna for help. Then I remembered what I hadn't done. "Do I need to put up the pool fence?"

Orna glanced at Bella, then back at me. "Bella can swim, but …" She trailed off, her eyes darting around as if searching for something.

"But what?"

"Well, I'm not so sure about the dog," she finished.

My mouth dropped open. *The dog?*

Bella's eyes widened, the first real reaction I'd seen from her.

Orna nodded, her clipboard bobbing with the motion. "Yes, Bella has a dog. It's part of the package deal. Danielle said you were okay with that."

Danielle stepped out of the kitchen and offered me a wrinkle of her shoulders and that little half smile that always got me. She handed a glass of ice water to Bella.

"Right," Orna continued, seemingly oblivious. I wasn't so sure. Oblivious might have just suited her purpose. "Well, I'll leave you to get settled. Call if there's any problem." She stepped around me to the door, then stopped and put her hand on my shoulder. "The first time's the scariest."

"We've done this before," I said. "It feels worse this time."

"Consider that a practice run, which you got through successfully." Orna tapped my shoulder like I was a toddler, then she was out the door, leaving us in stunned silence.

As the door clicked shut, I turned back to Danielle, my eyebrows raised. "The dog?" I mouthed silently.

Now Danielle gave me a full-blown smile. She turned to Bella, who was watching our silent exchange with a hint of amusement in her eyes.

"Bella," Danielle said gently, "what is your dog's name?"

Bella's posture relaxed. "Argos," she said, her voice soft but clear.

"He's in the backyard," Danielle said to one or both of us. "Bella, why don't you tell Miami about him while he puts up the safety fence?"

I nodded and headed for the back door. Bella followed, glass in hand. She waited on the patio while I hefted the mesh safety fence from its spot in the garage, grateful for Sal's foresight in having his guys lay the concrete mounting points. The late sun dropped low across the Intracoastal as I dragged the folded fence across the patio.

"What's that for?" Bella asked, her eyes following my movements. Argos sat at her feet, his mismatched eyes watching me warily.

"Safety fence," I grunted, unfolding the first section. "Gotta keep you two away from the water."

Bella's brow furrowed. "But you don't have a pool."

I secured the first panel. "A point I have made before, but we've got the Intracoastal right there." I nodded towards the glittering water beyond our yard. "Orna insists on the fence."

As I worked my way across the patio, Bella watched, absently scratching Argos behind the ears. "You done this much?" she asked.

"What's that?"

"Fostering?"

I stopped and glanced at her. "We did look after one little girl in an emergency, but officially you're the first."

"Noob. It shows."

"It does?"

"You're not super organized."

I noted she'd gotten chattier. Maybe she thought she had the upper hand in the situation, or maybe she was just more comfortable in the company of her dog.

"You got any tips?" I said, continuing with the fence.

"Not so far."

"Well, let me know. I'm always eager to learn."

She nodded and ruffled the dog's head.

I pulled the next fence section into place. "What's the story with your dog?"

"Argos is a mix," she said, taking a sip of her water but not dropping her eyes from me. "Like me, he's a mutt."

I glanced at the dog, noting his long body and bulging eyes. "What kind of mix?"

"Chiweenie," Bella replied. "Part chihuahua, part dachshund. But really, we don't know for sure. He's just Argos."

I nodded, wrestling with a particularly stubborn section of fence. "Nothing wrong with being a mutt." I stuck one of the fence poles into its predrilled hole in the concrete. "Best people I know are mutts."

Bella nodded, a small smile playing at the corners of her mouth. "Yeah, we're both one of a kind."

As I secured the last panel, I made a mental note to call Sal's guys about paying for the fence. They'd waved off payment on the proviso that I returned it after our first foster situation ended and the little girl went home. It looked like we'd be keeping it.

I wiped my brow, satisfied with the newly erected barrier, then ushered Bella and Argos inside. I wandered around the edge of the living room toward the bathroom—force of habit. When I had bought the house, it had an original 70s sunken living room, complete with shag carpet. A hurricane had later flooded the house, and in the rebuild, the sunken living space was raised, but I still navigated around rather than through where it had been, like it was sacred ground.

Bella followed me down the hall into her bedroom. I figured

Danielle and Orna had already given her the tour—it was hardly the Met. I washed my hands, then stopped by Bella's open door. She was creating a cozy spot for Argos near her bed. She fluffed a small blanket and put it in the plush doggie bed.

"You've got this down to a science," I remarked.

Bella shrugged. "It's not my first rodeo."

We wandered back out. The aroma of tomato and herbs wafted from the kitchen, where Danielle was busy preparing dinner. I caught her eye.

"Pasta bolognese," she said.

I opened the fridge and grabbed some iced tea, and took two glasses out. Then I went back for a third.

"Orna's recommendation," Danielle explained, stirring the sauce. "Apparently, it's a hit with most kids."

I nodded. Who didn't love spaghetti? After steak, it was the number one dinner of choice for baseball players the country over. As I poured tea, Bella appeared in the kitchen doorway.

"Can I help?" she asked, her tone cautious but willing.

Danielle smiled. "Sure. You can set the table if you'd like."

As Bella moved around the dining table, I noticed Argos padding into the living room. He hopped onto the sofa, his eyes never leaving Bella as she worked.

"Is it okay for him to be up there?" Bella asked, pausing mid-task.

Danielle glanced over. "Of course, it's fine. He looks comfortable."

Bella nodded, visibly relaxing. "Thanks. He likes to keep an eye on me."

"Dinner's almost ready," Danielle announced. "Why don't you wash up, Bella?"

Without argument, Bella headed to the bathroom. The sound of running water followed, and I had to hand it to her. She was handling the situation better than me. As I put the drinks on the table, it occurred that she was better at it because she had done it more than I had, and that brought a crease to my already wrinkled brow.

As we gathered around the table, the rich aroma of the sauce filling the air, I caught Danielle's eye. She gave me a small, encouraging smile. Maybe we could do this after all.

We sat down and ate. Pasta and garlic bread took everyone somewhere different. It sent me back to New Haven. Connecticut wasn't exactly Little Italy—most of the diners in our area were Greek—but my mother had come by a variation in *The Joy of Cooking,* which she called spaghetti with meat sauce. The garlic bread had been store-bought, and the cheese came from a little green container and smelled like a ballpark locker room. I'd eaten higher-quality food since, but I'd rarely had a better meal.

Bella sipped her tea and made a face, then took another sip and looked at me. "Why don't you have a dog?"

I twirled pasta onto my fork, buying time to formulate a response to Bella's question. "It's a big responsibility," I said finally, hoping that would suffice.

Bella nodded, seeming to accept my answer. But before I could relax, she hit me with another curveball.

"Why don't you have a kid? Are you infertile?"

I nearly choked on my mouthful of spaghetti. My eyes darted across the table to Danielle, who had frozen mid-bite, her expression a mix of surprise and something else I couldn't quite read.

Clearing my throat, I set my fork down. "It just didn't happen," I said, trying to keep my tone neutral. The subject was a sensitive one, and I wasn't sure how much to share with a kid we'd just met. "Why is it important?"

Bella shrugged, her eyes flicking between Danielle and me. "It's not," she said, picking up a piece of garlic bread. "It just helps to know the lay of the land."

The phrase struck me as oddly mature coming from a thirteen-year-old. I wondered how many homes she'd been in, how many times she'd had to quickly assess her new surroundings.

After we finished our meal, Danielle started clearing the plates.

I stood to help, but she waved me off with a smile. "You two chat," she said, disappearing into the kitchen.

Bella leaned back in her chair, her eyes scanning the living room. "So, no dog, no kid, no TV," she mused, ticking off each item on her fingers. "What do you guys do with your time?"

I settled into my seat with a shrug. "Well, we read a lot. And we talk. Sometimes we just sit on the patio and watch the boats go by on the Intracoastal."

Bella frowned. "That's it?"

"We work, too," I added. "I'm a private investigator, and Danielle's a cop."

Bella glanced at the kitchen with raised eyebrows. "Does she have a gun?"

"Not at home."

"But at work?"

"Yep."

"Cool."

"Not really."

She frowned. "Why?"

I leaned my elbows on the table. "Guns are serious business. Do you do shooter drills at school?"

She shrunk into her chair a little. "Yeah."

"Nothing fun about that."

"No."

"And it's the gun that's the not-fun part."

"But she's a cop."

"Which means she has to carry one, and she has to be well-trained on how and when to use it. Because using it has serious consequences."

I heard Danielle call across the kitchen island, "Maybe another topic, MJ?"

I nodded. "And we own part of a gym."

"A gym?" Bella perked up at that. "Like, with boxing and stuff?"

I nodded. "Boxing, weights, all kinds of training."

Bella seemed to mull this over, her fingers tracing patterns on the tablecloth. After a moment, she asked, "Are you a do-gooder?"

I sighed. I wasn't sure what I was. I mostly tried to do good, but I often failed. "When I was a kid, someone helped me when I really needed it. And when I was in college, someone else helped me. I guess I've never forgotten that."

"And you're a PI?"

I nodded.

"So, do you solve murders and stuff?"

"Sometimes," I replied, trying not to smile at her sudden interest. "But mostly it's less exciting things. Like finding lost pets."

"Huh?"

"I'm actually tracking down a lost dog at the moment."

"Don't people just put up posters? That's what I'd do."

"Me, too. But this is a show dog. She's worth a bit of money. And she didn't wander away. At least we don't think so."

"What happened?"

"She was stolen."

Bella glanced at Argos. His head was down, eyes heavy, and he turned an ear her way. "I don't understand people who do stuff like that."

"Me neither." Bella kept her eyes on her dog, but I saw the lids flagging. "Speaking of less exciting things, do you have any homework you need to do?"

Bella rolled her eyes. "You sound just like my mom," she groaned, pushing her chair back from the table.

"I'll take that as a yes," I said, watching as she stood up.

With a dramatic sigh, Bella headed towards her room. "Come on, Argos," she called, and the little dog trotted after her.

As they disappeared down the hallway, I heard her mutter, "It's not like there's anything else to do."

CHAPTER NINE

I spent the first half of the drive to Bella's school glancing at her in the passenger seat. She was slumped against the window, her backpack clutched to her chest like a shield. The morning was a touch cooler, and the sun glinted off her blonde curls, but her face was set in a scowl that could rival a thundercloud.

"So, uh, how'd you sleep?" I asked, trying to break the ice.

Bella shrugged, her eyes fixed on the passing scenery. "Fine, I guess."

I nodded. The silence stretched between us, thick and uncomfortable. I racked my brain for something to say, anything to break the silence.

"You like school?" I asked.

"Yep, school. Joy," she muttered, rolling her eyes.

I sighed. "Yeah, that's what I thought, too."

We drove in silence for a few more minutes, the only sound the hum of the engine and the occasional honk from other morning commuters on Route 1. I couldn't help but wonder if Bella's mood was just typical teenage angst or something more. Was she tired? Stressed about being away from home? I thought about asking about her mom but quickly decided against it.

Instead, I steered the conversation to safer waters. "So, tell me more about Argos," I said, glancing at her. "He seems like a cool dog."

For the first time since we'd left the house, Bella's expression softened. "He is," she said, a hint of pride in her voice. "He's the best."

"How long have you had him?"

"Three years," Bella replied, her fingers absently tracing patterns on her backpack. "He was a rescue. Nobody wanted him because he was all scrawny and had a weird eye."

"But you saw something in him?"

A small smile tugged at the corners of her mouth. "Yeah, I guess. He just… He needed someone, you know?"

The vulnerability in her voice was palpable. I cleared my throat, trying to keep the conversation light. "Well, you two make a great team. Though I gotta ask, where'd the name Argos come from?"

Bella sat up a little straighter, her eyes lighting up with interest. "You don't know the story of Argos?"

I shook my head. "Can't say that I do."

"Okay, so there's this guy Odysseus, right? He's, like, super important in Greece. He goes off to fight in this big war, the Trojan War, and he's gone for, like, twenty years. Can you imagine? Twenty whole years!"

I shook my head.

"So anyway, he finally makes it back home, but he can't just waltz in because there are all these jerks trying to marry his wife and take over his stuff. So he has to sneak in disguised as this old beggar dude." Bella's hands started moving animatedly as she got more into the story. "Now here's where Argos comes in. Odysseus had this dog when he left, just a puppy. But now Argos is super old, like ancient. He's been waiting for Odysseus this whole time, right? And he's the only one who recognizes him, even in his beggar disguise."

Her voice softened a bit, a touch of sadness creeping in. "But Odysseus can't blow his cover, so he has to ignore Argos. And Argos, he's so old and weak, all he can do is wag his tail and drop his ears.

He doesn't even have the strength to go to his master." I glanced at Bella as she paused, her eyes downcast. "So Odysseus has to just walk by, pretending not to notice. But he, like, sheds a tear when no one's looking. And then, well, Argos just dies. Right there. Because he finally got to see his master one last time after waiting for so long."

Bella fell silent for a moment, then added quietly, "That's why I named my dog Argos. Because he waited so long at the shelter, and I wanted him to know that someone would always come back for him."

We pulled up to the school just in time. My heart was in my boat shoes. I wiped my eye without her seeing, and Bella got out. I told her one of us would be there to pick her up, and she turned and shuffled away.

My mind lingered on Bella's story about Argos the whole drive back to my office. The kid had depth, that was for sure. *The Odyssey*? I recalled it from school, but only in the most general terms. The war, the Trojan Horse, the wind blowing him away just as he got near home. I didn't know there was a dog in the story, and now it seemed like a pretty important plot point.

I parked, strode into the building, and took the stairs two at a time. As I walked into the office, Lizzy glanced up from her computer, her face contorted in concentration. Maybe she was doing one of those captcha things where you had to click on all the bicycles or the crosswalks that were designed so you always got it wrong and had to do it over and over.

"Morning, boss," she said. "How's the new houseguest?"

I dropped into the chair across from her desk. "Complicated. But aren't they all?"

Lizzy snorted, finally pausing to give me her full attention. "Who are *they*? Girls, women? Foster children with nowhere else to go?"

"Teenagers."

She grunted. "So, what happened yesterday?"

"Her name's Bella. She seems like a nice kid."

"What about her missing dog?"

"Her dog isn't missing. He was there."

"So she got it back?"

"Got what back?"

Lizzy's eyes went wide like she was going to jump over the desk and throttle me. "The dog! The paper said her dog was missing."

I nodded like my head was on a spring. "Oh, you mean the kid from *The Post*?"

"Of course, that's what I mean. What in tarnation are you talking about?"

"Tarnation?" I laughed. "Who says that?"

Lizzy leaned forward and picked something up off her desk. "Miami, I have a stapler, and I am not afraid to use it." Then she added, "On you."

"Okay, okay. Bella is the girl we're fostering. She has a dog who is not missing. But I also went to see the girl who is missing a dog. Her name was Sophie."

I filled her in on my visit to Sophie Marshall's trailer park. As I spoke, Lizzy's fingers tapped at her keyboard, no doubt pulling up any relevant information she could find.

"So, we've got two missing dogs, both with show experience," Lizzy said, her painted nails tapping her chin as she scanned the screen. "But Lenny always said—"

"Two's a coincidence, three's a pattern."

"Exactly. So, are we looking at the start of a pattern?"

"I don't know," I said. "I mean, what's the angle? Dog shows don't exactly pay out big bucks."

Lizzy shook her head. "No, but breeding rights can be worth a fortune. Especially for a champion like Layla."

I mulled it over. "Could be. Evelyn Moreau made the point that there was money in it if you didn't have to cover the costs."

"How would you not cover the costs?" Lizzy nodded. "Oh, steal the dog."

"Exactly. But why take Sophie's dog too? Gaston's not exactly Westminster material."

"I looked up French Bulldogs," she said. "They can go for up to twenty thousand a pup."

"I'm in the wrong business."

"I've been saying that for years." She gave a knowing smirk.

We bounced theories back and forth for a while, but nothing quite fit. Something was missing, something we couldn't quite see yet.

The shrill ring of the office phone cut through our chat. Lizzy reached for it, her professional mask sliding into place. "LCI, how can I—"

She stopped mid-sentence, her eyes widening. I sat up straighter, instantly alert.

"I'm sorry, can you repeat that?" Lizzy said, her voice controlled. Then she said, "Yes, ma'am, don't worry. He'll be right there."

She dropped the phone into the cradle and then looked at me, mouth open.

"What?" I asked.

"Mrs. Kazarian. She just got a ransom demand."

CHAPTER TEN

R0N'S BEAT-UP RED TOYOTA COROLLA WAS PARKED HAPHAZARDLY near the door of the Kazarians' house, looking comically out of place among the luxury vehicles that dotted the circular driveway. I pulled in behind, wondering how that car was still running after all these years.

As I approached the front door, it swung open. The butler, whose name I couldn't remember for the life of me, ushered me inside with a curt nod.

"They're in the study, sir," he said.

Making my way across the vast entrance hall, the opulence of the place hit me all over again. I could hear muffled voices as I reached the study. I pushed open the heavy oak door to find a scene of controlled chaos.

Pixie Kazarian was perched on the edge of a leather armchair, her usually immaculate appearance slightly disheveled. Ron stood nearby, glancing my way as if he had been pacing back and forth. Detective Ronzoni was there too, his suit as wrinkled as ever. Different suit, same creases. He acknowledged me with a grunt. Aram Kazarian sat at his desk, his linen suit making us all look underdone.

"What happened?" I asked, scanning the room.

Pixie's eyes locked onto mine, her composure cracking. "Oh, Miami," she said, her voice trembling. "It's terrible. Simply terrible."

Ron stepped closer, placing a comforting hand on Pixie's shoulder. "Go ahead, Pixie. Tell Miami what you told us."

Pixie took a deep breath, her manicured hands clasped tightly in her lap. "I received a call about an hour ago. A man—his voice was so cold, so emotionless." She shuddered at the memory.

I moved into the room. "What did he say?"

"He said they had Layla," Pixie continued, her voice barely above a whisper. "My precious Layla. He said they'd kill her if we didn't pay."

Aram leaned forward. "They're demanding a hundred thousand dollars. In cash."

I made my impressed face. "That's quite a sum. Did they give you any proof of life?"

Pixie nodded, reaching for her phone with shaking hands. "They sent a photo. It's Layla. I'd know her anywhere. But she looks so frightened, so alone."

She held out the phone, and I leaned in to examine the picture. Sure enough, there was the Afghan Hound, her usually luxurious coat looking a touch matted but no worse than my hair after a big night out. The background was nondescript—it could have been a garage or a dungeon or backstage at the old Burt Reynolds theater.

"Did they give you a deadline?" I asked, handing the phone back.

"This afternoon," Aram replied, his voice tight with tension. "They said they'd contact us with drop-off instructions."

Ronzoni cleared his throat. "Mr. and Mrs. Kazarian, I must advise against paying the ransom. We have protocols for these situations—"

"Protocols?" Pixie interrupted, her voice rising. "This isn't some corporate takeover, Detective. This is Layla. She's family."

I held up a hand, trying to defuse the tension. "Did the caller say anything else? Anything that might give us a clue about who they are or where they're keeping Layla?"

Pixie shook her head, dabbing at her eyes with a mono-grammed handkerchief. "No, nothing. He was very efficient. The call lasted less than thirty seconds."

"And you're sure it was a man?" I pressed.

"Yes." Pixie nodded firmly. "His voice was deep, gravelly. Like he smoked too much."

I turned to Ronzoni. "Any luck tracing the call?"

The detective shook his head. "Burner phone. Untraceable."

"So what now?"

"Now we wait."

We waited in the study. I glanced at my watch, noting that an hour had crawled by. The tension in the room was palpable, like a thick fog settling over us all. Pixie hadn't moved from her perch on the armchair, her eyes fixed on her phone as if willing it to ring again. Aram paced tight laps behind his desk, hands behind his back.

Ronzoni cleared his throat, breaking the silence. "I need to step out, make some calls," he said, his voice gruff. "If we're going through with this, I'll need backup."

I nodded, watching as he lumbered out of the study. The door clicked shut behind him, leaving us in a momentary vacuum of silence.

My mind drifted to the logistics of the ransom. A hundred grand was no small change, even for folks like the Kazarians. I turned to Aram, who had paused his pacing to stare out the window.

"Mr. Kazarian," I said, keeping my voice low. "I hate to ask, but can you cover that kind of dough that quickly?"

"Of course," he said without hesitation. "I have a safe. It won't be a problem."

I tried not to let my surprise show. A hundred grand just sitting in a safe? Must be nice. My mind flashed to the measly fifty bucks I kept stashed in an old cookie jar at home, hidden behind the good china we never used. Different worlds, indeed.

Ronzoni stepped back into the study and made his way over to me. "Anything happen while I was gone?"

I shook my head. "All quiet on the western front, Detective."

He grunted, then fixed me with a look. "Jones, are you going to be a problem?"

I held up my hands. "This is your show, Detective. Ron and I are at your disposal."

Ronzoni nodded, a flicker of appreciation crossing his face.

The tense silence was shattered by the ring of Pixie's phone. She jumped, fumbling with it before answering and putting it on speaker.

A deep voice, almost robotic in its flatness, filled the room. "Listen carefully. Mr. Kazarian will drop the cash alone. No cops, no funny business. Or the dog dies." The voice explained the nature of the drop-off, then reiterated the *no cops* thing.

Ronzoni made a frantic hand gesture at Pixie to keep the call going. She swallowed hard before speaking. "We... We need more time. Please."

There was a pause, then the voice returned, cold and uncompromising. "Don't let your dog die."

The line went dead.

CHAPTER ELEVEN

I sat at a picnic table under the shade of sprawling oak trees, my eyes scanning the Meyer Amphitheater across the way. The park stretched out before me, a green oasis in the heart of West Palm Beach. The amphitheater's curved white roof gleamed in the midday sun, the grass at the base of the stage empty save for a few pigeons pecking at discarded crumbs.

To my left, EB Bradley's outdoor seating area buzzed with the chatter of lunch patrons, oblivious to the tension hanging in the air. I took a swig from my water bottle, trying to look casual while keeping an eye on the surroundings.

Detective Annabelle Faust sat beside me. She was reading something on her phone as she ate a chopped salad from a clamshell container. When we learned the location of the drop, Ronzoni knew he had a problem. Palm Beach was his turf, but the park was in West Palm—off the island and most definitely not part of his world. Technically, the West Palm Police looked after the city, but given the cross-jurisdictional turn things had taken, he begrudgingly decided to call in the county sheriff. I suggested that I knew someone in the sheriff's office who would be happy to stand back and let Ronzoni take the lead.

Happy might have been overstating it, but Detective Faust was nothing if not a pragmatist, and she wasn't going to take over an investigation—or the associated paperwork—without good reason.

She paused with a wad of lettuce on the end of her bamboo fork and spoke in her southern drawl. "Is that guy serious?"

"Ronzoni? Yeah, he's something."

I had to smile. Ronzoni stood out like a sore thumb on Flagler Drive, standing in the shade of a palm tree, his wrinkled suit and stiff posture screaming *cop on a stakeout*.

"He might as well be holding a sign saying *nothing to see here, folks*," Faust said.

I shook my head, wondering how many passersby had already pegged him for law enforcement.

"You really do get all the big cases, don't you?" She shoved the lettuce into her mouth. It looked like way too much green to me.

"I like this better than murder. Less at stake."

"You don't own a dog, huh?"

"Why do you say that?"

"If you did, you'd understand that the stakes are higher. Plenty of people mourn their pets more than their spouses."

I glanced toward a nondescript van parked on Narcissus Street, its tinted windows hiding what I knew to be a team of officers ready to spring into action. Ron was somewhere on the far side of the amphitheater, out of my line of sight, but hopefully blending in better than Ronzoni.

As I watched the scene, a nagging feeling gnawed at my gut. This setup was too obvious, too by-the-book. If our perp had any street smarts at all, they'd smell this trap from a mile away. I couldn't shake the feeling that we were wasting our time, that Layla's kidnapper was probably watching us right now, laughing at our clumsy attempt at a sting.

Something else was eating at me. The extortionist knew the Kazarians. I was sure of it. The fact that they had given so little time to get so much money suggested they knew Aram would have access to a large amount of cash. It didn't take Sherlock to know they were rich—the unemployment line on Palm Beach was a short one—but that didn't necessarily translate to cash on hand. It might have involved a trip to a bank vault or deposit box, but the caller had left no time for that.

But the short time frame was good strategy. It gave Ronzoni little time to arrange his crew, and the whole thing felt slapdash on our side. Ronzoni had been able to get a trace on the call—it had bounced off a cell tower on a building in Fern Street, just a hundred yards or so from where I now sat, which told us nothing.

I scanned the faces in the park, looking for anyone who seemed out of place or too interested in our little operation. But all I saw were joggers, families with strollers, and office workers enjoying their lunch break in the cooling breeze coming in off the Intracoastal.

I watched as Aram appeared from behind the amphitheater, walking along Narcissus Street with the gym bag full of money clutched tightly in his hand. I had assumed his safe to be in his study, but he had left us all in the office while he disappeared and returned with the gym bag of cash ready to go. Given the size of his house, he probably had an actual vault in the basement.

His gait was stiff, his shoulders tense as he approached the designated drop point. Even from this distance, I could see the nervous energy radiating off him. It was like watching a first-time actor stumble onto a Broadway stage—all wooden movements and no finesse.

He stopped by a trash can beside the amphitheater, his eyes darting around like a squirrel in a dog park. I could see the conflict on his face, even from my distant vantage point. It was as if he was mentally wrestling with himself, probably wondering if this whole ransom thing was such a good idea after all. He reached into the gym bag and pulled out a plastic bag containing the ransom money. The sunlight glinted off the plastic, making it look like he was holding a bag full of diamonds instead of cold, hard cash.

Aram hesitated, holding the bag over the trash can. From where I sat, it looked like he was having second thoughts about parting with a hundred grand. Can't say I blamed him—that kind of dough could buy a lot of designer suits or, in my case, a lifetime supply of beer and Mick's fish dip. But this wasn't the time for cold feet.

He lowered the bag into the can, but instead of dropping it and walking away like any self-respecting ransom-payer would do, he seemed to be fussing with it. I squinted, trying to get a better view. Was he arranging the money inside the can? It looked like he was trying to place it just so, as if he was worried about the cash getting dirty. For crying out loud, it was a trash can, not a five-star hotel safe.

I shook my head, suppressing a groan that threatened to escape my lips. Unless there was a dye bomb tucked in there—which I sincerely hoped there wasn't—no extortionist would give two hoots about the condition of the trash can, or if the cash had a little discarded Tabasco sauce on it.

"What the hell is he doing?" said Faust.

I felt like I was watching a slow-motion train wreck. Part of me wanted to rush over there and show him how it was done, but that would blow our cover faster than Ronzoni rolling in with sirens blazing. All I could do was sit tight and hope Aram would wrap up his impromptu trash can interior-decorating session before our whole operation went south.

I nearly stood and applauded when Aram finally stepped away from the trash can. He walked across the grass, heading in my direction. As he passed by, I caught a whiff of his expensive cologne mingling with the scent of nervous sweat. His eyes darted around, never quite meeting mine as he strode past my picnic table.

Aram continued onto Flagler Drive, his pace quickening as he put distance between himself and the drop point. I half-expected him to break into a run, but he managed to maintain some semblance of composure as he disappeared around the corner.

With Aram gone, an eerie calm settled over the park. The lunchtime crowd at EB Bradley's continued their chatter. A jogger passed by, earbuds in, completely unaware that she'd just run past a hundred grand sitting in a trash can.

I leaned back and stretched, trying to look casual while keeping my eyes peeled for any suspicious movement. Faust kept eating, but her eyes were everywhere. Ronzoni remained rooted to his spot, looking more like a statue than a detective. The van on Narcissus Street hadn't budged an inch.

Minutes ticked by. The sun inched higher in the sky, beating down on the amphitheater's white roof. A pair of pigeons squabbled over a discarded sandwich crust near the stage, their cooing the only sound breaking the silence.

I sipped my water, feeling sweat bead on my forehead. A gentle breeze rustled the leaves of the palm trees above me, offering relief from the heat. But the cooling effect did nothing to ease the knot of tension in my gut. The wait was excruciating. Every person who walked near the trash can sent a jolt of anticipation through me, only to fizzle out as they passed by without a second glance.

As I sat there, the sweat trickling down my back, a figure caught my eye. A man shuffled along the street, his stride unsteady and purposeless. At first glance, he looked like just another of West Palm's down-and-out crowd, the kind you'd expect to see panhandling near the Brightline station.

His clothes were a mishmash of castoffs—a faded Florida shirt hung loosely over stained khakis, both several sizes too big. A ratty baseball cap sat askew on his head, greasy hair poking out from underneath. His beard was unkempt, peppered with gray, and his skin had the leathery look of someone who'd spent too many years under the Florida sun.

As he approached the trash can, his movements changed. He started glancing around, his head swiveling like a rusty weathervane. It was the kind of obvious surveillance that would make even a rookie cop take a second look.

My muscles tensed as I watched him reach into the trash can. His grimy hand emerged clutching the plastic bag Aram had so carefully placed. Without missing a beat, he turned and shuffled off, rounding the corner of the amphitheater stage.

I held my breath, waiting for Ronzoni and his team to spring into action.

But nothing happened. The man disappeared from view, heading in the opposite direction from where Aram had gone.

Then all hell broke loose.

Ronzoni burst into action, moving faster than a garlic bulb in a suit had any right to move. He sprinted across the grass, his tie flapping over his shoulder like a disheveled superhero cape. The van on Narcissus roared to life, tires screeching as it peeled out along the street.

I pushed myself up from the picnic table, and Faust did the same, wiping her hands on a tiny napkin. I ambled across the grass with a mixture of curiosity and disbelief. How could our perp be so bad at this? It was like watching a Three Stooges routine play out in real time.

By the time we reached the scene, Ronzoni had the guy pinned against the amphitheater wall. The detective's face was red. Whether from exertion or frustration, I couldn't tell.

"Got you, you dirtbag," Ronzoni growled, fumbling with his handcuffs.

Faust dropped an eyebrow at me, I was sure in response to the "dirtbag" remark. Ronzoni was nothing if not a caricature.

Ronzoni yanked the plastic bag from the man's grimy hands. With a triumphant grin, he reached inside, no doubt expecting to pull out a stack of crisp hundreds.

Instead, what emerged was a deli container. The look on Ronzoni's face was priceless as he stared at the roasted chicken inside, his mouth opening and closing like a guppy out of water.

"What the ... What is this?" Ronzoni sputtered.

I turned back to the trash can, a sinking feeling in my gut. I sprinted over, reaching it before the others, and peered inside, my heart racing.

The can was a treasure trove of garbage. Crumpled napkins,

empty soda cans, half-eaten sandwiches. But there was no sign of the money. Not a single bill.

I pulled out my phone, dialing Ron's number. "Ron, did you see anyone else come by? Maybe grab something from the trash?"

"Just the guy Ronzoni nabbed." Ron's voice crackled through the speaker. "Why? What's going on?"

I looked back at Ronzoni, still holding the container of roasted chicken, his face twisted in confusion. "We've got a problem," I said into the phone. "A big one."

I watched as Ronzoni led the disheveled man to a nearby picnic table. The detective's face was a mix of frustration and resignation as he sat down across from our would-be extortionist. I edged closer, curious to hear what this guy had to say for himself. Faust remained mute, but her expression suggested she thought Ronzoni was the lead detective for the Keystone Kops.

Ronzoni patted the guy down, finding nothing, not even an ID, then they sat.

"All right, buddy," he began, his voice gruff. "What's your name?"

"Bernie," he said like it was a question, as if he wasn't sure.

"What were you doing in that trash can?"

Bernie blinked, his rheumy eyes darting between Ronzoni and the container of chicken sitting on the table between them. "Looking for my dinner," he mumbled, his voice rough as sandpaper.

Ronzoni's eyebrows shot up. "Your dinner? You mean this?" He pointed at the container, and the man nodded eagerly.

"Publix chicken. Best in town."

I couldn't help but smirk. Our master criminal was just a hungry homeless guy with impeccable timing.

Bernie leaned forward, his gaze fixed on the container. "You, uh, gonna eat that?"

Ronzoni sighed, pinching the bridge of his nose. "No, I'm not gonna eat it. It's evidence now."

The homeless man's face fell, and I felt sorry for him. Ronzoni called over one of his team to drive Bernie to a shelter, then he took out his wallet.

"Here," Ronzoni said, slapping a twenty-dollar bill on the table. "This officer is going to take you for a shower and a meal. I'm sure you won't stay there any longer than you have to, so keep this twenty for the next time you're hungry. And get something that hasn't been in a trash can, all right?"

The man's eyes widened at the sight of the money. He snatched it up, as if afraid Ronzoni might change his mind. "Thanks, Officer," he said, a toothless grin spreading across his face.

Ronzoni told his guy to ask the shelter if Bernie was known to them, in case they needed to track him down again. I watched the homeless man get taken away, then turned back to the container of chicken sitting on the picnic table. The smell wafting from it was pretty tempting, I had to admit.

"So, Detective," I said, nodding towards the container. "You are gonna eat that, aren't you?"

Ronzoni's lips twitched, almost forming a smile. "Nah, gotta put it in the evidence room. But it won't last long there. Our friend there didn't lie. Publix chicken is damned good."

"Ever the gourmand, Ronzoni."

"I may not know art, but I know what I like." He offered a defeated look to Faust. "Sorry to waste your time."

"Not at all, Detective. Best fun I've had all week." She winked at me. "Say hi to Danielle for me, Jonesy."

I didn't love the *Jonesy*, but I knew saying something would make it happen more often, so I just gave her a nod, and she walked away to her car.

I glanced around the park, noticing the other cops starting to disperse. The sting operation had been a bust, and now we had a bigger problem on our hands.

I turned back to Ronzoni. "So, you want to go tell Aram that he lost his money?"

Ronzoni's face hardened. "He's your client, Jones. You tell him."

I sighed. I wanted to throw it back in his face—this was his operation, after all. But I well knew Ronzoni's aversion to upsetting the locals, and this wasn't going to be a pleasant conversation. Aram had just lost a hundred grand, and we were no closer to finding Layla. I pulled out my phone, dreading the call I was about to make.

"Any ideas where the money might have gone?" I asked Ronzoni, hoping for a miracle. "I was watching Bernie with his chicken dinner."

He shrugged. "I suspect that was the plan. A diversion. The money could be anywhere by now. We'll check the cameras in the area, see if we can spot who made the pickup. Maybe we'll get lucky."

CHAPTER TWELVE

I left Detective Ronzoni to his dead ends and headed down to Okeechobee Boulevard, cruising past North Military Trail until I spotted the strip mall that Lizzy had found. The Goodwill sign loomed large, announcing itself as the anchor tenant. Every parking space was taken, which made me wonder if the thrift store was having a sale or if the Vietnamese restaurant was dishing out early bird specials.

With no spots available up front, I swung around to the back of the building. A wide expanse of blacktop stretched out before me, unmarked but spacious enough for a semi to pull a U-turn. The rear view of the strip mall was less than glamorous—a collection of unmarked doors, dumpsters, and a large roller for Goodwill deliveries. I parked my car at the back against a hurricane wire fence and stepped out, the asphalt radiating heat.

Counting the unmarked doors, I stopped at what I figured to be the back entrance to the cigarette shop. Two vehicles caught my eye on either side of the nondescript door—a sleek black BMW M-series that couldn't be more than a few weeks old, and a beat-up Honda Civic that looked like it might have been around when the Miami Dolphins were still relevant.

I walked around to the front of the strip mall, squinting against the glare. The Smokes and Things shop was wedged between a nail salon and a payday loan outfit, its windows plastered with cigarette brand logos, neon "OPEN" signs, and a collection of hookahs.

As I pushed open the door, an electronic buzz went off like I was on *Jeopardy*. The interior was dimly lit, a stark contrast to the bright day outside. Glass cases lined the walls, filled with an array of colorful vapes, pipes, and rolling papers. The unmistakable scent of tobacco hung in the air, mingling with the artificial sweetness of vape juice. It wasn't the most pleasant combination, like candy floss and beer.

Behind the counter stood a man with award-wining eyebrows. They were thick, perfectly groomed arches that seemed to have a life of their own. The irony wasn't lost on me that while his eyebrows were worthy of a shampoo commercial, his head was as smooth and shiny as a crystal ball.

"That your BMW out back?" I asked, leaning against the counter.

The eyebrows pointed down toward the bridge of his nose. "Yeah, Why?"

"Nice car."

The eyebrows flattened out again. "Sure is. Just got her last month. M5. Zero to sixty in two-point-eight seconds."

I nodded like that meant something to me, then got down to business. "I'm looking for Amanda. She around?"

The joy conveyed through his eyebrows disappeared, replaced by a suspicious frown. "Who's asking?"

"Name's Miami Jones. It's about her dog."

He grunted. "She's working."

"I can talk while she works."

Just then, a woman emerged from a back room, carrying a cardboard box. She was in her late thirties, with tired hazel eyes and unkempt brown hair. Her clothes were simple and worn—a faded T-shirt and jeans that had seen better days.

As she made her way towards a shelf, I stepped forward. "Amanda?"

She eyed me warily, her hands still gripping the cardboard box. "Yeah, that's me. What do you want?"

She said it like she got a lot of people asking after her and few reasons were good.

I introduced myself and explained I was looking into the theft of Gaston. Amanda's face remained impassive as she moved to the shelf and began stacking butane cans.

"What can you tell me about Gaston's disappearance?" I asked.

"Not much to tell," she said, her voice flat. "Dog was there one day, gone the next."

I watched her methodically arrange the cans. "Have you received any kind of ransom demand?"

Amanda snorted. "Ransom? If someone's asking me for money, they didn't do their homework very well."

I leaned against the shelves. "I spoke with Sophie at your home yesterday."

Amanda paused, her hand hovering over a can. She didn't seem particularly concerned about a stranger talking to her daughter alone, but some kids grow up faster than others. "Oh? And what did she have to say?"

"She mentioned a woman who yelled at her at a dog show. Know anything about that?"

Amanda shook her head, resuming her task. "Nope. I wasn't there. Some of us have to work for a living."

"Sophie said the woman's name was Vicki?"

Amanda's eyes flicked to mine. "Victoria McCaron. Henry's daughter."

"Henry? The man who gave Gaston to Sophie?" I asked, sensing we were getting somewhere.

"Damned dog," Amanda replied, her voice tinged with bitterness.

I raised an eyebrow. "I take it you're not a fan of Gaston?"

Amanda turned to face me, her tired eyes suddenly sharp. "Do you know how much a dog costs to keep? They eat. They crap. They cost money. The shows have entrance fees but don't pay any prize money. It's a scam, and I'm not a damned charity."

Just then, a buzzer rang. I glanced toward the door, but nobody came in. The guy behind the counter called out to Amanda, "Look after the store," before disappearing out the back.

"I'll hold back the rush," she replied. Amanda placed the last of the butane and took the empty box back behind the counter.

I followed her over and leaned on the glass by a sign telling me life would be better if I won the lottery. "Why did this Henry give your daughter a dog in the first place?"

Amanda sighed, her shoulders slumping. "Sophie's been going to those damn dog shows for years. First just to watch, then she was doing something, I don't know what. Brushing them or whatever. Didn't get paid. Anyway, the old fool thought she should have a mutt of her own."

"But Gaston isn't a mutt, is he? You can't show a mutt, can you?"

She shrugged. "I don't know, and I don't care. The kid will get over the dog soon enough. Life's tough. You gotta learn that."

Her words hung in the air, heavy with a bitterness that seemed to go beyond just the missing dog. I nodded, sensing that I wasn't going to get much more out of her. "Well, thanks for your time."

"You wanna buy something?" she said.

"I don't smoke."

"How about a lottery ticket? My boss won't be happy if you took up my time and didn't buy anything."

"I don't gamble."

"What are you, a damned saint?"

"Not even close. I just don't get any fun out of losing money."

"Tell me about it."

I bought a pack of gum and left, and I don't chew gum. I made my way out of the shop, the electronic buzz announcing my departure. When I reached the rear of the building, I noticed the owner's

BMW was still there, but there was no sign of the man himself. Maybe he'd gone back inside.

What caught my eye, though, was a van parked next to the beat-up Civic. It hadn't been there before, and it wasn't exactly inconspicuous. The windows were tinted dark, and the side of the van was adorned with a gaudy painting. The image was something else. Lightning bolts crackled across a stormy sky, and in the center stood a beefy, shirtless guy holding a sword aloft like some kind of lightning rod. It reminded me of old Meat Loaf album art, the kind that tried to cram an entire rock opera's worth of imagery onto a single canvas.

I couldn't help but smirk. The combination of machismo, power fantasies, and barely contained chaos painted on the side of a personal vehicle was some kind of statement. Somewhere out there, a psychologist was probably salivating at the chance to analyze the owner of that van.

CHAPTER THIRTEEN

That evening, we ate at Longboard Kelly's. Danielle was at ease at a table in the courtyard and Bella had never been, so she didn't care either way. But I kept glancing at the bar with a sense of displacement, like I was trying out a new fishing hole on an otherwise familiar river.

Muriel came over, her muscular arms on full display in her tank top. She fussed over Bella, asking her name and about the dog on the leash tied to the table. Bella, to her credit, answered politely but with a hint of wariness that I was starting to recognize as her default setting.

As we settled in with our drinks—iced tea for Danielle and me, a soda for Bella, a bowl of water for Argos—I began recounting the day's events. I told them about the ransom sting gone bad, how Aram had dropped off the money, only for us to find a container of roasted chicken instead.

"Wait," Bella interrupted, her eyes wide. "Someone has a hundred thousand dollars to blow on a dog?"

I nodded, realizing how absurd it sounded when put that way. "I suspect he thought the cops would get it back."

Danielle chimed in, "It's probably insured."

I frowned, feeling a bit sheepish. "Can you insure a ransom drop?"

"You can insure anything," she said, sipping her tea. "Ron will tell you, it's just a question of what the premium will be."

That got me thinking. "What about a dog? Could you insure a dog?"

"Anything, MJ. Anything."

"We've got pet insurance for Argos," said Bella.

"You do?"

"Yep. In case he gets sick. The vet recommended it when we took him in for his first checkup."

I watched Bella over the rim of my glass. I hadn't expected a foster kid to have pet insurance. Insurance sounded grounded and functional, not whatever a foster situation looked like. I decided I needed to reevaluate my theories on what the home situations of these foster kids looked like, because, as I thought about it, Bella didn't fit the mold I had created in my head. She was well clothed and well spoken. She had a nice dog bed and an iPad and a phone. All I really knew was the little Orna had told us: her mom was in rehab for a week or two.

Bella shook her head, muttering something about rich people that I chose to ignore. I continued with my story, describing the confused, homeless man and Ronzoni's frustration, and Muriel returned to take our orders. Danielle ordered us mixed salads with grilled chicken breast, and Bella got a burger and fries. I knew who got the better of that deal.

As we were halfway through our meals, a familiar face appeared in the courtyard. Sophie Marshall, the young girl I'd met at her home at the trailer park, was scanning the tables with determination.

"Sophie?" I called out, waving her over. "What are you doing here?"

She approached our table, her shoulders relaxing. "I was looking for you, Mr. Jones."

"How'd you find me?"

"I took a bus downtown to your office, but it was closed," she explained. "So I went to a lawyer's office in your building, and he said you'd probably be here. I walked over."

I glanced at Danielle, who wore a concerned expression that mirrored my own. "Where's your mom, Sophie?"

"At work." She shrugged, as if it were the most normal thing in the world for a young teenager to be wandering around downtown alone at night.

"Well, since you're here, how about some dinner?" I offered.

Sophie hesitated, her eyes darting between us and the exit. I could see the wheels turning in her head, weighing her options.

"Come on," I encouraged. "It's just dinner."

Finally, she nodded and pulled up a chair. I made quick introductions. "Sophie, this is Danielle, and this is Bella. Bella's staying with us for a bit."

Sophie's eyes lit up as she noticed Argos under the table. "Is that your dog? He's cute."

Bella beamed. "Yeah, this is Argos. He's a chiweenie."

"Part chihuahua, part dachshund. That's cool," Sophie replied, her voice softening as she reached down to pet Argos. "You're gorgeous."

I watched as the two girls began to chat, their initial hesitation melting away as they bonded over their shared love of the mutt.

As the girls talked, I caught Danielle's eye. We shared a silent conversation, both of us wondering what had brought Sophie to Longboards.

I watched as Muriel approached our table again, notepad in hand. "Anyone for another round?" she asked, her eyes lingering on Sophie.

We refreshed our drinks, and I handed Sophie a menu and prompted her to order something.

She scanned it, and I got the sense she was looking at the prices rather than the items. "I'll have a hot dog, please," she said. "And a lemonade."

"Is that all you want?" I asked.

"I'm not that hungry."

Danielle put her hand on my knee under the table to let it go, and Muriel jotted down the order and headed back to the bar.

"So, why were you looking for me?" I asked Sophie.

She reached into her backpack and pulled out a baseball. Even in the dim light of the courtyard, I could make out the signature scrawled across its surface. My eyebrows shot up in surprise.

"Is that—" I started, but Sophie nodded before I could finish.

"It's signed by Miguel Cabrera," she confirmed, holding it out for me to see.

Bella leaned in, curiosity etched on her face. "Who's Miguel Cabrera?"

I couldn't help but smile. "Only one of the greatest players to ever wear a Marlins uniform. He was a key part of their 2003 World Series win, and he went on to become one of the best hitters in the game. Triple Crown winner, multiple batting titles, the list goes on."

Sophie nodded along as I spoke, clearly familiar with Cabrera's accolades.

"Where did you get this?" I asked, examining the ball.

"It was my dad's," Sophie replied, her voice softening.

I handed the ball back to her, noting the care with which she held it. "And why did you bring it to me?"

Sophie looked me straight in the eye. "As payment."

I blinked, caught off guard. "Payment? For what?"

"To find Gassy," she said, her voice firm and determined. "You like baseball, don't you? I thought maybe you'd take this in exchange for helping me find him."

I watched as Sophie held the baseball, her fingers tracing the signature.

"Who's Gassy?" Bella asked, glancing between Sophie and me.

Sophie's expression tightened. "Gaston. He's my dog. He was stolen."

Bella's eyes widened. "Stolen? Are you serious? That's totes lame. Miami, you have to help her!"

I sighed. "I'm already working on a case—"

"What, so only rich people get help from you?" Bella cut in, her tone sharp.

I was taken aback by the philosophical depth of her question. That was going to keep me awake at night. I glanced at Danielle who seemed to be enjoying the exchange.

"What I mean is," I clarified, choosing my words carefully, "I'm already looking for a missing dog. So, while I'm asking around about that one, I can keep an ear out for Gaston too."

Both girls' faces lit up at this compromise.

Sophie thrust the baseball towards me again. "Here, take it."

I shook my head, gently pushing her hand back. "Keep it, Sophie. It was your dad's."

"My dad's gone," she said, her voice flat.

"All the more reason to hold onto it," I insisted.

Bella's gaze shifted to Sophie. "Your dad's gone?"

Sophie nodded. "Yeah. Left when I was little."

"That's busted." Bella's face dropped. "Mine's gone too."

"Sorry. When did he leave?"

"He died," Bella replied, her voice quiet. "Eighteen months ago."

"That sucks," Sophie said.

"Yeah," Bella agreed, looking down at Argos. "Life's a bitch and then you die."

Muriel snorted, having appeared with a hot dog and fries. "Well, that's pretty heavy. I was going to suggest ice cream, but it sounds like we need to bring out the big guns." She disappeared behind the bar and returned with two plates of Mick's key lime pie. "On the house. Just don't tell Mick."

I zipped my mouth and picked up a fork.

Over the best key lime pie outside of Key West, we ate in silence for a while. Sophie asked if I had gotten anywhere with finding Layla before stuffing some hot dog, fries, and key lime pie into her mouth.

I shook my head, setting down my fork. "Not yet. We're still working on it."

Bella piped up, her mouth full of pie. "Tell her about the hundred grand."

Sophie's eyes went wide. "What about the hundred grand?"

I sighed, realizing I was about to shatter Sophie's worldview. "Well, Pixie got a hundred-thousand-dollar ransom for Layla's return."

"Wow, that's a lot. Poor Pixie. She must be so upset."

"She is," I confirmed.

"I don't have a hundred grand," said Sophie.

I didn't say that now, neither did Pixie. Instead, I said, "Me neither."

Sophie nodded. "I know Pixie, but she doesn't show Layla herself. Evelyn Moreau does that. I'd like to do that someday."

Bella frowned. "You mean be rich?"

"No." Sophie laughed. "I mean handle dogs, like Evelyn does."

I smiled at her enthusiasm. "You know, I could show you Evelyn's facility sometime if you're interested."

Sophie's face lit up. "Really? That would be so cool!"

Bella chimed in, "Seeing all the dogs would be awesome. But I wanna know what these people do that makes them so rich they can hire someone to show their dogs."

I leaned back in my chair. "Well, Aram, Pixie's husband, is in fashion. I was told he does collaborations, but I'm not entirely sure what that means."

The girls exchanged a look before bursting into laughter.

"Oh, Miami." Bella giggled. "Collabs are, like, when brands work with famous people or influencers to promote their stuff."

Sophie nodded. "Yeah, social media influencers are fire right now. They're, like, super important for marketing."

I felt suddenly old. "Back in my day, Aram's brand worked with some big pop bands and actors. You know, like INXS and Molly Ringwald."

What I got in return were blank stares.

"Anyway," Bella said, turning to Sophie, "being an influencer would be totally lit. Like, imagine getting paid just to post pics and stuff?"

Sophie nodded enthusiastically. "For reals. We'd be living our best lives!"

Each of the words was familiar, but the order they came out rendered them meaningless. I saw the grin on Danielle's face, so I stuffed my mouth full of pie. We finished our dinner and offered Sophie a ride home.

As I walked out of the courtyard behind three women, I glanced back toward the bar. No one was sitting there, but through the ghosts of Miami and Ron, I saw Mick, arms crossed, dark eyes watching me like I might already be lost to him.

CHAPTER FOURTEEN

T HE NEXT MORNING, I STROLLED INTO THE OFFICE, THE SMELL OF FRESH coffee hitting me as soon as I opened the door. Lizzy was already at her desk, typing away furiously on her computer. I pushed into my office and found Ron lounging on the sofa.

"Morning, MJ," Ron called out, raising his water bottle in greeting. "Got some news for you."

Lizzy followed me in, handing me a cup of coffee.

I settled into my chair, blowing on the hot drink. "Let's hear it."

Ron leaned forward, his eyes twinkling. "A guy I know gave me the name of the head judge for the upcoming Grand Canine Classic. It's being held at the Expo Center."

"And?" I prompted, taking a sip of my coffee.

"My guy says the judge will be there this afternoon. According to him, if there's anything happening in the dog world, this judge will know about it."

I nodded, mulling over the information. It wasn't much, but it was a lead. "Good work. We'll check it out."

Lizzy cleared her throat, drawing my attention. "I've got something too."

"Of course."

She swiveled her chair to face me and picked a lump of mascara from the corner of her eye. "I've tracked down Victoria McCaron, the woman who may have abused Sophie at a local dog show."

"That was quick. What did you find?"

"Well, it turns out she's not just some random dog show attendee. As you suggested, she's the daughter of Henry McCaron, and there's a fair bit about him online. He's been involved in dog shows for decades. Quite the local celeb. But nothing lately."

I leaned back in my chair. "Interesting. Any idea why she'd have it in for Sophie?"

"You'll need to ask her that."

I decided that since I couldn't do anything for my paying client until later, I might as well follow up on Sophie's case. Victoria McCaron worked a stone's throw from my office, so I opted for a stroll.

The walk down Rosemary Avenue was pleasant, despite the humid Florida air. Palm trees swayed gently in the breeze, their fronds casting dappled shadows on the sidewalk. I passed by the fountain where kids often played, splashing in the water to beat the heat until security came to chase them out. The upscale shops and restaurants were just starting to come to life, with early birds sipping lattes at outdoor tables and window shoppers peering into boutique displays.

I found Victoria's office nestled among the mix of businesses in Rosemary Square. The promotional goods company occupied a modest space, its walls lined with shelves showcasing an array of useless items emblazoned with corporate logos. Pens, USB drives, stress balls, and tote bags competed for space with branded portable chargers and eco-friendly water bottles.

There were several people at work in the open plan space, so I asked the first person I came to for Victoria. She pointed to a desk where a woman with shoulder-length dark hair was hunched over a computer, her brow furrowed in concentration.

I cleared my throat to get her attention. "Victoria McCaron?"

She looked up, her green eyes narrowing. "Yes?"

"I'm Miami Jones. I was hoping we could talk privately."

"Why?" she asked.

I lowered my voice. "Well, you might not want to discuss abusing a kid in front of your co-workers."

Her eyes widened, and she led me to a small break room. She busied herself with a coffee machine, popping in a capsule. She didn't offer me one, but I'd had my fill.

I leaned against the break room counter, studying Victoria's tense posture. "So, about you yelling at Sophie Marshall at the dog show?"

Victoria's head snapped up. "Who told you that?"

I shrugged. "Does it matter? You either did it or you didn't."

She sighed, and her mouth tightened. "Look, that dog Sophie has? It belonged to my father. He just gave it away to her, and it's rightfully mine."

"Is your father dead?" I asked.

"Not yet," she replied, a hint of bitterness in her voice. "But I don't see why some little kid should get the dog and not me."

"It's just a dog. I was told you don't really care for dogs, anyway."

Victoria's eyes flashed. "I could have sold it. That dog is worth five or ten grand."

My eyebrows climbed higher, and I studied Victoria's face. "Maybe your dad wanted the dog to be with someone who actually wanted to show it," I suggested.

Victoria shrugged, her shoulders tense. "I don't care. I don't care about any of it."

But I wasn't buying her indifference. Her eyes were bouncing around the room to avoid looking at me, and her jaw was too tight. The coffee machine spluttered to end its cycle.

"What do you want, anyway?" she said. "That whole thing at the park was ages ago."

"I want to know who stole Sophie's dog."

She was raising the coffee cup to her mouth again but only got halfway there. "Who what?"

"Stole Gaston from her home."

She gave a mirthless laugh that stopped in her neck. "And you think *I* did it?"

"I don't know who did it. I'm talking to anyone who knew the dog and the kid."

"Well, it wasn't me." She lifted her coffee cup to her lips, taking a long sip. Her knuckles were white against the ceramic mug.

"You said yourself he's worth a lot of money."

"I'm no thief."

"Sometimes people take things because they believe the thing was theirs in the first place."

Victoria harrumphed.

"Who would you sell a dog to, anyway?" I asked.

"I don't know." She put the coffee mug down and ripped open a packet of sweetener. "Maybe I'd put an ad in the paper."

"People still do that?"

"Online then. Look, it doesn't matter. I didn't take the dog, okay? Yeah, I said some stuff, but what I said wasn't wrong." She busied herself stirring the drink.

"What was wrong was yelling it at a kid who isn't responsible for whatever's happened in your life."

"Thank you, Dr. Phil."

I decided I'd pushed enough for now. "Thanks for your time, Victoria," I said, heading for the door.

As I walked back to my office, I mulled over our conversation. Would Victoria actually steal Sophie's dog? Did she have any legal claim to it? I couldn't see it, and she didn't strike me as the ransom type. Then again, I wasn't even sure if the two dognappings were even linked. One was high society, one was not. One was high-tech, one was not. I was starting to doubt finding one dog would lead me to the other.

The cool air of my office hit me as I pushed through the door. Lizzy looked up from her desk, her lips pressed together.

"You forgot your phone," she said, holding it up.

I shrugged. "So?"

"So, Detective Ronzoni called," Lizzy replied, her eyebrows raised. "Somebody stole another dog."

CHAPTER FIFTEEN

BACK TO THE ISLAND. IT WAS BECOMING A THING. I PULLED UP ON Sunrise Avenue, outside the most discreet donut shop in Florida. The street was a long row of neat little stores that all had the same taupe signage, as if the colors red and yellow had been banned. Ronzoni's unmarked sedan was parked haphazardly at the curb. As I stopped behind him, he rolled down his window.

"Park there and you'll get a ticket," he grumbled.

I sighed and pulled around to the Publix grocery store lot, then walked back to meet him.

"Any progress on the ransom situation?" I asked.

Ronzoni's face tightened, clearly not keen to admit defeat. "What do you know?"

"Met someone who might have a connection to the dog taken in West Palm," I offered.

He waved his hand dismissively. "Don't care about that case. Not my jurisdiction."

"Three cases isn't raising any red flags for you?"

"Of what?" Ronzoni asked, his brow furrowing.

"A serial dognapper."

Ronzoni's eyes widened, and he shushed me, glancing around as if afraid the locals might overhear our loose chitchat.

I followed Ronzoni into the Donut Den, and my senses were assaulted by the overwhelming aroma of sugar and fried dough. It was like a sugar rush and a heart attack had gotten together for a fling.

The shop was nothing like the dingy donut joints I remembered from my youth. This place screamed high-end, with its polished marble countertops, gleaming glass display cases, and artisanal light fixtures. The walls were adorned with framed photos of elaborate donut creations, each one looking more like a work of art than something you'd stuff in your face.

Behind the counter, a stocky man in his mid-forties was serving a customer. His light brown hair was mostly hidden under a baseball cap emblazoned with the Donut Den logo—also in taupe—and his friendly smile seemed genuine as he chatted with the woman on the other side of the counter.

"And how's Travis getting on with his piano lessons?" he inquired, arranging a dozen assorted donuts into a stylish, logo-emblazoned box.

"Oh, Kevin, he's quite the little maestro," the woman gushed. "He loved those music note-shaped sprinkles you put on his birthday donuts last month."

Kevin beamed. "Well, you tell him to keep practicing, and maybe we'll do a whole keyboard of donuts for his next recital."

As the woman made her purchase, I turned my attention to the menu. Only it wasn't a board—it was a massive television screen mounted above the counter. The high-definition display showed mouth-watering close-ups of donuts rotating in a mesmerizing dance of glazes and toppings.

I scanned the prices, initially thinking eight dollars seemed reasonable for a dozen. Then I realized that was the price *per* donut. These weren't just donuts; they were small, edible luxuries, each one probably containing enough calories to fuel a marathon runner for a week.

As the customer left, Ronzoni stepped forward, his wrinkled

suit somehow looking even more rumpled in the pristine surroundings of the Donut Den.

"Kevin Thompson?" Ronzoni asked, flashing his badge. "I'm Detective Ronzoni, and this is Miami Jones. We'd like to ask you a few questions about what happened last night."

Kevin's smile faded, replaced by a worried frown. "Of course, Detective. It's about Charlie."

"Who's Charlie?" I asked, eyeing a particularly decadent-looking maple bacon donut in the display case.

"Charlie's my golden retriever," Kevin explained. He gestured to an empty plush dog bed near the front window. "That's where he usually lies during the day. The kids who come in after school love to pet him."

I wondered what kind of allowance these kids must get to afford eight-dollar donuts as an after-school snack.

"Can you walk us through what happened last night?" Ronzoni prompted.

Kevin nodded, leading us behind the counter and through a swinging door into the kitchen. The scent of sugar intensified, mingling with the tang of cooking oil. Stainless steel dominated the space—mixers, proofing cabinets, and a massive deep fryer that could probably cook enough donuts to feed an entire police force.

"I was closing up," Kevin began, pointing to another dog bed tucked in a corner near the back door. "Charlie was back here while I cleaned. I was taking out trash, wiping down surfaces—you know, the stuff you do when the shop is quiet." He paused, swallowing hard. "When I turned around, Charlie was gone. The back door was open."

I glanced at the heavy metal door. "Was it locked?"

Kevin's face flushed. "It usually is, but when I'm cleaning and taking out trash, sometimes I leave it unlocked. It's hard to open with one hand, you know?"

Ronzoni scribbled in his notepad. "Did you see anyone suspicious hanging around?"

Kevin nodded. "I didn't see anyone, but the video camera did."

"You got video?"

"Yes."

"And it worked?"

"Sure. I can show you."

Kevin ushered us to a small office that seemed to suck the joy out of the air. It was a stark contrast to the cheerful donut shop, with its bland walls, metal filing cabinets, and a desk buried under stacks of papers. A sad-looking potted plant drooped in the corner, clearly longing for sunlight and water.

Kevin settled into an office chair and opened a laptop that was dusted with flour. The screen flickered to life, showing a surprisingly good view of the back alley.

"Here's the footage from last night," Kevin said, hitting play.

We watched as a man in a ball cap strolled down the lane, stopping by the back door. He was well-tanned with dark hair, though it was hard to make out details in the late afternoon shade on the video. The man pointed something at the camera.

Ronzoni leaned in, squinting. "What's that he's holding?"

"Looks like a remote control," I suggested.

Kevin shrugged. "I'm not sure."

The video continued, showing the man pull something from his pocket and open the door. He disappeared inside for a moment, then reappeared, waving something low to the ground.

A golden-furred shape lumbered out the door, following the man's hand.

Ronzoni frowned. "What's he got now?"

I smirked. "Looks like a steak."

Kevin nodded glumly. "Charlie would follow anyone with a good New York strip."

"Not partial to donuts, then?"

We watched as Charlie followed the man out of frame. The door closed, and the thief grabbed the dog's collar, using the steak to lead him away down the lane.

Ronzoni sighed. "Well, that was easy."

Kevin pulled up another video on his laptop. The screen now showed the front of the store from behind the counter. It was bustling with activity, clearly the after-school rush.

"This is just before Charlie was taken," said Kevin. "I came out front when I heard the door. It's the same every weekday."

"Where'd all these kids come from?" I asked, surprised. "I didn't know there was a school nearby."

Kevin shook his head. "There isn't. Palm Beach isn't exactly teeming with youngsters. But Bak and Dreyfoos schools have a bus that drops off next door at the Publix. The kids come in for an after-school snack."

"Why don't they just go to Publix?" I wondered aloud.

Kevin looked offended, his eyebrows furrowing. "Maybe because they don't care for grocery store baked goods?"

I held up my hands in mock surrender. I wondered if the local rotisserie chicken shop made the same argument.

As we watched, the man in the baseball cap entered through the front door, positioning himself at the back of the group of students. He glanced up at the television menu, then took a long, deliberate look at the floor.

Ronzoni leaned in again. I wondered if he needed his eyes checked. "What's he looking at?"

"The dog bed," I replied, noting the empty cushion near the window.

I turned to Kevin. "If the whole point of the bed is for Charlie to be out front, why wasn't he there?"

Kevin pulled the cap from his head and ran a hand over his head. "The kids came in all at once. I called for Charlie, but he must have been asleep in the back."

Kevin closed the laptop, and for a moment, he stared at a calendar on the wall. The month's picture was a basketful of Labrador puppies. The silence in the small office was broken only by the distant hum of the refrigeration units in the kitchen.

"Kevin," I said, leaning against the filing cabinet, "have you heard about the other thefts?"

Ronzoni shot me a glare that could curdle milk, but I ignored him.

Kevin's brow furrowed. "Thefts? I heard about Layla. Poor Pixie must be beside herself."

"Sophie Marshall's dog Gaston was also taken," I added, watching his reaction carefully.

Kevin shook his head. "I'm not familiar with either of them."

"They live in West Palm," I explained. "You probably wouldn't know them."

"Actually, I live in West Palm too," Kevin said, jutting out his chin. "My business is here in Palm Beach, but I commute. Though I do know Pixie from the circuit."

I raised an eyebrow. "The circuit?"

"The dog show circuit," Kevin clarified. "Actually, her husband was in the other day."

"Aram?"

Kevin nodded. "Yes, he came in to get a dozen for his team."

"Was that when you heard about Layla?" I probed.

"No," Kevin replied, shaking his head. "It was before that." Kevin stood and addressed Ronzoni. "There's one more thing. The deputy who came last night said you'd want to see it. Charlie wore a Bluetooth tracking device on his collar."

Ronzoni perked up. "Does that mean we can see where the dog is?"

Kevin shook his head, deflating Ronzoni's enthusiasm. "I don't think so. It hasn't moved since last night."

He brought up an app on his phone, and the screen showed a map with an icon representing a location. Instead of a golden retriever, it was a cartoon dog that more closely resembled a beagle. The icon was stationed on Route 710, somewhere near the Martin County line.

Kevin pointed to some text beneath the map. "This is the last known location."

Ronzoni scratched his chin, his brow furrowed in thought. "Maybe the perp took the collar off and threw the tracker on the side of the road. There's not much out there."

Kevin shook his head again. "If they had, it would still be pulsing and showing the position as current. But it's not. It's like it went out of range."

"Out there, it's possible," I mused, thinking about the vast stretches of nothing that surrounded that area. "And if they did take it off, they could have gone west toward the lake or even cut up toward Orlando."

Kevin's shoulders slumped, the weight of the possibilities clearly crushing him. "Charlie could be anywhere now. Or nowhere."

I pulled out my phone, ready to snap a picture of the screen. "Mind if I take a photo of the map?"

"You don't need to do that," Kevin said, straightening up a bit. "I can share the tracker with you."

A few taps and swipes later, and the dog's last known location popped up on my phone. I stared at the little cartoon pooch icon, wondering what story it could tell if it could speak.

Ronzoni thanked Kevin and said he'd be in touch. We stepped out of the Donut Den, the sugary aroma fading as we hit the fresh air. Ronzoni's car was still angled at the curb, miraculously ticket-free.

The detective turned to me. "Where'd you park?"

I jerked my thumb towards the grocery store lot. "Over there. You wouldn't let me park here, remember?"

Ronzoni grunted, fishing his keys out of his pocket. "We should check out that location where the tracker stopped."

"Thought that wasn't your jurisdiction."

"It's not," Ronzoni confirmed. "But you could take a look."

I shook my head. "Kevin's not my client, Detective. I've got my own missing dog to find."

Ronzoni leaned against his car, his wrinkled suit bunching up even more. "What's your take on all this, Jones?"

I crossed my arms. "Two missing dogs? That's a coincidence. But three? That's a pattern. And three pedigrees vanishing the week before a major show?"

Ronzoni's brow furrowed. "You think they're connected?"

"I think someone's got a plan," I replied. "And my gut is saying it's got something to do with this dog show."

CHAPTER SIXTEEN

The familiar sight of the massive county courthouse greeted me like a warning as I stopped outside my office building on Banyan. Ron was already waiting outside, shades on, soaking up the rays in a way that no one with his propensity for skin cancer should.

"Ready for a field trip?" I asked as he climbed into the passenger seat.

Ron nodded, his ruddy cheeks flushed with excitement. "Let's go to the carnival."

We drove out to the South Florida Fairgrounds, the sprawling complex coming into view as we approached. It was home to the annual county fair—rides and animals and cake competitions, and people wandering around cheek to jowl in the winter sun, eating calories by the thousand. For the rest of the year, the place felt vast and open and soulless, and I imagined developers standing off to the side, wringing their hands with the anticipation of what they could do with all that land. The Expo Center stood out among the other buildings, its modern architecture a stark contrast to the more traditional fairground structures.

As we walked towards the entrance, I couldn't help but notice the flurry of activity around us. Trucks were unloading equipment, and people bustled about with clipboards and walkie-talkies.

Inside, the cavernous hall stretched out before us, its sheer size impressive. The air was thick with the smell of fresh paint and new carpeting. At one end, a massive curtain was being raised, creating a separate space behind it.

"Must be for the prep area," Ron mused, his eyes scanning the room.

Along the sides, workers were erecting bleachers, the metal frames clanging as they were locked in place. The sound echoed through the vast space.

But what caught my eye was the green carpet being rolled out across the center of the hall. It unfurled like a ribbon of artificial grass across the concrete floor.

"Instant dog park," I said, nudging Ron.

Ron nodded, his eyes crinkling at the corners. "Or maybe they're just trying to protect the floor from the scuff marks of all those claws."

"And the other stuff dogs do."

A worker in a vest that glowed like a highlighter directed us toward the center of the hall where two men stood surveying the work. One was actively directing traffic, pointing and gesturing at various spots around the space. The other watched with an air of quiet authority.

"Oliver Grant?" I asked as we approached.

The observer turned to face us. He cut an impressive figure—tall and sturdy, with neat gray hair and sharp blue eyes that seemed to take in everything at once. He smelled like spice, and his tailored suit and polished shoes spoke of someone who took presentation a little too seriously.

"I am he," he said, extending his hand.

I introduced myself and Ron, then whistled as I looked around the massive space. "Quite an operation you've got here."

"The Grand Canine Classic is the largest show in Florida,"

Grant said with pride. "We're expecting over two thousand entries."

"And you're the chief cook and bottle washer?"

Grant smiled. "I'm the head judge and assistant coordinator. The gentleman there who looks like he's directing air traffic is the chairman of the organizing committee."

"How does it all work?" I asked. "The competition itself?"

Grant's eyes lit up. "Dogs compete first within their breeds. The winners advance to their respective groups—Sporting, Working, Terrier, and so on. Then the group winners compete for Best in Show."

I nodded, then got down to business. "We're looking into the disappearance of Layla and Gaston. You know them?"

"Of course. Pixie and Eve are fixtures on the circuit." His brow furrowed. "And young Sophie shows great promise with Gaston. She's been competing at local park events."

"There's been another theft," I said. "Kevin Thompson's golden retriever, Charlie."

Grant's eyebrows shot up. "Kevin too? That's disturbing news." He shook his head. "I know them all well."

"Do you have any thoughts on why this might be happening?"

"I can't conceive why anyone would."

"Could it be competitors trying to thin the field?" I asked.

"Unlikely," Grant said firmly. "They're in different groups—Layla's in Hound, Charlie's Sporting, and Gaston's Non-Sporting. Besides, while Layla has a real shot at Best in Show, Charlie's still young. Best case, he might win his breed and possibly his group. And Gaston?" He smiled fondly. "Sophie's doing well with him, but they're both young and still learning. I'd be surprised to see him advance past breed level at this point."

Someone dropped a scaffold pole, and all our heads shot toward the sound like we were meerkats. Oliver put his hand to his chest, and for a moment I thought he might be having a heart attack, but he let out a long, slow breath to gather himself.

"So, with regard to the missing dogs. What about resale?" I asked. "Is there a market for stolen show dogs?"

Grant's face contorted like I'd accused him of kicking puppies. "I wouldn't know anything about that."

"Come on," I said, softening my tone. "Someone in your position, head judge of major shows, consultant to top breeders—you must hear things. The word on the street, so to speak."

He brushed his already immaculate lapels, considering. "Well, there are black market buyers. Unscrupulous breeders who want championship bloodlines without paying stud fees or following proper protocols." He lowered his voice. "And then there are the puppy mills."

"Puppy mills?"

"Places where dogs are bred in horrible conditions, purely for profit. They're a national crisis."

I thought about the kids I saw at Stone's Gym, the ones who needed a safe place to escape their often horrible home lives. That was a crisis. Puppies? I wasn't sure they were at the same level, until my mind drifted to Sophie's expression talking about Gaston.

"How would someone get into that world?" I asked. "If they wanted to move stolen dogs?"

Grant's face reddened. "I wouldn't possibly know—"

"Come on," I pressed. "You're a man of the people. You've got eyes and ears everywhere."

He glanced around the vast space, then stepped closer. "There is a man. Or at least a name. Zazy. That's all I know—and I wouldn't know how to find him."

"What about the competitor angle?" I asked. "You said there was no point because all the dogs were in different groups, but maybe only one of them is the real target."

"This is a tight-knit community. People are here for the love of man's best friend. It's collegial, not cutthroat."

"There's always someone willing to win at all costs," I said. "The one who's not so collegial. The outsider."

"Well, if you're looking for the outsider, you're talking about Chris Wozinski. He certainly doesn't mind ruffling a few feathers."

"What about …" I looked at Ron. "What the other guy's name?"

"Graham Albright."

Grant straightened up, clearly ready to end this line of questioning. "Yes, I know Albright."

"We heard he likes to win."

"They all like to win."

"But some more than others. Have you heard anything about his canine resort?"

"There are always rumors about such places starting up. It's easier said than done."

"But a competitor to the Pawlace might want to harm their brand."

A worker wheeling stackable tables on a dolly appeared and Grant pointed him toward the far side of the curtain. "I don't see how that's happened. None of these dogs were taken from the Pawlace, and I've seen the facility. Security is tight, and if I know Eve at all, I'm willing to bet it's even better now."

"By association, perhaps? Eve is Layla's handler, after all."

"I don't see it. Eve is in demand. She could handle pretty much any dog she wants."

"So, with Layla out of the picture, she's available."

"There are easier ways to hire someone."

It was a good point. "So you think this Wozinski might push the boundaries this far, but you don't think Albright would?"

Grant clicked his tongue. "I think they both like to win very much, but I am not going to accuse someone of something I cannot prove."

I shrugged that off. "So you don't know anything about this new resort?"

"I don't think a dog-friendly hotel is quite the same as the Pawlace."

"Nevertheless."

Another section of green carpet unrolled in our direction and we had to move to the side. "I've heard something about Boca, but I've not seen anything with my own eyes," said Grant. "But you could ask him yourself."

"He's been hard to pin down so far."

"Graham's a very busy man. But he'll be at his cigar club tonight."

"How do you know?"

"I'm meeting him and a few others connected to the show for pre-dinner drinks."

"Maybe we should drop by."

"It's really not a drop-by kind of place. Members only."

I smiled. Those were my favorite places to drop by.

CHAPTER SEVENTEEN

I DROPPED RON BACK AT THE OFFICE SO HE AND LIZZY COULD FIND OUT anything about this mysterious Zazy character. I cruised north on I-95 and then cut up 710, watching Palm Beach County's urban sprawl thin out into patches of scrubland. The tracker app on my phone showed Charlie's last known location in the middle of nowhere, where civilization gave way to swamp and sugar cane.

I felt like I was driving into old Florida. The kind of place where gators sunned themselves on banks and herons stalked through shallow water. No gleaming condos or perfectly manicured golf courses out here.

The icon on my phone grew closer. A sign announced the J.W. Corbett Wildlife Management Area—a vast expanse of cypress swamp and pine flatwoods. And ahead, endless rows of sugarcane stretched to the horizon, rustling in the warm breeze.

I slowed as I approached the spot where Charlie's signal had gone dark. There wasn't much here—just a weathered pole with a faded number marking the mile. Two unpaved tracks branched off the main road. One disappeared right into the dense woods of the wildlife area, while the other cut left through the cane fields, probably used by the plantation workers.

I stopped in the middle of the road and killed the engine when the app showed my little blue dot right on top of the beagle's face. The silence was heavy, broken only by the whisper of cane leaves and the distant cry of a hawk. I could see for miles in either direction. No buildings, no traffic—just wilderness and agriculture colliding at a lonely intersection.

Either they'd dumped the tracker here and kept going toward Indiantown, or they'd turned off onto one of these tracks. But which one? The dense woods could hide anything, and those cane fields went on forever.

The dashboard thermometer read eighty-two, but stepping out of the air conditioning felt like walking into a sauna. The water used to grow the sugarcane hung in the air as if it was dispersed as an aerosol. Hard to believe Palm Beach Gardens, with its manicured lawns and pristine shopping centers, was just minutes away. My phone showed full bars—whatever happened to Charlie's tracker, it wasn't due to lack of signal.

The stillness closed in on me. No traffic noise, no planes from the nearby Gwinn airfield, just the buzz of cicadas and the occasional rustle of something moving through the underbrush. The air was thick with the musty sweetness of decaying vegetation mixed with the sharp tang of wild citrus. A red-shouldered hawk circled overhead, riding the thermals, probably eyeing something small and edible in the grass below.

I walked to the intersection where the dirt tracks met the highway. Something caught my eye in the tall grass—a flash of weathered wood half-buried in weeds and vines. I pushed through the scratchy grass, feeling the sweat already soaking through my shirt. The object was firmly wedged, and it took some yanking to free it from years of accumulated growth.

It was an old wooden sign, the paint mostly worn away by countless Florida summers. But the text was still legible: *Feed the Lion.* I turned it over in my hands, but the back was blank except for some rotted spots where moisture had done its work.

A lion? Out here? Then again, this was Florida. The state where people kept tigers in their backyards and monkeys in their apartments. I'd learned long ago to never say never when it came to the Sunshine State's capacity for weirdness.

I tossed the sign back into the grass and checked my watch. I had places to be. The traffic always built on Route 1 when the school run was on, and today I had the joy of being part of it.

The school parking lot was a traffic jam as kids streamed out the front doors. Bella emerged from the crowd, her blonde curls bouncing as she jogged to the car.

"Feel like going to a dog park?" I asked.

"Can we get Argos?" she asked, barely getting settled in her seat.

"That would be the point."

Her face lit up. "Hey, we should get Sophie too!"

I shifted uncomfortably. "I don't know about that."

"Come on, she lost her dog. She probably misses having one around."

"Tell you what—we'll swing by and see if her mom's okay with it."

We collected Argos from the house and headed to the trailer park. Bella pressed her face against the window as we cruised past the rows of manufactured homes. "People live here?"

"Sure."

"They look like vacation places."

"Some of them are. Some are just homes." I glanced at her as I eased around the park. "Where do you live?"

"Right now, with you."

"I mean usually."

"In a condo on a lake in West Palm."

We found the Marshall residence, where Amanda was pulling her keys out and dropping her phone into her purse at the door.

"Gotta do some food deliveries," she said, eyeing us suspiciously. "Can't do ride-share anymore. They say my car's too old."

"Mind if Sophie comes to the dog park with us? I'll bring her back after."

Amanda's eyes narrowed. "As long as I don't have to pay for anything."

She scurried away, and Bella let herself in as if she lived there. I stepped onto the threshold but went no further. It was a small space, a kitchen and dining area and living room all crammed into one, probably with a couple of bedrooms off a tight hallway at the back. It was tidy but lived-in.

"Soph!" called Bella.

Sophie came from the rear of the home and smiled. "What are you guys doing here?"

"We're taking Argos to the dog park. Wanna come?"

Sophie looked at me.

I nodded. "Your mom said it was okay."

The smile got wider.

The dog park sprawled across an acre, divided into sections for small and large breeds. We settled Argos into the small dog area where a dozen or so canines of various sizes romped and played.

I found a bench in the shade while the girls wandered the enclosure. A pair of Jack Russell terriers bounded past, followed by their huffing owner. A poodle mix pranced around them, its carefully groomed coat collecting burrs and grass.

Bella and Sophie moved from dog to dog, asking owners for permission to pet them, learning names and breeds. Their laughter carried across the park as they discovered each new furry friend. For a moment, they were just two teenage girls without a care in the world. No thoughts of absent fathers or harried and lost mothers.

Sophie took Argos's leash and demonstrated the proper show-handling technique to Bella. She held the lead high and trotted in a circle, but Argos had other ideas. He darted left and right, nose to the ground, investigating every interesting scent. Sophie tried to keep him in line, but he zigzagged like a drunk sailor following a treasure map.

Sophie giggled. "I don't think this is his thing."

"Maybe he's more of an agility dog," Bella suggested.

They led him to the small obstacle course in the corner—a few jumps, a section of concrete tunnel, and some weave poles. Sophie tried to coax him through the tunnel with treats while Bella waited at the other end. Argos sniffed the entrance, backed away, then flopped down for a belly rub instead.

"I don't think he's cut out for competition," Sophie said, unleashing him.

Argos took off like a shot, racing around the enclosure with newfound freedom. The girls chased after him, lost in the simple joy of playing with a happy dog.

After Sophie and Bella had run Argos ragged, we found a shady spot near a sprawling banyan tree, and I bought ice creams from a van that played a tinny version of *New York State of Mind* through worn speakers. The girls sat cross-legged on a wooden bench, carefully managing drips in the late afternoon air, while Argos watched expectantly, tongue hanging out the side of his mouth.

Sophie kept glancing my way between licks of her chocolate cone. Finally, she cleared her throat. "Would you take me to see Henry?"

"Henry?"

"The man who gave me Gaston."

"Victoria's father?"

She nodded, focused intently on her ice cream.

I thought back to Victoria's attitude in the break room, her bitterness about her father giving away *her* dog. "I'd have to check with your mom first."

Sophie's shoulders slumped. "She doesn't like Henry much."

"Why's that?"

"Because of my dad." She swirled her tongue around the cone's edge. "She doesn't really trust people. Men especially. She thinks Henry wants something from me."

"Does he?"

"No." She shook her head firmly. "He just loves dogs and showing them. He taught me everything I know."

"Where does Henry live?"

"He used to be in Wellington, but he's not there anymore. He's in the hospital now." Her voice got quiet. "I don't know which one."

"I know someone who can find out."

As the girls finished their ice creams, I pulled out my phone and typed a quick message to Lizzy and asked her to work her magic.

CHAPTER NINETEEN

I tugged at my collar, feeling like an imposter in clothes that hadn't seen daylight since the last charity polo match Danielle dragged me to. I drove off Singer Island and back through downtown, then out into Palm Beach. The Leaf Lounge was discreetly tucked in off Worth Avenue like a testament to old money, its limestone facade glowing amber in the evening light.

Inside, dark wood paneling and leather chairs created intimate spaces where Palm Beach's elite gathered. Crystal decanters caught the light from brass wall sconces, and everywhere I looked, people wore outfits in which no sane person would ever garden. It was everything Longboard Kelly's wasn't.

"How'd you swing this?" I asked Ron as I met him in the reception foyer.

"Cassandra knows the owner." He smoothed his tie, looking more at home than I felt.

I made to run my hands through my hair but decided to leave it the hell alone. "She knows everybody."

"They might be all richer than Midas, but in the end, Palm Beach is still just a small town."

We followed a hostess up a curved staircase to the members' lounge. The rich aroma of premium tobacco wrapped around us like an expensive scarf. Leather club chairs clustered around low tables, occupied by men and women in evening wear, tendrils of smoke rising from their cigars like spirits ascending to heaven. The hostess pointed out the man we were there to meet.

Graham Albright dominated the far corner of the room. His massive frame filled a wingback chair, bald head glistening, commanding attention like a general surveying his troops. A perfectly groomed mustache twitched above his smile as he gestured with a thick cigar, holding court with a small group of admirers. His bold striped orange suit made my conservative blazer feel like something from a discount rack.

"Mr. Albright?" Ron's voice carried across the room.

Albright waved his hand, and his audience dispersed like subjects dismissed by their king. I noted that Oliver Grant wasn't among them. Perhaps he'd left earlier for dinner, or maybe we'd spooked him. "Mr. Bennett, we met, did we not?"

"I was trying to recall where."

"Majorie Wallingshaw's Fourth of July thing."

Ron smiled. "I believe you are right."

"How's Cassandra? Still slumming it on Ocean Boulevard?"

"Living the dream," Ron said.

"Sit, gentlemen. You'll need proper drinks for this conversation." Albright snapped his fingers, and a server materialized. "The Macallan '89 from my private stock."

I settled into a leather chair that was so comfortable I almost reconsidered my bar stool at Longboards. "Nice place."

"I like it. He offered a tight smile. "I'm Graham Albright."

"This is Miami Jones," said Ron. "He's my ..."

"Partner in crime," I said.

"Been in town long?" Ron asked.

"The family will be down after Thanksgiving," said Albright. "But I'm back and forth every week."

"To where?" I asked.

"New York," he said, as if we were discussing the Palm Tran bus.

The waiter returned with a silver tray holding three tulip-shaped glasses of whisky. He was dressed in a black shirt, pants, and vest, so he almost disappeared into the background, even when he was standing right there. I wondered if that was the point of the uniform.

After placing the three glasses and a small pitcher of water on the table, the waiter retreated. Albright took his drink, and I used that as my cue to pick up mine. There was no ice, but I knew enough to know that was some kind of heresy. A drop of water opened the liquor up, but Albright closed his eyes and sniffed it, then took a small sip.

I again followed his lead. I rolled around the heavy crystal glass. The aroma burned the hairs in my nose but seemed to complement the scent hanging on the air. I didn't close my eyes—it wasn't Mick's fish dip—but I did sip. It was like nothing I'd ever tasted before. This was not your father's Johnny Walker Red. I suddenly knew what the phrase *smooth as molasses* meant. The taste lingered but changed as it did, from an initial hint of oak to a finish that offered something reminiscent of fig.

"No burn there," I said. I thought Ron might have blushed.

Albright smiled. "No, sir. Do you get the tobacco on the nose?"

I stared at the glass as if it spoke to me. "Orange," I said.

"Yes, yes," said Albright. "The Glencairn glass really brings out the complexity of the aromas. Much preferable to a tumbler."

Albright took another sniff, but not a second taste. He held the glass by the short stem. These were not shots of vodka.

I rolled the liquid around my glass. "So, I understand you're in hotels, Mr. Albright."

"Graham, please. And yes. Banking was the family business." Albright's mustache twitched. "Dull as dishwater. I wanted to build something of my own." He waved his hand again, and the server appeared from the ether. Albright ordered a dozen oysters for the table, then he turned back to me. "Started with one run-down hotel in Palm Beach. Turned it into the first Albright Retreat. Now we have properties from Park City to Acapulco."

"All dog-friendly?" I asked.

"The most luxurious pet amenities in the business. Doggy day spas, room service menus for four-legged guests, the works." He took a sip of his drink, so I mirrored him. "Competition drives excellence, wouldn't you say? Take the show circuit—Pixie thinks she's untouchable with that Afghan of hers, but my Borzois are gaining ground."

"Sounds personal."

"Everything's personal. *It's only business* is a lie. Business, showing, life itself—we're all rivals in the end. If you'll pardon the pun, it's a dog-eat-dog world. It's genetically encoded in us." He chuckled. "I started showing dogs to promote the hotels. Now I'm hooked. The pageantry, the prestige, all of it."

"Speaking of Pixie's dog—"

"Ah yes, terrible business. Though I can't say I'm surprised, given everything."

"You're not worried about your own dogs?"

"Already moved them to a secure facility."

"Where's that?"

"If I told you, it wouldn't be secure."

"The Pawlace?" asked Ron.

"No, not the Pawlace." He grimaced. "Ghastly name. Must have a word with Eve about that."

"So, Boca Raton?" I said.

His mustache twitched. "Where did you hear that?"

"I picked it up along the way. So, I take it Evelyn doesn't look after your dog?"

"No. I currently have other arrangements."

"I hear she's quite in demand, despite handling exclusively for Pixie."

"She does quite well, though I suspect that may change soon enough."

"Why's that?"

"The Kazarians ..." He trailed off, studying his scotch. "Let's just say their star isn't burning quite as bright these days."

The oysters were delivered on a platter of ice. Blue Points, according to the invisible man. There was a vinaigrette in the center of the display. Albright encouraged us to dig in, then he took a half shell and gulped the bivalve down. I waited for Ron to grab one, then I followed. It was fresh and salty, like all good things from Connecticut.

Once we had sampled the seafood and sipped some more scotch, I got back to the point. "What are you telling us? That Aram's struggling?"

There was nothing more than a subtle raising of Albright's eyebrows.

"He doesn't look like he's hurting," I said. "I've been to his place. It's a hell of a pad."

"I didn't say he was never a star. I said he's not burning so bright."

"I thought his line was high-end. Doesn't he have all these collaborations with celebrities?"

Albright dabbed his mouth with a napkin. "He used to be all that. That's why our companies worked together. There was synergy. He'd partner with celebrities, athletes, musicians. Limited-edition fashion lines with their names attached. But most of that was years ago. Decades even. And his last deal ..." He shook his head.

"What happened with his last deal?" asked Ron.

"I don't know the particulars. Not sure anyone does yet. But we were set to host the launch party at my Hamptons property. Some big musical act was going to perform, debut their joint streetwear collection. A big secret revealed. Then, boom, the entire thing got canceled out of the blue."

I frowned. "Canceled?"

Albright's mustache twitched again. It was a tell. All I had to learn was whether it meant he had a royal flush or was bluffing, and I could clean him out at the poker table. If I ever took up cards.

Then Albright's jaw tightened. "Event canceled, leaving me with a host of expenses and him a line of creditors from manufacturers to advertising outlets. I understand Aram had already produced the entire inventory. Millions tied up in clothes I'm told he can't sell."

"Couldn't he rebrand it?" Ron asked.

"Maybe, but fashion moves fast. Last season's styles are worthless, and any collaborator will ask questions about what went wrong." Albright swirled his scotch. "So, he's got warehouses full of dead stock, no new collection in production, and bills piling up. As for the house, well, such appearances can be castles built on sand. And there's this club—from what I hear, he hasn't paid his membership dues in months."

Ron leaned back against the soft leather. "And now his wife's dog has been stolen."

Albright's laugh filled the room like thunder rolling across the ocean. "If you want to run with that narrative."

"What narrative?" Ron asked.

"That the dog is missing." Albright's mustache twitched again. "Did he tell you how much the insurance was worth?"

"What insurance?" I asked. "Pet insurance?"

"Hardly." He set his glass down with a soft clink. "Our dogs become more valuable if they win events. Their litters or stud fees go up. I, for one, cover mine for loss of future earnings. They cost plenty to raise. I know they'll have insurance on Layla."

"For how much?"

"I couldn't say exactly." Albright's eyes gleamed in the dim light. "But my best Borzoi is insured for a quarter of a million."

That put an interesting spin on things. "So, your dog is a Borzoi?"

"Yes. Magnificent beast."

"What group is that?"

"In the AKC? Hound group."

I nodded. "Same as Layla."

"Yes. Your point?"

"No point, just interesting to know."

We finished our drinks and oysters, then Albright checked his watch. "Gentlemen, I have a call with Asia. You understand."

No one brought a bill. No one lingered for a tip. We just got up and left. Albright got in the back of a Rolls Royce as his driver held the door open. I got my ride delivered by the valet.

On the drive home, I turned it over in my head. Could Aram be behind Layla's disappearance? The ransom demand didn't track—that cost him an extra hundred grand, not exactly helping his financial situation. But maybe there was more to it.

I thought about Albright's Borzois and how his chances at Best in Show just got better with Layla out of the picture. The man certainly knew his way around the dog show circuit; he liked to win. He said it himself: it was a dog-eat-dog world.

CHAPTER TWENTY

THE INVITATION HAD ARRIVED BY COURIER LATE IN THE EVENING, AND Lizzy left it on my desk for me to collect the following morning. Heavy cream cardstock with gold embossing invited *M. Jones Esq.* and companion to the soft opening of *Barkingham Palace* at Albright Boca. No confirmation on who had sent the invitation. Just a scrawled question across the bottom: *Do you have a dog?*

Oliver Grant's handiwork, I figured, given the flourishes in the handwriting. The timing was too perfect after our chat at the Expo Center.

Danielle confirmed that Bella had a thing called a student-free day and would not attend school. It sounded like a snow day without the snow, and I really didn't see the point, but an idea coalesced in my little brain, so I showed the invitation to the kid.

"We're going to a palace?" Bella's eyes lit up when I showed her the invitation.

"A dog palace," I said. "And we've got the perfect cover." I nodded toward Argos, who was sprawled on the couch like he owned it.

On the drive down to the Albright Boca resort, I began to wish I'd washed the car. I explained the purpose of the trip was for me to gather evidence, and for Bella and her dog to enjoy the facilities.

"Do you think Layla's there?" she asked.

"I don't know. Three dogs are harder to hide than one—if it's the same person—and I was taught this theory a long time ago that the best place for a grain of sand to hide is on the beach. You get me?"

"Yeah. Lots of nice dogs. You won't notice a few more."

I didn't add that this theory only worked if the dogs were still alive.

At the resort, a circular driveway swept past manicured palms to a portico that would make a Caesar jealous. Bella pressed her face against the window while Argos panted happily in the back seat, oblivious to the grandeur. I followed the signs away from the regular lobby to a separate entrance that had the feeling of an afterthought, with red ropes and carpet telling me where to stop.

"This place is insane," Bella whispered.

A doorman in a crisp white uniform stepped forward as we pulled up. His practiced smile faltered when Argos stuck his head out the window, tongue lolling. The mix of chihuahua eyes and dachshund body seemed to short-circuit his training.

"Welcome to Barkingham Palace," he managed, though his tone suggested we'd taken a wrong turn. Bella and I had already agreed to try to minimize the number of eyerolls we did when we heard the name. These guys really needed a better marketing department —or maybe they didn't. Maybe puns sold.

A woman in a tailored navy suit strode across the marble floor toward us, iPad clutched to her chest like a shield. Her silver hair was pulled back so tight it looked painful.

"I'm Ms. Devereaux, the property manager." Her accent sounded like someone from Dayton trying to impersonate an English aristocrat, and it ended up halfway between Dick van Dyke in *Mary Poppins* and a Red Sox fan. Her gaze dropped to Argos, who was sniffing the doorman's shoes. "And this is?"

"This is Argos," Bella announced proudly. "He's a chiweenie."

Ms. Devereaux pursed her lips like she was sucking a milkshake through an uncooperative straw. "Do you have a reservation?"

I handed her the invitation, and she looked at it like I had found it wrapped inside a bar of chocolate. Her perfectly manicured fingers tapped the iPad screen. "Ah, media, I see. We'll list him as an…" She paused, fingernail tapping her lip. "Artisanal breed blend. We do have certain standards to maintain."

She glanced at Argos's mismatched eyes and the gray on his chin, and I was sure her eyes narrowed. The doorman shifted uncomfortably. But I knew we were in. That was the thing about the rich. Once upon a time, they used to dress rich, like a Brooks Brothers catalog before Brooks Brothers ended up in every mall. Now the wealthy wore track pants and unkempt stubble to the opera and were unrecognizable from the riffraff like me.

Ms. Devereaux led us through a lobby that gave the Breakers a run for its money as she rattled off features like she was selling time shares to billionaires.

"Our canine guests enjoy personalized crystal water bowls, imported Egyptian cotton bedding, and a dedicated butler service." She gestured to a wall lined with oil paintings. "And this is our pawtrait gallery, celebrating our most distinguished visitors."

The paintings showed various dogs posed like European aristocracy—a German shepherd in military regalia, a poodle draped in pearls, a Great Dane looking thoughtful beside a globe. Bella stifled a snicker.

A group of women with perfectly coiffed hair clustered near a seating area, their show dogs arranged at their feet like living accessories. A Borzoi's nose lifted in our direction, followed by its owner's equally disdainful gaze. Their whispers carried across the marble.

"Each suite features climate-controlled sleeping quarters," Ms. Devereaux continued, her eyes darting to Argos as he trotted along, tail wagging. He stopped to sniff an oversized crystal vase, and she flinched like he might mark his territory on the Ming dynasty.

"Our *exclusive* clientele expects the highest standards." She glanced at Argos's mismatched eyes. He responded with a happy pant, tongue lolling out the side of his mouth, completely missing her point. "We cater to championship bloodlines and distinguished pedigrees."

Argos was a better partner than I gave him credit for. He kept all eyes on him, which gave me the opportunity to scope out the place and answer the two questions I had: was this place a big enough competitor to the Pawlace to make stealing Layla a viable brand issue, and if Albright was behind the theft, would he be so bold as to hide the three dogs in a canine resort?

"The spa offers aromatherapy, massage, and coat treatments using only organic products." Ms. Devereaux's voice grew tighter as Argos investigated a decorative plant. "Though perhaps some of our services wouldn't be appropriate for all guests."

She led us into a spa area that made Stone's locker room look like a truck stop bathroom. Italian marble gleamed under crystal chandeliers, and the air carried hints of lavender.

"This is Pierre, our master groomer." She gestured to a tall man in crisp whites who looked like a pastry chef. "He formerly oversaw the dogs for the Monégasque royal family."

Pierre glided forward, cologne trailing in his wake. "Bonjour." He studied Argos with the intensity of an art critic at the Louvre. "And who is zis little unique specimen?"

Bella beamed. "This is Argos. He's a chiweenie."

"Ah, Argos. The dog of Odysseus." Pierre's eyebrows arched. "Did you know Princess Charlene of Monaco has a chihuahua rescue?"

"Argos is a rescue."

Pierre reached for a bottle with a label I couldn't pronounce. "We shall use ze organic chamomile blend from ze Alps."

Ms. Devereaux hovered nearby as Pierre guided Argos into a

marble basin. The dog didn't look eager and tried to back his way out.

"Ze water temperature is precise for maximum comfort," Pierre explained, working up a lather in Argos's black fur.

That was when Argos decided to share the experience with everyone. He shook like he was trying to achieve lift-off, sending a spray of alpine fresh water in all directions. Pierre jumped back, but not fast enough. Ms. Devereaux caught the brunt of it, her silk blouse now sporting wet patches that spread like blood stains.

I bit the inside of my cheek to keep from laughing. Bella didn't even try. Ms. Devereaux's face turned the color of overcooked lobster as she dabbed frantically at her damp blouse. Her fingers flew across her iPad screen, muttering something about *admission protocols* and *breed verification requirements.*

Pierre maintained his composure, though his perfect hair now drooped over one eye. "Zis little one is—*comment dit-on*—spirited?"

After the spa, Ms. Devereaux hustled us toward what she called the "social hour" in a grand salon overlooking Lake Boca. An LED disco ball cast rainbow patterns across marble floors while floor-to-ceiling windows framed the water view.

Waiters in white jackets circulated with silver trays of what looked like fancy dog biscuits. One stopped beside us, lowering his tray. "Today's selection includes duck liver pâté squares and wild-caught salmon crisps."

Argos ignored the offered treats, his attention locked on something else—the edge of the top cocktail napkin on the tray lifting in the breeze from a nearby air vent. Before I could grab his leash, he lunged, attacking the napkin like it had personally insulted his mother.

The tray clanged across the floor as the entire pile of napkins broke skyward, just out of reach as Argos bounced and snapped at them. He chased one toward a podium where two Pomeranians sat getting their photos taken, sending them scattering. Their yips seemed to trigger something in the other dogs—suddenly every pooch in the place was after floating napkins.

A standard poodle with an elaborate continental clip bounded past, its elderly owner stumbling behind. Two Yorkies in designer sweaters broke formation and joined the chase, their diamond collars glinting as they weaved between legs.

Ms. Devereaux's horrified gasp cut through the commotion like a knife. She clutched her iPad tight, face growing redder by the second.

I used the distraction to scan the room, looking for any sign of Layla or the other missing dogs. The kennels would be the obvious place to hide them, and this chaos gave me a chance to peek behind some doors. Through the mayhem, I spotted a service entrance partially hidden behind a decorative screen.

I caught Bella's eye and nodded toward Argos. "I need a minute."

She nodded, getting my meaning. "Ms. Devereaux, what's that drink station over there? The one with all the fancy glasses?"

The manager looked on the edge of hyperventilating. "Oh, our signature doggy mocktail bar." Ms. Devereaux's posture straightened, as napkins finally landed, dogs lost interest, and owners and handlers wrangled control. "We offer a full menu of refreshing beverages."

While Bella led Ms. Devereaux toward the bar, I edged closer to the service entrance. A Yorkshire terrier darted past, still chasing a stray napkin, providing the perfect cover as I slipped through the door.

"So what's the difference between the bark-tinis and the tail-garitas?" Bella's voice carried through the door as it closed behind me. I had to hand it to the kid—she was a natural.

The service corridor stretched ahead like a hospital hallway, all function and no frills. My footsteps echoed off polished concrete floors despite my attempts to move quietly. The fluorescent lighting was a jarring change from the opulent front-of-house.

Boarding suites lined both sides, each with an LCD screen

nameplate mounted beside the door. Through small windows, I could see plush beds and flat-screen TVs mounted on walls, but no occupants. The rooms sat empty, waiting for their wealthy guests.

Around a corner, a heavy steel door blocked my path. A keycard reader glowed red beside the handle. Through the door's glass pane, I spotted an outdoor training area—the usual agility courses and a small show ring, with cameras in every corner, and what looked like motion sensors.

Footsteps echoed from behind. I ducked into a supply closet, leaving the door cracked just enough to peer out. The chemical smell of cleaning supplies stung my nostrils.

A staff member in crisp whites appeared, leading a German shepherd on a leather lead. The dog's nails clicked against the floor as they passed. "Come on, Baron," the handler cooed. "Time for your afternoon constitutional."

Once they were through the heavy door, I returned down the corridor and checked a few more rooms. No sign of Layla or the other missing dogs, but security cameras covered every angle of the hallway. Getting in and out undetected would be nearly impossible—either the dogs weren't here, or if they were, someone knew.

I slipped out of the service corridor and into what looked like a maintenance area. The door clicked shut behind me with a finality that suggested I'd made a wrong turn.

"Can I help you, sir?"

A security guard watched a van back up, delivering some kind of food product. His uniform was pressed, and his expression suggested he'd rather escort me out than help. His name tag read *Burns*.

"Sorry, I was looking for the restroom." I patted my stomach and grimaced. "Too many bark-tinis, I guess."

His eyes narrowed. "The drinks are for the dogs."

"Now you tell me."

"And the facilities are clearly marked in the main salon."

"Right. Got turned around." I shrugged. "This place is bigger than my house."

He didn't crack a smile. "Let me show you back."

We emerged into the main area, but Bella, Argos, and our tightly wound host were nowhere in sight. The salon had cleared out, napkin carnage swept away as if it never happened.

"Where did everyone go?" I asked.

"Pool time," Burns huffed. "Your party should be there."

"Pool?" I pictured Argos's reaction to his spa treatment. "That should be fun. Say, you wouldn't happen to have any Afghan Hounds staying here?"

"No Afghans."

"What about Golden Retrievers?"

He shook his head.

"French Bulldogs?"

"Two of those." His brow creased. "Why?"

"I know what breeds my beagle gets along with."

"Well, we're not fully operational, but when we are, they'll separate bigs and smalls."

I wasn't sure if he meant size or personality.

I followed the security guard to the pool area. He pushed a door open but didn't follow me through. A beach-entry pool stretched before me, ringed by owners in resort wear and their pooches as if lined up for a swimming race. At the shallow end, a handler tried to coax Argos into the water while Bella watched, hands on her head.

Argos had other ideas. He yanked backward, shooting between the handler's legs like a furry bullet. His escape route took him along the pool's edge, darting in and out through ankles and legs as he went. Like dominoes, owners, handlers, and their perfectly groomed charges toppled into the water. The dogs looked like they were finally having fun—the humans, not so much.

Bella turned to Ms. Devereaux, whose face had achieved a shade of purple I didn't think possible. "See? I told you he doesn't like swimming."

Ms. Devereaux herded us toward the exit like she was a border collie and we were covered in fleece. We marched double-time across the marble floor, and she kept glancing over her shoulder as if afraid we might make a break for the spa.

"That was awesome," Bella declared, practically skipping. "Best day ever."

A row of dogs pressed their noses against the glass through the floor-to-ceiling windows. A St. Bernard's tail thumped like a drum. Next to it, a Cavalier King Charles spaniel tilted its head, watching Argos with undisguised envy. Even the stuck-up Borzoi from earlier looked wistful, like it was remembering a time before proper breeding demanded proper behavior.

"Mr. Jones." Ms. Devereaux's voice had taken on a pleading quality. "Please understand, we're still working out some minor operational details. We'd appreciate your keeping that in mind when writing your article."

I paused. "Article?"

She tapped her iPad screen. "For *Vanity Fair*?" Her forced smile wavered. "That is who you're with, correct?"

"Oh. Right. Of course." I nodded. "Don't worry, I'll note that you're still in beta testing."

Her relief was visible. "We do appreciate balanced journalism."

Argos trotted through the revolving door with the same happy swagger he'd arrived with, completely oblivious to the trail of wet footprints, scattered napkins, and ruffled dignity he left in his wake. His tail wagged at the doorman, who took an instinctive step back.

The valet brought my car around, and Argos hopped in like he hadn't just gotten an entire resort's worth of show dogs to remember what being a dog felt like.

CHAPTER TWENTY-ONE

I dropped Bella back home. She spoke to Danielle in rapid fire, like she had downed a barrel of Red Bull. My wife gave me a look as if I'd electrocuted the kid but offered to make her lunch while I left to answer some more questions.

I headed over to Trey Ellis's office in a small business park off 45th Street. His company occupied the end unit of a single-story building with dark-tinted windows and a discrete sign reading *Ellis Security Solutions*.

Inside, the reception area looked like any other office—bland artwork, uncomfortable chairs, fake plants. But through the glass partition, I could see racks of servers and testing equipment. Three techs hunched over workstations, in focused concentration.

Trey met me in his office, which was surprisingly sparse except for the multitude of monitors displaying lots of numbers and graphs that defied my comprehension. I noted that he was wearing a Tommy Bahama shirt. I dug his style.

"Check this out," I said, taking out my phone and pulling up the photo of Kevin Thompson's laptop screen showing the dognapper in the lane. "The guy points something at the camera before breaking in. Looks like a remote control."

Trey squinted at the screen, then shook his head. "Remember what we talked about at lunch? About Wi-Fi jammers?"

He disappeared into a back room and returned with a black plastic box about the size of two decks of cards. He handed it to me. There was no screen and no button, just a very basic on-off switch, the sort of thing I remember from remote-control cars as a kid. "This is what he was using. Sends out a signal that disrupts Wi-Fi connections. Runs on a phone battery."

"But he was pointing it directly at the camera," I said, handing the box to him.

"Amateur move. These aren't like TV remotes—you don't need to aim them. The signal broadcasts in all directions." Trey turned the jammer over in his hands. "Not very powerful, but enough to knock out security cameras and alarms if you're close enough."

"So our guy knows enough about security systems to use a jammer, but not enough to know how to use it properly?"

"Exactly. Like someone who learned just enough to be danger-ous." Trey set the device on his desk. "And like I said the other day, these things are easy to get online."

"So you can pick one up at Radio Shack?"

"Radio Shack closed years ago."

"You know what I mean."

"We'll you can't buy them in legit stores—they're illegal. The FCC hates them. It's not like a de-authentication attack—that's targeted at a particular MAC address—"

He might as well have been drawing hieroglyphs on the wall. I had no idea what he was saying, and he saw that in my face because he waved both hands like he was erasing a blackboard.

"Forget it. The point is, it's cheap, and you can get one easy enough." Trey picked up the device again. "That's why these things are popular with criminals. But this guy clearly watched too many heist movies."

"And these things are illegal?"

"It's a federal crime to have one."

"But you've got one."

Trey rolled the device around in his hand. "We only use it for testing, and this little thing only has a range of about twenty yards."

"And that's legal?"

"No, technically not."

"You probably don't want to go showing that around too much," I said.

"I didn't go get it from the display case out front, you know what I mean? And Sally says I can trust you."

"He said the same thing about you."

"Then I guess we can trust each other."

"No guessing about it."

He smiled without opening his mouth, just a little hint of acknowledgment that some facts were carved in stone. Then a thought hit me.

"But the camera kept recording anyway."

Trey frowned. He didn't do wrinkles like me. "It did?"

"Yeah. That's how we got this shot."

"This is the estate?"

"No, this is a different one—the Donut Den in Palm Beach. The guy grabbed another dog."

"Do you know what kind of system the shopkeeper has?"

I pulled up another photo on my phone, this one showing Kevin's security setup.

Trey glanced at the image and let out a short laugh. "That's because the Donut Den has a hardwired system. This one uses old-school coaxial cables running to a DVR with local storage. Wi-Fi jammers can't touch that."

"So our dognapper came prepared with the wrong tool for the job?"

"Exactly." Trey set the jammer back on his desk. "This is why I always tell clients to go hardwired with both local recording and cloud backup. Sure, it costs more upfront, but it's way more reliable. This dog thief clearly doesn't know much about security systems."

"So the jammer worked at the estate," I said. "But this little box only works over about twenty yards, you say?"

"Give or take, depending on other signals and obstructions."

"So he would have had to knock out the camera at the rear of the property, where the doghouse is."

"If you say so."

"But there's a camera on the main house showing the backyard with the doghouse in the frame. It's way more than twenty yards away."

"How big is this place?"

"I don't use the word *estate* lightly."

"Well, you could have two of them, I suppose."

"But we never see anyone who shouldn't be in the house. So …"

"Inside knowledge," Trey said.

I nodded and packed that thought away for later. "So then he hits the donut shop …"

"But he didn't know about the hardwired cameras," Trey said.

"Could be someone who heard about the setup second-hand."

That sparked something. Kevin had mentioned Aram coming in for donuts. For his team, he'd said.

"The thief also knew exactly when to come," I said. "He knew about the rear door being unlocked during cleanup."

Trey nodded. "Local knowledge."

"But not technical knowledge." I leaned back and crossed my arms. "I wish we could see where he went after he left with Charlie."

"You probably can," Trey said. "This happened in Palm Beach, right? Every business has cameras these days. You know what direction the guy went, so you can follow the trail."

"That's good thinking. You'd make a decent investigator."

"Deductive reasoning is a big part of my job."

"Let's hope Palm Beach businesses aren't too cheap to pay for wired security."

"They'd have some nice stuff, I'd imagine. It pays to get something decent when you care about what you might lose."

I thanked him and was about to stand when I had another thought. They were coming thick and fast, like home runs with Shohei Ohtani at the plate.

"One more thing," I said, pulling out my phone again. "The donut shop owner had a tracker on his dog's collar. It went offline out on 710, but I had a decent phone signal out there."

Trey took the phone and studied the map, showing Charlie's last known location. "These Bluetooth trackers don't work like cell phones. They piggyback off other people's devices."

"What do you mean?"

"The tracker itself doesn't connect to cell towers. It connects to nearby phones running the tracking app, and those phones relay the location data to the cloud." Trey handed the phone back. "So when the signal disappeared, it wasn't because of poor cell coverage—it was because there weren't any compatible phones within range."

"How close would a phone need to be?"

"In ideal conditions, maybe two hundred feet max. Less if there are buildings or walls in the way. In populated areas, that's not usually a problem—there are enough phones around to maintain coverage. But out in rural areas, well ..." He gestured at the app and the last known location.

"So the tracker didn't die, and it wasn't jammed. It just couldn't find a friendly phone to talk to."

"Probably. The battery might be dead. They only last about a year in those things."

I thought about that empty stretch of road where the signal died. No houses, no businesses, just sugarcane and swamp. The perfect place to vanish with a stolen dog.

CHAPTER TWENTY-TWO

Trey's explanation rattled something loose in my brain. I steered the SUV back toward North Military Trail, thinking about security camera trails.

I rolled past the trailer park's entrance and its faded sign, heading straight for Amanda's place at the back. The Marshalls' trailer sat baking in the mid-afternoon sun. No car in the carport meant she was at one of her jobs, and Sophie would have been laboring through algebra class unless her school had also decided to declare a beach day.

No problem. I already knew they didn't have a security camera.

I cruised along the narrow streets, scanning the homes. These weren't luxury manufactured homes with pristine lawns and automatic watering systems. But even here, technology had crept in. Video doorbells and Wi-Fi cameras dotted the façades like electronic gargoyles. Some pointed at front doors, others toward the street.

The residents might not have much, but they protected what they had.

I counted six cameras on my first pass, making mental notes of their coverage areas, but I was looking for something specific.

Three houses down from Amanda's place, I found it. A double-wide with coral siding and a rusted Ford F-150 in the drive. Through the window, I caught movement—someone was home. But more importantly, mounted under the eave was exactly what I'd hoped to find: a security camera with a clear view of the street leading out to the park exit.

I pulled up to the curb and killed the engine. The double-wide's façade looked even worse up close, like sunburned skin ready to slough off. I walked up the cracked concrete path and knocked on the metal door.

Nothing.

I knocked again. I waited longer than necessary. But I heard movement inside, the soft shuffle of slippers on linoleum.

After what felt like an eternity, the door creaked open. A tiny woman peered out, wrapped in a cream cardigan despite the heat. Her silver hair was set in perfect pin curls, like she'd just come from the beauty parlor.

"Can I help you, dear?"

I introduced myself and mentioned Sophie's missing dog. Her face softened.

"Oh, that poor girl. Come in, come in. I'm Betty." She looked exactly like a Betty should look—gentle eyes, apple cheeks, and hands that had probably baked a million cookies. She led me through a living room filled with family photos and ceramic angels to a kitchen that smelled of coffee and something sweet. "Have a seat. Would you like some coffee? I just made blondies."

I sat at a small Formica table while Betty bustled around, pulling out mugs and a jar of instant coffee. "Is that your truck outside?"

"Oh no, that's Harold's."

"Your husband?"

"Forty-seven years," she said with a soft smile.

"He's not home?"

"Oh, yes. He's on the mantle."

I swiveled toward the living space. A wood mantle over an electric heater made to look like a fireplace. An urn on top.

"He passed eight years ago." She set a plate of blondies in front of me. "Cancer."

"I'm sorry for your loss."

"Thank you, dear, but I'm over all that business. He was here, he loved me, we enjoyed a lifetime together, and then his time came. We should all be so lucky."

I couldn't have put it better. Betty placed a mug of hot water in front of me and then sat down opposite.

"I noticed the security camera outside," I said.

"My son installed it. He's always worried about me being alone." She stirred a spoonful of instant coffee into our mugs. "He can see everything on his phone."

"Do you have access to it?"

"I do, somewhere." She disappeared into the living room and returned with a smartphone. "I never look at it, though. These new gadgets. I can do the video phone call thing with the grandkiddies, but that's as far as I need to go." She handed me the phone. "Maybe you can figure it out."

I found the security app and opened it. Two camera feeds appeared—one showing her living room, the other her front yard. I focused on the external camera. I scrolled back through the footage, searching for the day before I first met Sophie. There was a row of images at the bottom that represented a video of every time the camera had sensed motion and come on. Most of them were cars driving by. Betty went out to check the mail. More cars. There was nothing out of the ordinary. As I scrolled back and forth, I realized I didn't know the exact day Gaston had been taken.

"What day was that?" I muttered.

"The day Sophie's pup disappeared?" She gazed at the urn while she thought. "That was Friday."

"Friday? No, that can't be right."

"Definitely Friday, dear. Poor thing came knocking on all our doors looking for her pup. I remember because I was watching my programs. *The Wheel* was on." She shook her head. "I don't like that new boy as much. I miss Pat."

"Give him time," I found myself saying.

"Perhaps you're right."

The day didn't sound right—that would put it before Layla's theft. But I scrolled to Friday, anyway.

The footage played normally until it cut off. Not cutting to black, just cutting out. Nothing. Just like at the Kazarians'. Ten minutes later, it happened again—in and out, motion waking the camera before the feed died.

Someone with a jammer driving in, and then, ten minutes later, driving out.

I found a share button and sent the video to myself and Lizzy. Then I returned Betty's phone and sipped my coffee. It was horrible, but I drank it, anyway. The blondies were worth it. We chatted for a half hour, mostly about how the Palm Beaches had changed over the years. Then I thanked her for the coffee and cake and headed out. But I didn't get far.

As I moved toward the exit, the community center caught my eye, so I pulled in. The squat cinderblock building looked like it had been dropped there in 1975 and forgotten. A bulletin board by the door displayed notices in various states of fade and curl, including a Fourth of July BBQ flyer that might have witnessed the fall of the Berlin Wall.

But mounted above the entrance was a security camera that looked equally ancient—a beige box with a glass eye.

Inside, fluorescent lights buzzed overhead. A woman sat behind a desk, her silver-streaked hair pulled back in a tight bun that matched her no-nonsense expression. A nameplate read *Mrs. Henderson—Park Manager*.

"Can I help you?" Her voice had the weary tone of someone who'd asked that question too many times today.

I explained about Sophie's dog and Betty's footage. "I was wondering if your security system might have caught something. It's not Wi-Fi, is it?"

"Wi-Fi?" She laughed. "Five minutes ago it was VHS tapes."

"So it's an older system?"

"Honey, this thing's so old it probably filmed the moon landing."

"Could I take a look?"

"You got a warrant?" She offered a frown but didn't seem fully committed to it.

"I'm not a cop. Just trying to help find a kid's dog."

"There are privacy concerns—"

"If you prefer, I could call the sheriff. Of course, they'll want to check every camera in the park. Probably have to do a full inspection while they're here. Fire codes and all that."

Mrs. Henderson's lips thinned. "Follow me."

In a back room, she showed me a setup that looked like my dad's old garage TV, where he watched football games. The security feed played on a tiny screen inside a big square box that sat on top of what could have been a DVD player's grandfather.

Now that I had the date from Betty, we found the footage easily. Cars rolled in and out of frame, their plates impossible to read at this distance and quality. The angle of the shot meant we saw the vehicles front or rear, but as they turned, they moved out of frame. Around the time of Betty's first outage, a van that might have been brown entered. Ten minutes later, it left.

I watched it again, noting every vehicle that entered during that window, then checked them off as they departed. Only one vehicle's timing matched the video outages perfectly—that brown van.

"Mind if I get a copy of this?"

CHAPTER TWENTY-THREE

I mulled over Albright's comments about Aram's financial troubles as I headed across Bingham Island Bridge. The fashion mogul's canceled events and mounting debts raised questions, but was Albright just trying to undermine a competitor? I suspected Pixie's handler might know something about it.

The Pawlace sprawled before me like a Mediterranean resort. The normally serene campus buzzed with activity. Delivery trucks clogged the circular drive while handlers led dogs of every imaginable breed across the manicured lawns. A woman in designer workout wear clutched the leash of a tiny Yorkie like it might sprout wings and fly away.

I found a spot between a Mercedes G-Wagon and a van marked *Premium Pet Transport*. The parking lot looked like a luxury car dealership had merged with the pound.

Inside, the lobby teemed with anxious pet owners and more relaxed-looking canines. A harried receptionist tried to explain their enhanced security measures to three different people at once. Through the floor-to-ceiling windows, I spotted more dogs being exercised in the training rings than I'd seen at the dog park with Sophie and Bella.

One thing was for sure: Eve's business was booming, thanks to the wave of paranoia sweeping through Palm Beach's dog-owning elite. Nothing sold security like fear, and three missing show dogs had the whole community running scared. The Pawlace had become a five-star fortress for four-legged friends.

The receptionist recognized me when I asked after Evelyn and pointed me toward the grooming area. I found Evelyn on her knees, scrubbing a stainless-steel grooming station with the focus of a crime scene tech. Her auburn ponytail swung as she attacked a stubborn spot.

"Business is good," I said.

She looked up, wiping sweat from her brow. "Everyone's spooked. Can't say I blame them."

"How are things with the Kazarians?"

"Fine." She stood, tossing the cleaning rag into a bucket. "Pixie's been calling twice a day. She's at her wit's end."

"And Aram?"

"What about him?"

"He keeps up with the bills?"

"Never missed one." She narrowed her eyes. "Why?"

"Just asking." I leaned against the gleaming counter. "What are Layla's chances at the Canine Classic?"

Evelyn curled her lip like she was giving it some thought. "The Classic? If we get her back, she could win Westminster. She's that good."

"I've been hearing two theories about who took her. Either black market breeders or show circuit rivals."

"There's definitely a black market." She picked up the cleaning bucket. "But you can't show those dogs anywhere legitimate. The minute someone scans their chip, game over."

"How does that whole chip system work?"

She glanced at her watch. "I've got to get to a thing. Ask Dr. Ndiaye—she handles all our microchipping. I'll show you."

I followed Eve across the pristine grounds, past the bone-shaped swimming pool where a German shepherd paddled after tennis balls. Evelyn dropped the cleaning bucket in the bed of a pristine pickup truck and continued on.

"How many dogs are you boarding now?" I asked, dodging a golf cart loaded with grooming supplies.

"Triple our normal occupancy." Eve led me down a covered walkway lined with flowering jasmine. "Someone should have stolen a dog a long time ago." She stopped and her jaw dropped open. "I didn't mean that. I don't need this much business, honestly."

I nodded like I got her point.

We passed the training rings where handlers put various breeds through their paces. A massive Great Dane pranced like a ballet dancer, while a tiny Pomeranian strutted with the attitude of a heavyweight champ.

"You must have some idea who'd want to steal show dogs," I said. "Black market breeders? Puppy mills?"

"Nobody I'd know personally." She shook her head. "That's a different world."

"What about competitors?"

Eve stopped walking, her face thoughtful. "Three different breeds in three different groups have been taken. So either it's someone who only sees one of those dogs as their real competition, or ..."

"Or?"

"Or it's someone with a dog in another group entirely. Someone looking to eliminate the strongest contenders for Best in Show."

"Albright?"

"Graham?" She snorted. "He's ruthless in business, but he plays fair in the ring."

"Does that extend to creating a competitor for your facility?"

Evelyn's mouth extended in a tight smile. "You mean Bark-ingham Palace?"

"You know about it?"

"It's not that big an industry."

"So maybe he's trying to discredit you through Pixie and Layla."

"How? Layla wasn't here. If she had been, she would never have been taken. Look around. This is good for me, and Graham would know that. Besides, there's a difference between a world-class training facility and a ballroom with astroturf laid in it so you can visit your pooch while you're on vacation."

"And McDonalds started with one restaurant."

"True. They also pioneered franchising, so I'll tell you something no one else knows. Graham and I are in discussions for the Pawlace brand to take over the running of the doggie resorts at his hotels. Barkingham Palace has taught him that he doesn't want or need to be in the canine business."

"He doesn't grab me as being a quitter."

"He's not. He's a pragmatist. And a businessman. He knows our brands complement each other."

"So a collaboration?"

"You could call it that."

I wouldn't normally, but it seemed to be the word du jour. "So, not Graham. Then who?"

Her eyes narrowed. "If you want someone truly clinical and cutthroat, you want Chris Wozinski."

Evelyn left me outside the veterinary clinic's glass doors and strode away with the same name Oliver Grant had suggested still hanging on the air. Inside, the waiting room buzzed with activity. A Bernese Mountain Dog sprawled across the cool tile floor while its owner filled out paperwork.

The walls displayed Dr. Ndiaye's impressive credentials—Cornell University veterinary degree, specializations in equine medicine and theriogenology, certificates from various canine health organizations. Photos showed her working with different animals ranging from Norwich terriers to thoroughbred horses, her caring touch evident even in still images.

"I'm sorry, but Dr. Ndiaye is fully booked today," the receptionist said, barely glancing up from her computer. Her name tag read *Jennifer*.

"Hey, Jennifer. I'm investigating three missing dogs. Evelyn sent me over. Said the doctor might be able to help with some questions."

Jennifer's demeanor shifted. "Oh, you're the one looking for Layla? Let me see what I can do."

While she tapped at her keyboard, I noticed a corkboard near the entrance. Among the usual pet-sitting flyers and vaccination reminders was a *Missing Dog* poster. Sophie's carefully printed handwriting described Gaston, complete with a photo of him looking like a loquacious prize fighter.

"I see Gaston's poster," I said to Jennifer. "But not Layla's."

She shrugged. "No. Bad publicity."

"Why? The dog didn't go missing from here."

"But everyone associates her with us." Jennifer lowered her voice. "Ms. Moreau is very particular about the Pawlace's reputation. Everything has to be perfect."

The Bernese Mountain Dog had wandered over and was now sniffing my shoes with great interest. I reached down to scratch behind its ears while Jennifer made a call.

After a short wait, Jennifer waved me through to the treatment area. "Two minutes," she said.

"Only need one."

The back area was a whole other world. Stainless-steel examination tables gleamed under bright LED lights. Recovery cages lined one wall, each containing a drowsy patient. The sharp scent of antiseptic couldn't quite mask the underlying animal odors.

I recognized Dr. Ndiaye as soon as I saw her colorful head wrap, a splash of vibrancy against blue medical scrubs. She cradled a Yorkshire terrier on a table while examining its leg. Her amber eyes flicked up through colorful frames to acknowledge me, but her hands never stopped their work.

"You must be Miami Jones. Evelyn mentioned you might stop by."

"Thanks for seeing me. I'm looking into these missing dogs—"

"Layla. Yes, I've heard." She set the Yorkie down, and it immediately curled against her palm. "How can I help?"

"Tell me about microchips. Can they track a dog anywhere?"

"No, they're not GPS devices." She reached for a sealed packet on a nearby shelf. "This is what they look like before insertion. About the size of a grain of rice." She held it up to the light. "We inject them between the shoulder blades. They're passive—they don't emit any signal until they're scanned."

"Like a scanner at the grocery store checkout?"

"Different technology, but that's the idea. There are a number of registries that maintain databases of the ID numbers. When a scanner passes over the chip, it reads the number, and we can look up the owner's information."

"Could someone remove it? To hide a dog's identity?"

Dr. Ndiaye's expression darkened. "It would require surgery and anesthesia. The chips are designed for one-way insertion. Removal is complicated—they can migrate under the skin over time, and there's scar tissue to deal with." She gestured at the surgical suite visible through a window. "You'd need proper medical equipment, expertise."

"A corrupt vet?"

"At least someone with strong medical knowledge. But there's an easier way—you can simply deactivate them in the registry."

"Turn them off?"

"No, the chip itself doesn't turn on or off. The data just becomes inactive in the database. The number would still read on a scan, but the record would possibly be out of date, or, depending on the registry, unable to be retrieved."

"So you could essentially wipe the dog's existence away."

"Possibly, but there's a problem. All the dogs that were taken are pedigree show dogs."

"So?"

"So, in order to show a dog at an American Kennel Club event, it must be registered with the AKC. That means the microchip is in their database. So even if the owner record was out of date, you would still be able to know who the dog was."

"What kind of car do you drive?" I asked.

She pushed her glasses up her nose. "A Lexus. Why do you ask that?"

"Just curious if vets drive the same cars as doctors?"

"Do they?"

"Doctors favor Mercedes, except plastic surgeons. They love Porsches."

"How is this relevant to anything?"

It wasn't. I just wanted to know that it was her vehicle that I saw her put supplies in when I saw her sneaking around the rear of the facility during my previous visit. Supplies that might be used to look after a dog offsite. Or three dogs.

"Thanks for your help," I said, turning toward the door. Then stopped. "One more thing—do you know Chris Wozinski?"

"Chris Wozinski?" Dr. Ndiaye's amber eyes met mine. "I wouldn't say I know him."

"What would you say?"

"He's around the show circuit."

"Does he bring his dogs here?"

"No. He has his own facility." She focused back on the terrier on the table. "So I've heard."

"Is this facility on the island?"

"No," she said. "I don't think so. But he may have a home here."

"What's your take on him?"

"My take? He's brilliant, and he genuinely cares for his animals." Something flickered across her face.

"I sense a *but* coming."

She adjusted the stethoscope hanging around her neck, choosing her words carefully. "His approach to genetic testing as a breeding tool raises concerns. It's actually a moral issue that plagues the entire show dog industry." She gestured at a nearby chart showing canine skeletal structures. "We've created breeds through selective inbreeding. But at what cost? These practices can lead to genetic anomalies, health issues."

"Like what?"

"Take French Bulldogs, for instance. We've bred them to have those cute flat faces, but many struggle to breathe properly. Some breeds have tails docked purely for aesthetic reasons. Is that ethical?"

"I wouldn't want my tail docked," I said, reaching for the door handle.

"Mr. Jones?" Her voice stopped me. "Will you find them? Layla, Gaston, and Charlie?"

I turned back, surprised. "You know all three dogs?"

"Only Layla comes here, but I work as a vet at local shows. I've met them all. So will you? Find them?"

I looked her in the eye and sighed.

"I hope so," I said.

CHAPTER TWENTY-FOUR

I walked across the campus, squinting against the glare bouncing off the Pawlace's cream-colored walls. A warm breeze carried the scent of salt air from the Intracoastal, along with the distant barking of dogs at play in the exercise yards.

The pieces weren't fitting together neatly. Three dogs stolen, all show quality but from different categories. Someone tech-savvy enough to jam security systems but amateur enough to point the jammer like a TV remote. Microchips that could be deactivated but would still give away the dogs' identities if they ever showed up at another competition.

I watched a handler lead a pair of Afghan Hounds across the manicured lawn, their coats flowing like silk in the breeze. These weren't street mutts being grabbed for quick cash—these were calculated thefts of specific dogs. But for what? Did black market breeding make sense if you couldn't register the puppies? And taking out show competition seemed extreme.

I reached my SUV, the heat from the black paint almost burning my hand as I grabbed the door handle. The whole thing felt off, like I was missing something obvious. Three dogs, three different owners, three different categories—but one common thread I hadn't found yet.

I slid into the driver's seat, the leather creaking as I started the engine. The air conditioning blew across me, letting my thoughts settle.

Through the windshield, I watched a woman in designer shades lead her perfectly groomed poodle to a waiting Range Rover. The contrast hit me hard—here were people spending more on dog grooming than some families made in a month. Back at Stone's, we had kids who couldn't afford a meal, let alone proper boxing gloves, yet they showed up every day, determined to make something of themselves.

The steering wheel was hot under my palms. A memory flashed of the lanky teenager I'd watched working the speed bag a few days ago, complete focus despite the worn-out gear. He had more grit in his little finger than half the people I'd seen on the island with their designer dogs and climate-controlled kennels. But, I reminded myself, that didn't mean the people here loved their pets any less.

I pulled out of the Pawlace parking lot, merging into the steady flow of luxury cars and service vehicles that characterized Palm Beach traffic. The sun filtered through rows of royal palms lining the street, their fronds casting shifting shadows across my hood. The familiar landmarks of wealth—boutiques, galleries, and carefully maintained hedges—scrolled past my windows as I headed toward the Palm Beach Police Department.

I pulled over in front of the police station, finding a spot between two patrol cars. The Mediterranean style that dominated Palm Beach was evident here too. Officers moved with purpose through the sliding doors, their pressed uniforms and polished badges catching the afternoon sun.

Behind the front desk, an officer with sergeant's stripes shuffled through a stack of papers. He glanced up long enough to give me a tired nod.

"You want me to call him?"

I shook my head. "I texted."

The sergeant went back to his paperwork. The lobby buzzed

with activity—phones ringing, radios crackling, the steady stream of officers and civilians moving through security.

I'd barely taken a seat in one of the hard plastic chairs when Ronzoni appeared from a side office. His tie hung loose around his neck, and dark circles under his eyes suggested he'd been at it since dawn. His extra-wrinkled outfit showed signs of a day or three spent hunched over reports.

"Jones." He waved me toward the back. "Let's talk."

I followed Ronzoni into his office, the tang of old Chinese food and burnt coffee hitting me like a Louisville Slugger. Case files littered his desk, threatening to avalanche onto the floor. The bulletin board behind him had grown since my last visit—photos of missing people now shared space with pictures of Layla and Charlie.

Ronzoni flopped into his chair. "You look like you've got something."

"Maybe. What'd you find on the ransom?"

He leaned back, the chair creaking under his garlic-bulb frame. "Dead ends. Every security camera in a three-block radius of the amphitheater shows nobody of interest."

"Out of action, like the donut shop?"

"No, they were working. They showed nothing. None showed the actual trash can, but we looked for comings and goings and saw nothing but us." He grabbed a stack of papers. "Interviewed twenty-seven people who were in the park. Nobody saw anything unusual except our homeless friend, and he was more interested in that chicken than helping us." Ronzoni's face darkened. "We checked traffic cams leading out of downtown. Nothing. It's like whoever took that money vanished into thin air."

"What about the homeless guy?"

"You heard him. He was just looking for food. We checked him out—he's just a homeless guy." Ronzoni threw his hands up in despair. "Three dogs, one ransom attempt, and all I've got is an empty chicken dinner container in evidence." Ronzoni let out a heavy sigh. What about you? Got anything?"

"Maybe. You know anything about a Chris Wozinski?"

"Should I?"

"Name came up in conversation with Eve Moreau. Apparently, he's making waves in the show circuit with his approach to breeding. Uses genetic testing. Real cutting-edge stuff."

Ronzoni's brow furrowed. "Tech guy?"

"That's the whole dossier, so far."

Ronzoni's chair squeaked as he sat up straighter. "You think he's involved?"

"No idea."

"But why steal show dogs?" Ronzoni asked. "What's the endgame?"

"Maybe it's not about the dogs themselves. Maybe it's about who wins when they're gone."

Ronzoni turned to his computer, his thick fingers beating at the keyboard with the precision of a distracted woodpecker. The screen's glow highlighted his face as he pulled up the driver's license database.

"Well, that's interesting." He squinted at the screen. "Only Chris Wozinski in Florida lives in Port St. Joe."

"That's not our guy. Word is he lives here in Palm Beach."

"Let's try something else," he said, his tongue sticking out as he typed. "Okay, he's got a business license. And let's see ..." He typed again. I watched him work, wondering if this was how Lizzy did her work, and how the two of them might fare in a database-off. "Yep, his business owns a property on the island."

"A store?"

"A residence."

"How does a business own a house?"

"Real estate investing? Otherwise known as a tax dodge."

"But he's not a resident?"

"Lots of that here. New York. New Jersey. Getting a few Texans these days."

"Can you get me an address? Where's this house?"

Ronzoni leaned back, his face pinching with discomfort. "You know I can't share that kind of information without probable cause. Right now, all we've got is speculation and Eve Moreau's opinion."

"Come on, Detective. Three dogs are missing."

"But I can go see him, and I suppose there's no constitutional amendment says you can't tag along."

CHAPTER TWENTY-FIVE

Ronzoni's unmarked car wound through the side streets off North County Road, past hedges and gates that screened mansions from view. Chris Wozinski's place sat back from the road, nestled among towering royal palms. No gates, just a simple shell driveway that curved toward a modern beach house.

The house spread low across its lot, weathered cedar siding and walls of glass catching the light. Native plants and sea grapes created privacy without the usual Palm Beach ostentation.

The doorbell chimed inside. Footsteps approached, and the door opened to reveal a lean man in his early fifties, red hair going lighter at the temples where most men went gray. He wore designer running shoes and expensive athletic wear that looked tailored, as if there was such a thing.

"Chris Wozinski?" Ronzoni held up his badge. "Detective Ronzoni, Palm Beach Police. This is Miami Jones."

A small crease appeared above his nose. "Yes?"

"We're investigating the disappearance of a couple pedigree dogs on the island, and your name came up as someone with information on the dog show industry."

"Came up where?"

"In our inquiries." Ronzoni put his badge in his jacket pocket. "Perhaps we could talk inside?"

"Come in." Chris ushered us inside and led us into an open living room. Floor-to-ceiling windows framed a stunning ocean view, while pale wood floors and white walls created a sense of endless space.

"Water?" Chris asked, heading toward the kitchen. "Just got some fresh lime and mint from the garden."

We both nodded, and I looked around the room. The space felt lived in despite its pristine appearance—a laptop on the coffee table, running shoes by the door, dog toys scattered across the floor.

A massive dog padded into the kitchen, its tawny coat gleaming in the sunlight. Chris gave it a pat as he prepared our drinks. The dog wagged its tail before moving to a thick rug by the windows, where it settled with a view of the beach.

"That's a beauty," I said. "What is it?"

"She's a Saluki, and yes, she is a beauty."

As we moved toward the sofas in the living room, I asked him what he did for a living.

"I have a number of ventures," he said. "Mostly technology. My latest is an AI-driven system to predict heart attacks in susceptible patients without the need for a full CT scan."

"You in Silicon Valley?"

"No, Austin."

"You prefer Texas?"

"No. I prefer the Bay Area, but Texas is cheaper for labor right now."

I frowned. "Right now?"

He nodded. "That will change. Things always do. I'm actually looking at New Mexico for my next venture."

We sat on sofas looking out to the beach. Ronzoni leaned forward, his tie dangling precariously close to his water glass. "Have you heard about the recent dognappings?"

Chris nodded, his expression neutral. "You said a couple. But three dogs are missing, if I'm not mistaken, not two."

Ronzoni didn't mention he didn't care about anything that happened off island. "You're not concerned."

"Should I be? My dogs are well protected." He gestured toward a sleek panel on the wall that I assumed was a security system.

"We understand you're a pedigree breeder," Ronzoni said.

"Not exactly." Chris set his glass down. "I breed to show, not to produce puppies for sale. There's a difference."

"I hear you do things differently," I said.

Chris offered a tight smile. "If by *differently* you mean, do I live in the twenty-first century? Then, yes." He pulled his laptop closer. "For generations, breeders have relied on gut instinct and traditional wisdom. But data doesn't lie."

He turned the screen toward us. Charts and genetic markers filled the display. "Modern technology lets us identify optimal breeding pairs, track hereditary traits, and predict show success with remarkable accuracy."

"Clinical," I said.

"Exactly." He smiled. "The data is clear. Terriers have dominated Westminster Best in Show. Wire fox terriers, in particular, have won more than any other breed. It's not chance—it's mathematics."

The Saluki lifted its head, watching Chris with devoted eyes.

"Sounds like *Moneyball*," I said, thinking back to the Oakland A's revolutionary approach to baseball statistics. Billy Beane was into the data when I had been with the A's.

Chris sipped his water. "Exactly. Sabermetrics methodology took gut instinct out of baseball recruitment and focused on what the data said. I look for the aspects that win rather than those that are popular mythology. The art within the data."

I glanced at the elegant hound lounging by the window. "But that's not a terrier."

"No, she's not." Chris's expression softened as he looked at his dog. "That's Terra. She's the reason I got into dogs in the first place." He paused, watching her stretch and resettle. "She's magnificent. But that's what I mean. If I showed what I loved, I would compete and lose. A Saluki has never won their group at Westminster, let alone Best in Show."

"Why is that?" Ronzoni asked. "She looks like a dog the queen might have."

Chris nodded. "Yes, that's true. Salukis have been favorites of royalty in the Middle East and Europe for centuries." He gestured toward Terra, who remained regally indifferent to our conversation. "But if you're referring to the late Queen of England, then no —she favored Pembroke Welsh corgis."

The tech mogul leaned back, his designer athletic wear creasing and un-creasing in ways that suggested expensive clothes were immune to wrinkles. "Now, corgis have won their group numerous times but never Best in Show." He was clearly a smart guy, but there was a good dose of mischief in his eyes. "But the point is, I don't enter to lose. I enter to win." He tapped his laptop screen. "So I currently show wire fox terriers. The data supports no other conclusion."

I leaned forward and held my water between my knees. "You don't mind pushing boundaries to win."

"No, I don't." Chris's smile remained steady. "I'll use every advantage I have."

"Even if that means taking out other potential Best in Show candidates?"

The temperature in the room seemed to drop. Chris's eyes narrowed, though his posture remained relaxed. "Are you accusing me of something, Mr. Jones?"

"Just asking questions."

"What exactly is your business here?" He set his glass down with a soft *clink.*

"I've been hired to find Layla."

"Ah, Pixie." Chris leaned back, understanding dawning on his face. "Okay. Well, to answer your question—yes, thinning the herd would help, but it's not within the rules." He gestured toward his laptop. "And I push boundaries. I don't cheat. Besides..." He shrugged. "An Afghan Hound will never beat a genetically perfect terrier for Best in Show."

"What about Charlie?" I asked.

Chris let out a genuine laugh. "A golden retriever? No. Really, no. Beautiful dog, great with kids, but way too dopey in the ring to win." He took another sip of his lime-infused water. "And before you ask about the French Bulldog—the little girl's dog?" He shook his head. "Neither of them are ready for the Canine Classic, let alone Westminster. Maybe one day, but not now. Taking out that dog would be a waste of resources."

We sat in silence for a moment, sipping our drinks. Through the wall of windows, waves rolled onto the beach, and a pelican dove into the surf. Terra lifted her head to watch the bird, then settled back into her sophisticated lounging.

Ronzoni shifted in his seat. "So why wouldn't Terra win Best in Show? She's pretty impressive."

Chris's eyes softened as he looked at his dog. "Salukis are incredibly intuitive, with high emotional intelligence. If I'm stressed, she knows and shares my stress. And show floors are stressful places."

Terra lifted her head at the mention of shows, or perhaps the thought of food, and padded over to her person.

"That's why Salukis don't win," Chris continued, reaching over to caress behind Terra's ears. "They're never their best selves under pressure. The noise, the tension, the expectations—they feel it all. Most people don't understand that. They think a dog is just a dog."

I watched Terra lean into Chris's touch, her whole body relaxing. The bond between them was obvious, making his choice to show terriers instead of his beloved Saluki even more telling. Here was a man who'd choose data over emotion every time.

"A wire fox terrier," Chris said, "doesn't care if you're nervous. Doesn't pick up on the crowd's energy. Just struts around like it owns the place, which is exactly what the judges want to see."

I set my empty glass on the coffee table, letting the *clink* punctuate the silence. "You seem to know every angle of the business. Ever come across the dark side?"

Chris's eyebrows lifted. "Dark side?"

"A guy like you who pushes boundaries, you must get glimpses of the other side of the fence."

He shifted in his seat. "What exactly are you asking about?"

"Black market breeders, puppy mills. That sort of thing."

Terra pressed closer to Chris's leg. He absently stroked her head, his eyes fixed on me.

"I want to be clear," I said, holding up my hands. "I'm not accusing you of anything. Just curious what you might have heard."

Chris's jaw worked for a moment. Terra's tail thumped softly against his leg, the only sound in the room besides the distant surf.

"The show world isn't as pristine as the public thinks," he said finally. "But I stay away from that side of things. My methods might ruffle feathers, but they're all above board. Everything I do can be tracked in databases and verified through DNA testing."

Ronzoni asked, "But you've heard things?"

"Of course, I've heard things." Chris's hand stilled on Terra's head. "When you're successful, people approach you with opportunities. Usually at shows, after hours. Always very careful with their words." He shook his head. "I shut them down fast. My reputation is worth more than whatever they're offering."

He grabbed a device that looked like a phone and hit something on the screen. The sliding glass door eased open all by itself, and the flyscreen door replaced it. The sound of the waves amplified, and the salt aroma wafted in.

"There are always bad actors," Chris said, letting his hand drop from Terra's head as she wandered back toward the new smells coming from outside. "Puppy mills are real, and yes, a purebred show dog would make an excellent breeding animal. That's why I keep my facility's location private and maintain strict security."

"Your security's not Wi-Fi-based, is it?" I asked.

"It's military grade. I know, because I sold the military their latest on-base systems." A ghost of a smile crossed his face.

"Anyone around here fit that puppy mill profile?" Ronzoni asked.

Chris shook his head. "They wouldn't need to be local. These networks often operate across state lines to confuse record-keeping. There's no national database of dogs."

"Dr. Ndiaye mentioned something like that," I said.

"You know Dr. Zara?"

"Layla is a client," I said. "But you're not."

"Like I say, I have my own facility."

"But you know Dr. Ndiaye?"

"I keep my ear to the ground for good people. A first-class team doesn't build itself."

"You've offered her a job?"

"I didn't say that."

I nodded. "What did she think of your methods?"

"I don't believe I said I had discussed them with her."

"*You* didn't."

He lifted his chin and watched me along his nose like it was the barrel of a rifle. "She had reservations about the facility. But that's why I want her. I want those opinions. I choose to not live in an echo chamber."

"Fair enough. But whoever took these dogs needs somewhere to keep them. The thefts happened over more than a week. First Layla, then Gaston, and now Charlie."

"Actually," Chris interrupted, "I believe Gaston was taken first."

Ronzoni nodded. "That's correct. *The Post* confirmed they spoke to the young girl before Pixie reported her dog missing."

My mind flashed back to Betty at the trailer park, her security footage confirming that my earlier thinking was incorrect. "They must be keeping them somewhere nearby."

"They could drive each one to Georgia or Louisiana, hell, even California, one at a time," Chris said.

"Seems like a waste of resources."

"It would be."

I leaned forward. "So, do you know anyone? Because we're coming up empty here."

Chris glanced out at the beach. "I've heard a name," he said, dropping his voice. Terra's ears perked up at his change in tone. "But you didn't hear it from me."

"Okay."

"Zazy."

The name hit me like a fastball. That name kept coming up.

"Who is this Zazy?" I kept my voice neutral, not wanting to spook him.

Chris shook his head. "Could be a man, could be a woman. But whenever someone talks about the darker side of breeding, that name comes up."

Ronzoni put his glass down. "Thanks for sharing that with us, Chris." His tone had shifted from casual to cop-mode in an instant. "We appreciate your time."

Ronzoni stood and extended his hand. Chris shook it firmly.

"I hope everything goes well for you at the show," I added.

Chris managed a small smile.

Back in the car, Ronzoni and I exchanged looks. "Zazy," he muttered, like he was tasting the word. "I'll run it through our database, see what comes up."

I nodded. "Good. I wanted to know more about this guy."

Ronzoni started the car. "This is my investigation, Jones. I'll decide what I want to share."

"You wouldn't even have the name without me, Ronzoni."

"And the taxpayers of Palm Beach thank you."

CHAPTER TWENTY-SIX

I left Ronzoni at the station and headed straight for the Publix lot down the road. The mid-afternoon siesta time offered plenty of spots.

My phone buzzed as I reached for the door handle. Lizzy's number flashed on the screen.

"Got something for me?" I asked.

"I found Henry McCaron." Her voice carried that tone she used when delivering less-than-great news.

"The hospital?"

"That's just it—he's not in a hospital." Lizzy paused. "It took longer to track him down because he's in hospice care."

My hand dropped from the car door. "Hospice?"

"Yes. He's dying, Miami." The gentleness in her voice matched the gravity of her words. "Do you still want the details?"

I leaned against the door, feeling the heat through the window. "More than ever, I think."

"I'll text it to you."

I heard her, but my mind was on poor Sophie—first her dog, and now this. "Thanks, Lizzy. You're the best."

"I know," she said, and hung up.

I walked down Sunrise Avenue to the Donut Den. Kevin's shop sat quiet now, the lull before the after-school storm.

I didn't go in. Instead, I turned down the service alley that ran beside the building. The security camera that caught our dognapper hung from the wall, its lens pointed down over the back door where Charlie had been led away.

The alley continued past dumpsters and utility meters. About fifty feet along, it opened into a loading dock area—the kind of space delivery trucks used during business hours but sat empty otherwise. A perfect spot to park without drawing attention. The high walls of the surrounding buildings created shadows even in daylight.

I followed the path the dognapper would have taken with Charlie, emerging onto Sunset Avenue. I had no idea which way the guy would have gone. Across the street, a row of upscale boutiques and galleries lined the sidewalk. During business hours, their customers' luxury cars would have provided perfect cover for a getaway vehicle.

I crossed Sunset Avenue, dodging a Bentley that crept along, looking for parking. A bell chimed as I pushed through the door of Salon de la Mer. The air conditioning carried hints of lavender and something chemical.

A receptionist peered over tortoiseshell glasses. "Can I help you?"

"I'm looking for the manager."

"That would be me, darling." A tall man swooped in from behind a styling station, his fitted shirt matching the blue high-lights in his artfully tousled hair. He extended manicured fingers. "I'm Brioche."

"Like the bread?"

"Exactly like the bread, honey. And you've arrived just in time." He circled me slowly, fingers combing through my hair. His face fell into an expression of theatrical despair. "Don't worry, I can fix this."

I gently pulled away from Brioche's hands. "I was hoping to ask about your security cameras."

"Our what?" His fingers twitched, clearly wanting another pass at my hair.

"I'm looking for footage from two nights ago. A dog was stolen from across the street."

"Oh, the donut man's dog?" said Brioche. "Such a sweetie. Always so well-behaved, unlike some of our clientele's little monsters."

"You know Charlie?"

"Of course."

"You don't happen to know Pixie Kazarian, do you?"

He sniffed. "No. She gets her hair done at Claude's."

His tone carried enough disdain to fill an Olympic swimming pool. I filed away the territorial nature of Palm Beach hairdressers for future reference.

"About those cameras—" I started, but Brioche was back to examining my hair.

"Honey, when was the last time you had a proper cut? This is criminal."

"There are lives at stake here, Brioche."

His hands paused mid-fuss. "I don't know."

"For heaven's sake, Brioche," called a woman from under a dryer. "There are lives at stake. Show the man whatever he needs."

Brioche handed me back to the receptionist as he returned to his client's hair. She led me to a sleek computer terminal behind the counter and pulled up the security system interface.

"It's pretty straightforward," she said. "Just use these arrows to scroll through different times."

I leaned over the counter, watching as footage rolled across the screen. The camera faced the street, capturing a slice of sidewalk and road at an angle that missed most of the loading area.

"Anyone leaving that back area would have to turn left to show up here," I said, mostly to myself.

Brioche hummed in agreement from his station where he was transforming his client's hair into what looked like modern art.

I found the timestamp from the day in question and started scanning. Palm Beach's afternoon crowd passed by in fast-forward —women in designer resort wear, men in pastel polo shirts, the occasional service worker hurrying to catch a bus.

"There's a lot more foot traffic than I expected," I noted.

"Honey, this is the new Worth Avenue," Brioche replied without looking up from his work. "That new wine bar opened across the street."

I continued searching but saw nothing larger than toy poodles and designer purse dogs. No sign of our dognapper or Charlie.

"I don't think this is going to help," I said, straightening. "But thanks for letting me look."

"You're welcome, darling." Brioche appeared at my side. "Now about that hair—"

"Thanks, but I'm good." I headed for the door.

"*Good* is not the word I would use!" he called after me. "Come back when you're ready to take your appearance seriously!"

I let the door close behind me, running a hand through my perfectly fine hair.

I checked the angles from this side of the street and walked down the block to Palm Beach Dental Associates, pushing through glass doors into an atmosphere thick with antiseptic and that uniquely dental mix of fluoride and fear. The waiting room gleamed with the sterility of an operating theater, all chrome and white surfaces.

A receptionist in pale blue scrubs sat behind a sliding glass partition, her eyes fixed on a computer screen. The rhythmic whine of a drill filtered through the walls, accompanied by the soft hum of voices.

She didn't look up from her screen. "Can I help you?"

"I need to see your security footage from two days ago."

That got her attention. She peered at me through the glass. "Are you with the police?"

I pulled out a business card and slid it through the opening. "Private investigator. There's been a series of thefts in the area."

She picked up the card, examining it like it might bite. "I'll have to check with the doctor."

She disappeared down a hallway toward the sound of dental work. The drill stopped, replaced by murmured conversation.

A moment later, she returned with a tall man whose frame seemed constructed entirely of right angles. His white coat hung from his shoulders like a flag on a windless day.

"I'm Dr. Peering," he said, his voice carrying the kind of grave undertone usually reserved for announcing bad news. "What's this about?"

"I'm Miami Jones," I replied. "I'd like to look at your security footage."

He regarded me with the same detached interest morticians reserved for their clients. "And you are?"

"I just told you. Miami Jones."

"No, I mean, what is your authority here?"

I watched the dentist's face harden and thought of Lenny. My old friend and mentor always said you could never trust a man who put his fingers in your mouth for a living. Looking at Dr. Peering's rigid posture and clinical gaze, I could see his point.

"This is a police matter," Dr. Peering said. "Have them return with a warrant."

He turned to leave, his white coat swishing with self-importance.

"You know Pixie Kazarian?" I called after him.

He paused mid-stride. "Pixie? Yes."

"She's a patient?"

"She is." His words carried the careful measure of someone who understood patient confidentiality laws.

"Well, she's my client." I let that sink in. "I'll be sure to let her know how helpful you were in trying to get Layla back."

Confusion flickered across his face. He clearly had no idea who

Layla was, but Pixie's name carried enough weight to make him reconsider.

"Let him in," he said to the woman in scrubs, then he strode away.

This receptionist must have trimmed her nails because she worked the keyboard silently as she navigated through the security system. The footage showed the same stretch of street I'd been watching at the salon, but from a different angle. This view captured more of the loading area, though the afternoon shadows made details harder to pick out.

"There." I pointed. "That's the time stamp we want."

She clicked play, and we watched the scene unfold. I leaned closer, expecting to see our ball-capped friend leading Charlie away from the Donut Den.

"Wait, go back about thirty seconds."

She reversed the footage. I studied the screen, searching for any sign of man and dog. Instead, a brown van rolled out from beside the loading dock, its windowless sides offering no glimpse of what —or who—might be inside.

"Can you zoom in on that van?" I asked.

The image grew larger but grainier. No license plate was visible in the shadows, and the vehicle itself was so generic it could have been any one of thousands in South Florida. Except I had the idea of a brown van lodged in my mind.

Then the receptionist used the space bar to progress the video a frame or two at a time. In slow motion, the van turned into the street.

I squinted at the screen. The painted lightning bolts caught my eye first, followed by the muscled figure wielding a sword against a stormy backdrop.

"Stop it there," I said.

The receptionist's finger hovered over the keyboard. "Is that guy holding a sword?"

"Sure is."

"He looks like He-Man." She tilted her head, studying the

gaudy artwork. "Though he's going to get electrocuted standing out there in all that lightning."

The mural was as subtle as a monster truck rally, but it triggered something in my memory. I'd seen this van before, recently.

"The police will be coming by for a copy of this footage," I said, straightening up from the counter. "It would be better if they didn't need a warrant. Your cooperation will be appreciated."

She nodded, already reaching for a sticky note to write down the timestamp.

I stepped out onto the sidewalk and stood in the heat radiating off the buildings. That van. Where had I seen it? The memory crystallized behind the cigarette shop, parked next to that beat-up Civic. The same brown van with its over-the-top mural of lightning and muscles.

CHAPTER TWENTY-SEVEN

THE SHERIFF'S OFFICE ON GUN CLUB ROAD LOOKED EXACTLY AS IT HAD the last hundred times I'd been there. A massive center dedicated to the incarceration of human beings. It was an edifice to the failure of a society if ever there was one.

I didn't know what Ronzoni might be prepared to share with me, but I had my own ways of finding out things. Some were official, others less so.

I asked for Detective Annabelle Faust at the duty desk and waited for a few minutes until she arrived. She wore a blue button-up shirt and hadn't bothered to put on a jacket, so her holstered weapon was on display, a reminder for me to mind my manners.

"Coffee?" Faust said. She didn't wait for an answer, already moving toward the cart just outside in the shade of the building.

"I'm good." It was getting way too late in the day for coffee if I planned on sleeping anytime in the next week. I watched her order something that probably had more ingredients than syllables.

"Soy vanilla latte, extra hot," she told the barista, then turned to me. "You look like you've been busy."

"Three missing dogs now."

She nodded and then turned away until the barista handed over her beverage. She took her first sip and dropped that right eyebrow of hers. "The ransom drop was a waste of my morning. I did you a favor showing up for that circus."

"This is different." I watched a uniformed deputy order a black coffee I was sure he could have gotten inside for free. We've got two dogs taken in Palm Beach, and now one in West Palm."

"Riviera Beach, technically." She lowered her cup. "Which means none of them are my responsibility."

"Are you sure?" I asked. "Two different cities makes it a county investigation."

"Only if they're linked, and you haven't shown me anything to suggest that. It's just three dogs, for crying out loud, Jones."

"But where there's three, there might be more." I paused, watching her sip her drink. "I'm not asking you to investigate. Just wondering if you know anything about puppy mills or illegal breeding rings in the area."

Her brown eyes narrowed. "What exactly do you think I do for a living?"

"Investigate stuff."

"Not stuff, Jones." She squared those tight runner's shoulders. "I investigate major crimes—armed robbery, murder. I don't do puppies. You do puppies."

"I do," I said. "Because fourteen-year-old girls can't do it for themselves."

She eyed me for longer than was necessary. "Your client is a fourteen-year-old girl?"

"More or less."

"Not some rich Palm Beach socialite?"

I had to hand it to her. She had me pegged. "Look, I just need to know if you have any intel on this. I heard a name."

Faust's wrinkle under her left eye deepened as she studied me. "I suppose I can plug in a name."

I followed Faust back into the building and through the maze of cubicles, dodging desk corners and rolling chairs. The office space was all beige walls and fluorescent lights that made everyone look slightly ill.

Her desk setup reminded me of a day trader who'd fallen on hard times. Multiple monitors hung from metal arms, their screens covered in a film of dust, the desktop and chair scratched and worn. Manila folders teetered on the edge of a filing cabinet like a game of bureaucratic Jenga.

Faust dropped into her seat with the familiarity of someone who spent more time there than at home. She didn't offer me a chair, so I leaned in over her shoulder.

Her fingers hit the keyboard like she was accusing them of something, the clacking mixing with the ambient office noise. As she worked, she squinted at the display.

Her right eyebrow shot up. "Well, well," she muttered, scanning the records. "Your boy Zazy's been busy. Armed robbery, grand theft auto, three separate domestic violence orders ..." Her southern drawl made it sound like she was reading off ingredients for Betty's blondie recipe. She shook her head, ponytail swaying.

When she reached the animal cruelty charges, her voice hardened. "Ran a puppy mill outside Phoenix. Got shut down after multiple violations. Dead animals found on site." She turned to me. "You can pick 'em, Jones. This guy's a nasty piece of work."

The harsh overhead lighting cast sharp shadows across her face as she spun back around and continued scrolling. Each new charge painted an increasingly darker picture.

I leaned forward, and Faust's hair touched my cheek, so I pulled back some. Faust's posture shifted subtly. I could see the investigator in her taking over. It might not have been a murder case, but people were still getting hurt. People like Pixie and Sophie.

"Got a photo of this charmer?" I asked, and Faust clicked through to another screen.

The image was a classic mug shot, and no one looked good in a mug shot. Even the Hollywood actors who were done for drugs or DUI looked washed out and subhuman. But this guy was something else. Black hair pulled back in a ponytail, his cheeks craggy and all kinds of angles, with a goatee that appeared to have been left to its own devices. Something about the shape of his mouth caught my attention—the way it stretched horizontally without curving, like someone trying to smile without showing their teeth. This guy wouldn't have looked better if Annie Leibovitz had taken the shot.

"Could be our guy from the donut shop, if he grew a goatee," I mused. "Or shaved one off. Hard to tell from that security footage. Any local address?"

Faust shook her head, scrolling through more records. "Nothing in Florida. Last known was Arizona, before the mill got shut down." She turned in her chair, fixing me with those sharp brown eyes. "If you want me to dig deeper, I need probable cause. You got anything concrete linking him to these dogs?"

I thought about the van with its ridiculous mural, the jammed security cameras, the missing pets. All circumstantial. "Not yet. He's just a name. Can't confirm if he took them, where they might be, or if the dogs are still, you know …" I left the last part unsaid.

"Still alive," Faust finished for me. Her face hardened. "Sounds like you've got work to do, Jones."

"Thanks for this." I straightened up and stretched out my back.

"Don't thank me yet," Faust said, already turning back to her screens. "Come back when you've got something I can use."

I left the office and walked back across the crowded parking lot. I needed to find that brown van—the one thing that might tie Zazy to these thefts. And I knew where to look.

CHAPTER TWENTY-EIGHT

I EASED INTO THE STRIP MALL PARKING LOT IN THE TWILIGHT AND cruised past the Goodwill. Easing around the back, I spotted the tobacco store's back entrance wedged ajar with a cement block, the dented Honda where I'd seen it before. The brown van with its absurd painted artwork and the gleaming Beemer were nowhere in sight.

I parked out front and went inside, and the *Jeopardy* buzzer went off. Amanda looked up from behind the counter, where she was restocking display shelves with vape supplies. Did they take liquid, or were they cartridges like the bug-repellent device I had sitting on the back patio? I had no idea.

The dim lights served to make everyone look sallow, but the shadows across Amanda's tired face were not just one bad night's sleep in the making.

"Your boss around?" I asked.

"No." She didn't look up.

"The guy with the Meat Loaf van. Tell me about him."

Her shoulders tensed. "Don't know much to tell."

"But you know him?"

"He deals with my boss." She shoved another box onto the shelf. "I mind my own business."

"Even when he might have stolen your daughter's dog?"

That got her attention. She spun around, eyes narrowing. "What are you talking about?"

"The van was spotted near where at least two of the dogs were taken. Including Gaston."

"Listen," she said, voice sharp. "I need this job. I'm not getting mixed up in whatever you think is going on."

"Your daughter's heartbroken about that dog."

"He did me a favor if he took it. I don't need to be paying for no dog. "

"So you do know him."

"I told you—he deals with my boss. That's all I know, and that's all I'm saying." She turned back to the shelves. "Now, unless you're buying something, we're done here."

I leaned against the counter, watching her rigid posture. "Okay, but when the police start digging—and they will—they'll find a connection between this van and your workplace. They'll talk to Sophie, who'll tell them how much you hated paying for that dog. Makes for a tidy little case."

Amanda's hands froze on the shelf. She set down a box with deliberate care.

"You think I'd do that to my own kid?" She turned, eyes flashing. "I work three jobs to keep food on the table. Yeah, I complain about the dog—it's one more expense we don't need. But steal it?" She shook her head. "Who do you think I am?"

"Someone who might want to tell me about the van's owner before this gets messier."

"I told you, he deals with my boss." Her voice cracked. "That's all I know."

I studied Amanda's face, every muscle being pulled toward the floor like she was aging right in front of me. She was caught between protecting her job and caring for her daughter. Maybe the two things weren't as separate as I had thought. But I could see in her expression that she was lying.

"Look, just give me the guy's name. Is it Zazy?"

"Zazy?" She shook her head. "No. Luis. Luis Romero."

"Are you sure?"

"Yes."

"Does he go by Zazy?"

She frowned again. "How would I know? I'm telling you, I don't know the guy."

"Why have I seen him here?"

Amanda's eyes darted toward the door, then back to the shelves. Finally, she sighed. "He provides cigars."

"Cigars?" I raised an eyebrow. "Like he delivers them?"

"Kind of." Her voice dropped. "He delivers Cubans. Technically, they're illegal."

"Contraband cigars." I almost laughed. "Seriously?"

"Yes." Amanda's posture remained rigid. "My boss sells them under the counter to a few special customers. People who know."

"Are they that much better than the local thing?"

She shrugged, returning to her restocking. "I don't know. I don't smoke them. But they smell the same." A slight pause. "Some people just like prestige things, don't they? Sometimes it's not about being better. It's about having something they're told they shouldn't have."

She had a point—tell someone not to do something and suddenly that was all they wanted to do. Like those *Keep Off the Grass* signs that made you want to sprint across the lawn doing cartwheels. Human nature was funny that way.

"Look, I appreciate the help," I said.

"Will you go after my boss?"

"I'm not a cop, Amanda. But don't worry—I'm not interested in busting anyone for a few cigars. That's not my thing."

Amanda's shoulders relaxed, though her eyes still held that wary look.

"I just want to find these missing dogs. So, I wouldn't mind knowing where I could find this Luis. Any ideas?"

She hesitated, then seemed to make up her mind with a sigh.

"He works at some fancy place called the Leaf Lounge. You know it?"

I nodded. I knew it. The Leaf Lounge. The pieces clicked into place—the cigars, Albright's comments, the connection between Palm Beach's elite and the shadier underbelly. A high-end cigar club would be the perfect place to move contraband smokes, and to overhear all sorts of interesting conversations about valuable dogs.

I turned to leave but stopped at the door. "One more thing."

Amanda was watching me go, and I saw the wariness creeping back into her expression.

"Sophie wants to visit Henry McCaron. Would you let me take her?"

Her face hardened. "I don't like that guy. What's his angle with a young girl like that?"

"He's in hospice care," I said. "He's dying. He's not going to do anything except maybe say goodbye."

Amanda's hands stilled on the shelf. I could see the conflict playing across her features.

"Look, he means something to Sophie. If he passed and she never got to see him…" I let that hang in the air. "Do you really want her to hate you for keeping her away?"

Amanda's shoulders slumped. She lifted just her head and looked at me through old eyes. "Fine. You can take her."

"Thank you."

"But," she added, "you have to promise not to tell anyone about my boss and, you know, the other stuff." She gestured vaguely at the shelves.

I shook my head. "I'm not interested in your boss or what he sells."

"Then you should come back later tonight. Luis usually comes on Wednesday nights because he doesn't have a shift at the lounge."

"Okay. Thanks."

"But make it look like you didn't know, will you?"

"I don't even need to come in."

Her jaw tightened, but she gave a short nod. "And Sophie, be careful with her, okay? I know you don't believe me, but she's the most important thing in the world to me."

"I've never believed anything more in my life." I nodded and stepped back into a brilliant sunset that really didn't fit the mood of the day.

CHAPTER TWENTY-NINE

I parked in the gap between Goodwill's delivery door and the hurricane fence, killing the lights but leaving the engine running. The AC fought against the thick evening air while I watched the rear of Smokes and Things.

Amanda's beat-up Civic sat where it had been earlier. The putrid security lights behind the shops flickered, casting weak squares onto the cracked asphalt.

Eight-fifteen came and went. The AC labored harder against the humidity until the windows started to fog. I cranked them down and killed the engine, letting in the symphony of crickets and distant traffic. The evening air carried traces of potential rain mixed with dumpster funk.

A sleek black BMW rolled in precisely at eight-thirty. The shop owner emerged, his carefully groomed eyebrows visible even in the dim light.

The Meat Loaf van announced itself before I saw it, the incongruous sound of Gloria Estefan and Miami Sound Machine thundering through speakers that caused the panels to vibrate. The gaudy artwork on its side was even more ridiculous in the security lights. The shirtless warrior holding his lightning rod sword against a stormy backdrop looked like he might have jaundice.

Luis hopped out wearing a black hoodie that seemed calculated to draw attention rather than deflect it. A nylon messenger bag hung at his side as he sauntered toward the back door.

He didn't bother checking his surroundings. Why would he? No one cared what happened behind discount stores after hours. The cops had bigger problems than contraband cigars, and the evening workers at surrounding businesses were too focused on closing up to care.

The shop owner held the door open, light spilling onto the asphalt. Their shadows stretched long across the parking lot as they disappeared inside.

I slouched lower in my seat, though I doubted either of them would notice me tucked deep in the shadows. After less than ten minutes, Luis returned alone, tossed his bag inside, and drove away.

I followed the van at a distance as it wound through West Palm's side streets. The mural made it easy to track without staying too close. Luis had a routine down—pull up, grab the messenger bag, disappear inside for roughly eight minutes. Like clockwork.

First stop was Smoker's Joint off Okeechobee, a dimly lit shop wedged between a karate gym and a place that sold cardboard boxes. Then Heavenly Tobacco near the turnpike, which looked anything but heaven-like with bar-covered windows. Stop three was some no-name joint in a strip mall that had seen better days, probably back when disco was king.

The final cigarette shop sat in the shadow of I-95, the constant whoosh of traffic almost drowning out the van's sound system. Gloria had given way to Celine Dion by this point. The contrast between "My Heart Will Go On" and the muscle-bound warrior on the van's side made me wonder if Luis picked his music purely to confuse anyone tailing him.

The next stop was Club Paradise. Not a smoke shop. This one was a strip joint. The neon sign buzzed and flickered, the *P* permanently dark but the pair of upturned legs a giveaway. A handful of cars dotted the parking lot. There was no paradise to be found in their dashboard lights.

Luis parked around back, away from the main entrance. This time, he emerged nine minutes later, the messenger bag noticeably lighter than when he'd gone in. He tossed it into the passenger seat and fired up the van, Bonnie Tyler filling the night air.

I hung back as he moved south around the airport.

The van swung into El Gallo's parking lot, the space lit by the diner's giant neon rooster. A cluster of yellow cabs lined one side of the lot, their drivers inside getting their midnight fuel of Cuban coffee and pastelitos. The *Open 24 Hours* sign cast alternating shadow and light across the asphalt.

Luis pulled into a spot away from the cabs but with a clear view of the entrance. He killed the engine, silencing Whitney Houston mid-chorus, and traded his messenger bag for a large duffel on wheels, the kind I recalled baseball players carrying their equipment in.

I positioned myself where I could watch both the van and the diner's entrance. The aroma of grilled meat drifted through my open window, mixing with the muggy night air and setting me off like Pavlov's pooch.

The minutes ticked by. Cab drivers came and went, paper bags of late-night sustenance in hand. A couple of cops stopped in, probably working the graveyard shift. The neon rooster cast its red glow across my dashboard as I waited.

Ten minutes stretched to fifteen. Then twenty. Luis hadn't emerged.

Either he was having the world's slowest midnight snack, or El Gallo wasn't just about Cuban sandwiches and café con leche. I drummed my fingers on the steering wheel, watching the entrance for any sign of movement.

Curiosity killed the cat, but boredom did too, so I pushed through El Gallo's glass door, the bell overhead chiming against the hum of conversation and clinking plates. The aroma of Cuban coffee hit me first, followed by fried plantains and garlic. My stomach growled, reminding me I'd skipped dinner.

A waitress with *Maria* on her name tag barely glanced up from wiping down the counter. "Coffee?"

"To go." I slid onto a vinyl stool to wait.

There was no Bunn flask. Cubans didn't drink that dishwater. The Moka pot gurgled and while Maria poured, I scanned the room. Red vinyl booths lined the windows, most occupied by cabbies killing time between fares. Four of them hunched over a card game at one table, stacks of coins and singles between them. A couple of truckers nursed cups of café con leche at the counter, their eyes fixed on their phones.

No sign of Luis or his duffel bag.

Maria set the coffee in front of me. It smelled like heaven but tasted like tar, and I pretended to sip it.

I passed over some cash and nursed the drink for a few minutes, watching the room's reflection in the chrome napkin dispenser. The card players erupted in Spanish curses as someone swept the pot. A cook emerged from the kitchen with medianoche sandwiches, a variation on a Cuban sandwich that sent both sweet and savory notes into the room.

Still no Luis.

I held up the paper cup to Maria, and she offered a smile, then I walked back outside. The van sat exactly where Luis had parked it.

I circled around to the back of the building, where dumpsters sat in complete darkness. The air felt thick enough to swim in. My eyes adjusted slowly, picking out shapes—stacked milk crates, cardboard boxes waiting for recycling.

A metal door marked "Employees Only" broke up the plain concrete wall. Light seeped out from underneath, a thin yellow line against the black asphalt.

I crept along the back wall, where a small window, grimy with years of kitchen grease and dirt, sat chest-high. I wiped a small circle with my fingers that only did something for one side of the pane and pressed my face close.

A room spread out before me. Four dining tables had been pushed together in the center, creating a makeshift workspace. Half a dozen men sat around them, methodically rolling cigars. Tobacco leaves and cellophane wrappers littered the tables. Spanish conversation mixed with laughter floated through the glass.

The scene looked more like a social club than a sweatshop. These weren't captive workers—they moved freely and joked with each other. One guy even had a small radio playing salsa music while he worked.

But no sign of Luis or his duffel bag. I was about to pull away when two heavy hands landed on my shoulders.

They spun me around, nearly lifting me off my feet. Two guys built like nightclub bouncers held my arms. One had a neck tattoo that looked like a barcode. The other wore enough gold chains to start his own pawn shop.

"Inside," Barcode rumbled, his accent thick with Little Havana.

They marched me through the metal door and down a short hallway that smelled of bleach and tobacco. The cigar rollers looked up as we entered, then returned to their work. No one wanted to make eye contact.

An older man rose from a desk in the corner, his white guayabera crisp despite the humid air. His silver hair was slicked back, and a gold tooth flashed when he smiled. He moved with the confidence of someone used to being in charge.

"Ah, a curious gringo," he said, spreading his arms wide like I was a long-lost relative. "Welcome to my humble workshop."

He gestured at the tables where the workers continued rolling cigars. "You want to learn about our business, huh? Well, my friend, take a look."

Barcode turned me toward the workers as if I wasn't capable of doing it myself.

"See how carefully they work? Each leaf must be perfect." The silver-haired man picked up a finished cigar, holding it under his nose. "The aroma, the construction—indistinguishable from genuine Cubans. And at a quarter of the price."

The pride in his voice was unmistakable. This wasn't just business to him; it was art. Illegal art, but art, nonetheless.

"They look like the real thing," I said, flexing against Barcode's grip on my arm.

"They *are* the real thing."

"Just not made in Cuba."

"Exactly."

"Some might call this counterfeiting, then," I pointed out.

The man shook his head gently. "I prefer to think of it as preserving tradition. These are family recipes, passed down through generations." He tapped the cigar against his palm. "The embargo merely forces us to be creative in our methods."

The silver-haired man moved to a workbench against the wall, and Barcode deposited me beside him. Boxes of labels and bands sat in neat stacks, each one a perfect match for famous Cuban brands. He held up a Cohiba band, the gold hologram catching the fluorescent light.

"Feel this," he said, pressing it into my palm. "The texture, the weight—exactly like the originals. You cannot tell the difference."

He pulled open a drawer filled with wooden cigar boxes, the Spanish text burned into the lids with precision. The craftsmanship was undeniable. Each box could have come straight from Havana.

"My box man, he is an artist." The man picked up an empty box, running his fingers over the wood grain. "He learned from his father in Cuba, worked for the state factory until he escaped. Now he works from his garage in Hallandale." He picked up a cigar band. "The old printing press we use came piece by piece from the island."

He demonstrated how the bands slipped perfectly onto the rolled cigars, how the box hinges moved without a sound. Every detail considered, every element refined through years of practice. "The boxes age in his garage for months. The wood must absorb the Florida humidity, just like in Cuba. When they arrive here, they are perfect."

I watched him seal a box. Then he turned back to survey the room like a proud parent.

"Why are you showing me all this?" I asked, Barcode's grip firm on my biceps.

His smile faded, the gold tooth disappearing. The pride in his voice gave way to something harder. "Because I need you to understand the care we take. The art we preserve."

The switchblade appeared in his hand like a magic trick, light dancing along its polished surface. He turned it over, letting me appreciate the craftsmanship of the handle, the precision of the mechanism.

"You see, my friend, what we do here is our cultural heritage. And as such, it must be protected." He stepped closer, the blade catching fluorescent glints. "We cannot allow curiosity to endanger what we have built."

His two enforcers tightened their grip on my arms. I could feel Barcode's breath on my neck, heavy with garlic from what I assumed was a midnight Cuban sandwich.

The silver-haired man took another step. "It is important you understand what we—"

"Miami Jones?"

The voice cut through the tension like that blade would have cut through my ribs. Everyone turned toward the metal door where a well-built man stood with a plate of bistec. It took me longer than necessary to place him. It had been ten years since I had last seen him.

The man with the knife paused, his eyebrows drawing together. "Julio, you know this person?"

Julio stepped into the room and put his plate on a side table. He moved toward us with an easy grace. He had been an athlete, and despite the extra wrinkles around his eyes, he still moved like one.

"Miami Jones, it is you." Julio's voice carried the same warmth

I remembered from when I had met him during a case a decade ago. Back then, he'd been the star at West Palm Jai Alai.

The silver-haired man's blade wavered. "You vouch for this man, Julio?"

I recalled his name was Diego Alvarez, but all the Jai Alai players adopted one-name monikers like Brazilian footballers.

Julio nodded, a smile breaking across his weathered face. "This man helped me and my brothers at the fronton. He saved my life. He's good people, Mr. Ruiz."

Mr. Ruiz studied me with new interest, the knife disappearing as quickly as it had appeared. "Is this true?"

"Ancient history," I said, noting that the grip the enforcers had on me had not slackened. "And I'm not here about your cigars. Your business is yours. I'm more interested in your delivery boy."

"Luis?" Ruiz's expression darkened. "What has he done?"

"He might be involved in some thefts."

Ruiz's face twisted like he'd bitten into a lemon. "Stealing? This is unacceptable. We will handle him—"

"Let me confirm it's him first," I cut in. "No need for anything drastic. I just need to know if he's involved."

The two guys holding my arms released their grip at a nod from Ruiz. I rolled my shoulders, working out the tension.

"You are sure about this man?" Ruiz asked Julio again.

"On my life," Julio replied.

Mr. Ruiz sat me at a table to the side where Julio ate his dinner. Julio explained that he had given up jai alai when his shoulder finally quit on him. Now he worked as a landscape gardener and came to the diner for the homestyle food and camaraderie.

"So what has Luis done?" he asked. I noted Mr. Ruiz paying close attention.

"Some dogs went missing," I said.

"Dogs?" said Mr. Ruiz. "That's it?"

"Expensive dogs."

Mr. Ruiz said something in rapid-fire Spanish that I didn't catch.

Julio said, "He doesn't like it when things attract unwanted attention. Luis should know better."

"I can't disagree with that, but I don't have proof he did anything yet." I rubbed my biceps. There was going to be bruising. "If I get it, there's no need for you boys to be part of the story."

Julio repeated this to Mr. Ruiz in Spanish despite the older man speaking perfect English.

Mr. Ruiz moved to a large crate by the wall and returned with a polished wooden box, the Cohiba logo burned into the lid. He pressed it into my hands with a tight smile.

"A gift," he said, "to commemorate our newfound friendship."

The box felt heavy, solid. Real Cuban cedar, or a damn good fake. Everything about it screamed authenticity, right down to the tax stamp.

"You're too kind," I said, knowing better than to refuse.

"Not at all." He patted the box. "Perhaps you will develop a taste for fine cigars." He walked me to the metal door, clapping me on the shoulder. "Take care, my friend. And about Luis…"

"If he did something, it had nothing to do with you. I was never here."

He smiled, and his gold tooth shone. I shook hands with Julio and walked out through the diner.

The night air didn't feel so humid after the confines of the cigar production room. There had been turnover in the parking lot—cabs had gone and been replaced by others that looked the same, and a semi-trailer truck idled in the far corner, both driver and vehicle fueled and ready for a long night following a tunnel of light they would never catch. Luis's van was nowhere to be seen.

I sat in my car for a moment looking at the late-night crowd of insomniacs nursing cups of coffee. Mambo music drifted out into the lot, competing with the buzz of the neon rooster overhead.

I placed the box of contraband cigars on the passenger seat, feeling the weight of Mr. Ruiz's gift and everything it represented. The night had given me more questions than answers, but at least I'd walked out with all my parts intact.

CHAPTER THIRTY

DANIELLE AND BELLA WERE ASLEEP WHEN I GOT HOME AND WERE STILL tucked in bed when I took off the next morning. I cruised past the main gate of the Pawlace just as the sun crept over the horizon. The morning dew still clung to the manicured lawns, and the only movement came from sprinklers making their rounds.

I had questions about Chris Wozinski's relationship with Dr. Ndiaye, and I wanted to catch her early, so I drove around the property near the employee's service entrance behind the surgery building.

I was prepared to wait, but Dr. Ndiaye's white Lexus sat backed into a spot near the rear entrance, trunk open, so I pulled over in the early shade of a stand of pines. She emerged from the building carrying bags of pet food and more plastic tubs. Nothing unusual for a vet, except for how she kept looking over her shoulder between trips, and the fact that the supplies were going out and not coming in.

I resisted the urge to slouch lower in my seat—the tinted windows of my SUV probably kept me hidden well enough, and although the car was obvious enough parked outside the gate, it was just another bland SUV in a land full of them. She made three more trips, each time checking the parking lot before loading items into her trunk. She moved like someone who'd done this before and knew exactly how much time they had.

On her final trip, she did a complete three-hundred-sixty-degree check of her surroundings, reminding me of surveillance footage of convenience store robbers casing the joint before going in. She closed the trunk gently, like she was trying not to make a sound despite being the only person around. Or at least, the only person she knew was around. Another quick glance in all directions, then she slipped into the driver's seat of her Lexus.

I kept three cars between us as Dr. Ndiaye crossed the bridge off Palm Beach island. The morning commuter traffic made it easy to stay hidden while she navigated west on Southern Boulevard.

The landscape changed dramatically as we left the coastal wealth behind. Gone were the perfectly trimmed hedges and spotless sidewalks. The manicured palm trees gave way to scrubland dotted with convenience stores and auto repair shops.

Past the turnpike, even those signs of suburban life thinned out. Fields of sugarcane stretched to the horizon on both sides of the road. The sharp contrast between Palm Beach's excess and western Palm Beach County's agricultural poverty hit home. On the island, people were concerned about which luxury car to drive. Out here, they worried about whether their decades-old pickup would start.

Belle Glade rose from the farmland like a town that time forgot. Where Palm Beach had gleaming high-rises and boutiques, the biggest thing in Belle Glade were the sugarcane stores, and most buildings had bars on the windows. Palm trees still lined the streets, but these weren't the carefully cultivated royal palms of Worth Avenue—these were wild, untamed specimens that had survived decades of hurricanes and neglect.

The town's nickname, Muck City, came from the rich, black soil that had made this region an agricultural powerhouse. But that same soil also marked the divide between the haves and have-nots. While Palm Beach had grown wealthy on the produce grown here, Belle Glade's farmworkers lived in squat cinderblock homes and shopped at Dollar General.

Dr. Ndiaye's pristine Lexus stood out among the dusty work trucks and ancient sedans, marking her as clearly as if she'd driven through with lights and sirens. I followed her as she turned onto Main Street, past stores that were all part of national chains.

The Lexus continued as if heading south out of town, but on the outskirts slowed before a large, low building that might have been some kind of agricultural sales facility. I turned down the side road where I pulled over beside a horse training ring. I got out and took in the trail that led around a large lake, then I walked back along the fence line and hid behind a tangle of bushes.

Dr. Ndiaye was going through the same process in reverse, carrying supplies into the building. She did several trips again, only this time she didn't bother looking around furtively, as if she knew she wouldn't be spotted out here. Pickups and a handful of sedans drove by on the Cross State Highway, but none seemed to pay her any mind.

The whole thing had the feel of a drug deal. The desolate location, the barren parking lot, the rundown state of the building. I got the sense that time wasn't all that had been forgotten in this place. People had been, too.

I tried to think of a good reason why the vet was out here all alone, because I already had a mind full of bad reasons. Some had something to do with moving stolen pet supplies or pharmaceuticals, but those thoughts were getting crowded out by the obvious. You brought dog food and supplies out to the edge of nowhere because you had dogs in the building that you didn't want anyone to know about.

Stolen dogs.

I couldn't make the pieces fit. Dr. Ndiaye seemed passionate about the animals she cared for. Were her misgivings about Chris Wozinski just baloney to deflect me from their relationship? Was she working for him to ensure he did win the next big dog show?

A lot of questions outside in the bushes. The answers were all inside that building. I gave the vet ten minutes. She didn't return to her car, so I crept toward the building, mindful of my capture the previous evening.

The problem with the structure was that it was built to withstand hurricanes and beating sun, and not to offer views of the interior to sneaky private investigators. There were no windows. None. The side nearest the road had two roller doors for deliveries that were both closed. The only opening on the side I watched from was the service door Dr. Ndiaye had used.

So I took door number one and only. It wasn't locked. I stepped into the darkness of an open area that bore the mild tang of horsehair. As I moved further inside, I picked up the sound of humans—the hum of indistinct chatter and tension. But chatter didn't come from two people doing a drug deal, and stolen dogs never sounded like a cocktail party. This was people, plural, and a good number of them.

I entered what turned out to be a cavernous livestock sale barn, my eyes adjusting to the dim light filtering through gaps in the metal roof. Dr. Ndiaye was setting up folding tables along one wall, arranging basic medical supplies and examination equipment. A line of people snaked from a makeshift reception area toward a door on the far side of the building, through which I could see a collection of old-model vehicles parked in the sunlight.

The crowd reminded me of a soup kitchen line, but instead of empty bowls, these folks clutched animals of all shapes and sizes. A weathered man in overalls held a scruffy terrier mix with a limp. Behind him, an elderly woman cradled a cat wrapped in a threadbare towel. A teenage boy struggled with a goat that seemed determined to eat his T-shirt.

Further down the line, I spotted chickens in carrying cages, a rabbit with an eye infection, and what looked like a three-legged pig. Most of the dogs were mixed breeds, their coats dulled by sun and dirt, a far cry from the pampered pooches at the Pawlace.

A young mother juggled a squirming toddler and a German shepherd with a visible wound on its flank. The dog's ribs showed through its coat, but its tail wagged hopefully.

Dr. Ndiaye's eyes locked onto me from across the makeshift clinic. Her professional demeanor flickered for just a moment before she marched over, her colorful head wrap a stark contrast to the agricultural surroundings.

"Mr. Jones, did you follow me here?" Her voice carried more irritation than anger.

"I did." No point lying about it. "What exactly are you doing out here?"

She grabbed my arm and pulled me toward an examination table where a scrawny puppy waited. "Since you're here, make yourself useful. Hold him down while I give him his shots."

I placed my hands gently but firmly on the pup's ribcage. Its heart raced under my palm as Dr. Ndiaye prepared a vaccine.

"These people can't afford regular vet care," she explained, expertly administering the shot. "Most clinics won't even see them without payment upfront. The nearest low-cost facility is in Fort Pierce."

The puppy barely flinched as the needle went in. Dr. Ndiaye's touch was that gentle.

"But these animals need care, and their owners love them just as much as any Palm Beach socialite loves their show dog." She caressed the puppy's head. "Maybe more, because they sacrifice so much to keep them fed. Did you know some of these folks skip meals to buy dog food?"

The pup's tail wagged as its owner, a weathered woman in a factory uniform, scooped it up and thanked Dr. Ndiaye profusely in Spanish.

Dr. Ndiaye smiled at the woman but then turned to me, her eyes flashing. "Why did you follow me out here, Mr. Jones?"

"I came to the Pawlace early to ask you some questions. Saw you sneaking around, loading supplies into your car." I shrugged. "I'm looking for stolen dogs, so I put two and two together."

Her jaw dropped. "You thought I stole those dogs? That I'm keeping them here?"

"You were taking stuff from the clinic."

She let out a short laugh and walked to a cardboard box near her makeshift examination table. She pulled out several packages of medications, holding them up so I could read the labels. *Sample —Not for Resale* was stamped across each one in bold red letters.

"These are donations from pharmaceutical reps. The Pawlace gets more than we can use, especially since most clients there can afford whatever their pets need." She set the packages down. "Many clients there write us checks to buy what we can't otherwise get. The food companies give us anything they don't give away during the shows."

A young boy approached, cradling a scraggly orange cat with a swollen paw. Dr. Ndiaye motioned him forward.

"Here, hold him like this." She positioned my hands on the cat's body and the scruff of its neck. "Gentle but firm. These farm cats aren't used to being handled."

The cat tensed under my grip but didn't struggle as she examined its paw. The boy watched anxiously, asking if the cat would be okay in Spanish. Dr. Ndiaye responded in kind, her voice soothing.

"Infected scratch," she explained while cleaning the wound. She glanced at me. "Probably from fighting over territory. Out here, cats are working animals—they keep the rats out of feed stores and barns. But they still need care."

I spent the next few hours holding various animals while Dr. Ndiaye worked her magic. A farmer brought in a sheep with an infected eye, its wool matted and dirty. The animal stayed surprisingly calm as she cleaned the infection and administered antibiotics. The farmer explained how the sheep had walked into a barbed wire fence, and Dr. Ndiaye showed him how to apply the medication going forward.

An elderly woman shuffled in with an ancient chihuahua mix that had trouble breathing. Dr. Ndiaye diagnosed a respiratory infection and provided medicine, but also spent time showing the woman exercises to help the dog's breathing. The woman's weathered hands trembled as she counted out dollar bills, but Dr. Ndiaye waved the money away.

I spent ten minutes lying on top of a working dog from one of the sugar plantations. The Belgian Malinois had cut its paw on something in the fields, and infection had set in. The dog's handler, a sunbaked man in dusty work clothes, explained how the dog helped patrol the vast fields at night. Dr. Ndiaye cleaned and stitched the wound while I kept the powerful animal still. Despite its obvious pain, the dog remained stoic, only whimpering once when she hit a tender spot.

Between patients, Dr. Ndiaye would sort through donations and organize supplies. She worked efficiently, never wasting a movement or a moment. The line of people and animals never seemed to get shorter, but she gave each case her full attention, switching easily between English and Spanish as needed.

As the last patient left—a mono-horned goat with an attitude problem—Dr. Ndiaye began packing her leftover supplies.

"So, what did you want to ask me about?" She folded a stainless-steel table. "Before you decided to follow me out here?"

"Chris Wozinski." I helped her stack some chairs. "You didn't mention he offered you a job."

Her movements stiffened. "Because it wasn't relevant."

"Everything's relevant in my line of work."

She turned to face me, her eyes narrowing. "I like working at the Pawlace. The facilities are excellent, Eve is fair, and the pay allows me to do clinics like this." She gestured at the now-empty barn. "Chris offered more money, yes. But money isn't everything."

"You said you didn't agree with his genetic testing and cutting-edge breeding programs."

"I don't."

"He suggested he would like an alternative point of view."

She snapped shut her medical bag. "He wants alternative ways to do the things he wants to do, not be talked out of doing them at all."

"Sounds like you've got it all figured out."

"I do." Her tone left no room for argument.

I helped Dr. Ndiaye carry boxes of leftover supplies to her Lexus. The cargo space was mostly empty now, the bulk of the medicines and all the food having gone.

"So what was with all the sneaking around this morning?" I asked.

"Eve doesn't like me doing these clinics," she said, arranging the empty tubs carefully. "Says it could hurt the brand if people found out we also serve regular farm animals."

"The horror."

"She worries clients might think their precious show dogs are getting the same treatment as working animals." Dr. Ndiaye shook her head. "As if good veterinary care should be different based on pedigree."

A young boy ran up with a chicken cradled in his arms. The bird's wing drooped at an odd angle. Dr. Ndiaye set down the box she was holding.

"Un momento," she told me, leading the boy back inside.

I watched through the door as she gently examined the wing, speaking to both bird and boy.

When she returned, she was wiping her hands on a paper towel. "Simple dislocation. Easy fix." She tossed the towel in a waste bin. "Eve would have a fit if she knew I was treating chickens. But I won't stop. My days off are my own, and these people need help, and their animals deserve care just as much as any champion Afghan Hound. So now you know my secret," Dr. Ndiaye said, opening the driver's side door of her car. "What are you going to do about it?"

I put my hands in my pockets and kicked at the dirt beneath my feet. "What do you need?"

CHAPTER THIRTY-ONE

WHEN I GOT TO THE MARSHALLS' PLACE, SOPHIE WAS ALREADY waiting on the tiny concrete porch, her backpack clutched to her chest like a shield. She bounded down the steps before I could cut the engine.

She slid into the passenger seat, her energy filling the car. "Is it far?"

"About twenty minutes." I navigated through the park's narrow streets. "You ready for this?"

She nodded, though her fingers twisted the straps of her backpack.

The hospice sat back from Military Trail, surrounded by landscaped gardens dotted with benches and water features. The building itself was single-story, looking more like a family home that had been held through several generations than any kind of hospital.

Inside, the air held that carefully cultivated blend of antiseptic and artificial freshness. Potted orchids lined the reception desk, their delicate blooms adding splashes of color. Somewhere, an essential oil diffuser puffed out lavender mist, mixing with the sharp bite of bleach and the underlying notes that reminded me this was still a medical facility.

A nurse led us down a hallway floored with vinyl plank where landscape prints hung at precise intervals. Sophie walked close beside me, her earlier enthusiasm dampened by the hushed atmosphere.

"He's been asking about you," the nurse said softly, pausing outside a room. Rather than a number or a patient name, the nameplate on the door read *Marigold*. "Just know, he tires easily now."

Sophie's hand found mine, surprising us both. I gave it a quick squeeze as we stepped into Henry's room.

Henry lay propped against stark white pillows, his skin nearly matching their pallor except for the gray undertones that spoke of failing organs. The flesh around his jaw had retreated, leaving shadows where vitality used to be. His hands rested on the blanket like fallen leaves, paper-thin and trembling slightly.

But those eyes—they sparked with recognition. The bright blue irises seemed to float in their sunken sockets, and a smile creased his weathered face as he spotted Sophie.

"There's my champion," he whispered, his voice carrying the scratch of disuse.

Sophie's grip on my hand tightened. She stood frozen halfway between the door and the bed, her shoulders rigid. I recognized that look—the same one I'd seen when she talked about her father. That mix of wanting to trust and being afraid to. The wariness of a kid who'd learned early that people left.

"It's okay," Henry said softly. "I don't bite."

Something in his tone broke through her hesitation. Sophie dropped my hand and launched herself at the bed, throwing her arms around Henry's neck. The force lifted his head from the pillow as he wrapped those fragile arms around her.

"Easy there, kid," I started to say, but Henry was already shaking his head at me, his eyes welling with tears.

I settled into a chair by the window as Sophie perched on the edge of Henry's bed. The old man's eyes never left her face as she launched into stories about past dog shows they'd attended together.

"Remember that Pomeranian that wouldn't stop barking?" Sophie smiled. "And you said it probably thought it was a lion?"

Henry's laugh turned into a wheeze, but his smile remained steady. "That judge nearly jumped out of his shoes every time it yapped."

They traded memories back and forth—training sessions in the park, an Australian cattle dog that kept trying to herd the other contestants, Sophie's first time in the ring with a borrowed corgi. The room felt lighter somehow, as if their shared joy had pushed back the sterile hospice atmosphere.

Then Sophie's voice dropped. "Gaston's gone, Henry."

The old man's face fell, those bright eyes dimming. "Gone?"

"Someone took him." Sophie twisted her hands in her lap. "While I was at school."

Henry reached out with trembling fingers to pat her arm. "Oh, Sophie. I'm so sorry."

"But Miami's going to find him." She turned those hopeful eyes my way. "Right?"

I shifted in my chair, the weight of that trust settling heavy on my shoulders. Finding lost dogs wasn't exactly my usual line of work, but looking at these two—the dying mentor and his young protégée—what felt like a frivolous case on the surface took on a whole other level of significance. I knew something about that mentor-protégé relationship. But for Lenny Cox, I would be… I didn't know. Nothing good. And that only served to add to the gravity of what I was doing chasing after a bunch of pampered pooches.

Henry studied me with surprising intensity for someone so frail. "You'll bring him home?"

I nodded, hoping I could make good on that silent promise. Three missing dogs, a mysterious van, and a shadowy figure named Zazy—the pieces were there, but I still hadn't figured out how they fit together.

Sophie launched into telling Henry about how Gaston had placed second in his latest park show, an achievement that had earned him a place in the Canine Classic before he disappeared, and I watched the old man's face light up with pride despite his obvious exhaustion.

Henry's gaze lifted from Sophie to me. His voice dropped, barely a whisper. "You should have seen her that first day at the show. Most kids just want to pet the dogs, play with them. Not Sophie. She watched how they moved, how the handlers guided them." His thin hands smoothed the blanket. "She asked questions about stance, about presentation. Real questions."

I nodded, remembering her at the dog park, teaching Argos show moves.

"The next show, she was there again. And the next. Walking around with a notebook, writing everything down." Henry's eyes brightened at the memory. "She helped anyone who needed it—holding leads, fetching water, cleaning up after the dogs. Never complained once."

"That's why you gave her Gaston?"

"One of my best puppies." He smiled weakly. "Sophie has the gift. Not just love for the animals—plenty of people have that. She understands them, works with them, not against them. Natural talent like that, you nurture it."

I thought about Amanda's trailer, the worn furniture, the multiple jobs she worked just to keep food on the table. A show-quality French Bulldog would eat better than most people in that park. And then there were the vet bills. But Henry had seen something special in Sophie, something worth investing in. Maybe he hadn't considered the financial burden he was placing on a single mother, or maybe he had and decided Sophie's potential was worth more.

"Most handlers, they're in it for the ribbons," Henry continued. "Sophie—she just wants to learn, to be better, and to help the dogs do the same. That's rare in someone so young."

Henry's words faded into a hacking cough that shook his bird-like frame. Sophie grabbed a tissue box from the bedside table, and Henry took one, pressing it to his mouth as the spasms continued.

"Sophie," I said, "could you go and find some water for Henry?"

She hesitated, but Henry nodded between coughs, and she slipped out of the room.

I waited until his breathing steadied before I spoke again. "Why didn't you give a dog to Victoria?"

Henry's eyebrows lifted. "You know Vicki?"

"We've met."

He sank deeper into his pillows, the coughing fit having drained what little energy he had. "I would have loved for her to get into the dogs, but she just wasn't interested." His fingers plucked at the blanket. "I didn't want to force her. It's something you do because you love it. She had to find her own thing she loved."

"Has she?" I watched his face carefully. "Found her own thing?"

Henry's eyes drifted to the window. "I don't know." The words came out barely above a whisper. "I really don't know."

I watched Henry's face, the afternoon light casting deep shadows in the hollows of his cheeks. The question had been sitting there since my conversation with Victoria, and now seemed the time to ask it.

"Would Victoria steal Gaston?"

Henry's eyes closed for a moment, pain flickering across his features that had nothing to do with his illness. "I hope not." He opened his eyes, focusing on some point beyond the window. "But I knew the girl, not the woman. Disappointment can make us see a world that isn't real." His fingers traced invisible patterns on the blanket. "My wife and I did what we could for Vicki, but she drifted away and never came back. She might think it's her versus Sophie, but Soph's fourteen. She wasn't born when Vicki started to break the strings that bound her to us."

He paused, gathering strength. "I don't know what she blames Sophie or the world for, but she believes the results of her choices are her parents' fault. But she had a good childhood, I think. Never missed a meal or a hug from her mother. She was never abused or mistreated like these poor kids you hear about. Things maybe haven't gone the way she planned with her life, but they never do, do they?"

"Not in my experience," I agreed, thinking of my own path from minor league baseball to private investigator. Life had a way of throwing curveballs when you least expected them. The batters that made it learned to make hay from the few easy pitches that came in between the tough ones.

Sophie returned with a paper cup of water, helping Henry take small sips. His color improved slightly, though exhaustion had carved deeper lines around his eyes.

We talked a while longer, Sophie sharing stories about the dog park and her attempts to teach Argos show moves. Henry smiled at that, though his responses grew shorter, his eyes fighting to stay open.

"I think we should let Henry rest," I said, catching Sophie's eye.

She started to protest, but then saw Henry's drooping eyelids.

"Okay." She stood, hesitating for a moment before wrapping her arms around Henry in a gentle hug. "I'll come back soon."

Henry patted her back weakly. "Thank you for coming."

Sophie stepped out into the hallway, leaving me to follow. But Henry's thin voice stopped me at the door.

"Miami." He beckoned me closer with one trembling hand. I leaned in, catching the medicinal scent that clung to his skin. "If you see Vicki, would you ask her to come visit?"

His eyes fixed on mine, carrying a weight his frail body no longer could. "If she won't do it for me," he whispered, "maybe she'll do it for herself."

I nodded, unable to find words that wouldn't sound hollow.

Henry settled back against his pillows, those bright eyes already closing as I turned toward the door.

CHAPTER THIRTY-TWO

W E LEFT THE MANICURED GARDENS OF THE HOSPICE IN SILENCE. SOPHIE stared out the passenger window, her earlier energy replaced by something heavier. The afternoon sun caught her profile, reminding me of Henry's wan face against those stark white pillows.

"What's your mom doing tonight?" I asked, merging onto Military Trail.

"Working at the tattoo parlor." Sophie's fingers twisted in her lap. "I've got a Kraft dinner, don't worry."

I thought about the empty trailer, about a fourteen-year-old girl eating mac and cheese alone while processing what we'd just seen. "Why don't you come to ours? Bella will be there."

Sophie shrugged, her shoulders barely moving beneath her floral top.

I pulled into our driveway, Sophie trailing me toward the front door. Danielle met us in the entryway, her eyes widening at the extra guest. Bella appeared at the end of the hallway. The smile on her face vanished as she caught the mood in Sophie's slack posture. Bella stepped forward and without a word put her arm around her friend, leading her away to the kitchen.

Danielle caught my arm as I closed the front door. "Did you get permission to bring her here?"

"I had permission to take her to a hospice to visit a dying man." I shrugged. "We're just on the way home."

The girls emerged from the kitchen with glasses of water, Argos padding alongside. They disappeared down the hall into Bella's room, the door clicking shut behind them.

I scrunched my face, glancing toward the closed door. "Should we—"

"Calm down." Danielle said, patting my shoulder. "They didn't take a rock band in there with them."

"But anything could be happening."

"They need their private space." She crossed her arms. "Just like you do."

"My private space is Longboards."

"Exactly." Danielle's eyes softened. "And they need theirs. Let them be."

I offered her a nod coupled with a sigh. Danielle touched my shoulder then moved back to the kitchen. I stepped out onto the patio, the evening air thick with humidity. The last light threw spears of gold across the Intracoastal as I pulled out my phone and dialed Ronzoni.

"Got something for you," I said when he picked up. "Remember the video from the Donut Den? Guy who took Charlie? His name is Luis Romero. Works at the Leaf Lounge, delivering contraband cigars on the side. There's security footage of his van at a dentist's office across from where Charlie was taken."

"The dentist just gave you the footage?"

"They let me see it. Let's say I name-dropped Pixie Kazarian. You might want to send someone over to collect it officially."

"All right."

I glanced up as a yacht mast passed by on the Intracoatal. "And next time you don't want to share with me, just remember this moment."

Ronzoni grunted. "I guess I can give you the overview on your friend Zazy."

"He's no friend of mine, and I know all I need to. It's Luis I'm concerned about right now."

"You want to grab him?"

"Thought you'd never ask."

"The Leaf Lounge, huh? Let me check if he's working tonight."

The line went dead.

I watched a gecko skitter across the patio screen, its shadow elongated by the retiring sun. My phone buzzed.

"He's off tonight," Ronzoni said. "Back tomorrow. Did a quick search. He lives in Lake Worth Beach."

"Not your jurisdiction."

"Exactly. And I want him on my turf when we have our chat. We'll grab him tomorrow at the club. But Jones, just remember—"

"I know. You're the cop. It's your show."

I hung up and glanced through the sliding glass doors as Danielle, Bella, and Sophie moved around the dining table, laying out plates and silverware. It was an image Rockwell would have envisaged if he was still around. A bucolic family scene that twisted my guts. Sophie's father had walked away, Bella's had died, and Danielle, who had saved me from myself after I lost Lenny, had been left unable to have kids of her own.

They worked in an easy rhythm, like they'd been doing this together for years instead of minutes. Bella showed Sophie where the napkins were while Danielle arranged serving bowls. I stepped inside, drawn by both the domesticity of the moment and the aroma of whatever Danielle had cooked up.

Over dinner, the conversation stayed light. School projects, teachers they liked and didn't, the latest social media drama. But I could see Sophie's mind churning behind her careful responses, processing everything that had happened. Her missing dog, her dying mentor, the ghost of her absent father—it was a lot for anyone to carry, let alone a fourteen-year-old kid.

After we cleared the plates, the girls took Argos out back. Their laughter drifted in through the screens as they played fetch in the gathering dusk. When full dark settled in, I grabbed my keys.

The drive to Sophie's place was quiet. She stared out the window, streetlights painting her face in alternating light and shadow. When I pulled up to her trailer, she climbed out and paused.

"Thank you," she said softly, then turned and walked away toward the dark house.

I waited until I saw lights inside, then I waited a little longer. Eventually, I felt like a stalker, so I did a U-turn and drove home.

I slept poorly, tossing and turning, the weight of three missing dogs and a dying man upon me.

A sharp knock jolted me awake. The bedside clock read 2:17 a.m.

I lay still, listening. Danielle's breathing remained steady beside me. Another knock, or had I dreamed it?

I slid out of bed and padded to the living room. Moonlight spilled through the windows, casting long shadows across the furniture. Nothing moved. No sounds except the hum of the bugs outside.

Shaking my head at my imagination, I turned back toward the bedroom. As I passed Bella's door, I paused. A habit I'd developed with the toddler we housed briefly before we even signed up to be foster parents—checking on her. I eased the door open.

The empty dog bed caught my eye first. My pulse quickened as I pushed the door wider. Bella's bed was empty, covers thrown back.

"Bella?" I whispered, then louder. "Bella?"

I rushed through the house, checking bathrooms, the kitchen, the patio. No sign of her or Argos. My hands shook as I flipped on lights.

I ran to our bedroom and shook Danielle's shoulder. "Wake up. Bella's gone."

She bolted upright. "What?"

"She's not in her room. Not anywhere in the house."

We threw on clothes, bumping into each other in our haste.

"Did she seem off to you earlier?" I asked, pulling on a shirt. "Acting strange?"

"No." Danielle pulled on her jeans. "She was fine at dinner. Happy even. You?"

"Nothing." I grabbed my phone. "She was just…normal."

I burst through the back door, scanning the yard again in the dim moonlight. Over the pool fence, nothing moved except palm fronds stirring in the breeze off the Intracoastal.

"Bella!" My voice carried across the water, echoing off the seawalls of the houses opposite. No response except a startled egret taking flight.

Danielle jumped in her car and headed down along the Intracoastal, while I made for Blue Heron. I stopped right in the middle of the road and was looking both ways when my phone buzzed. Danielle's voice trembled slightly when I answered.

"Nothing along the water. I'm heading north toward the state park."

"I'll take Palm Shores," I said, pulling out of the driveway.

"I'm going to call in a BOLO."

"Okay."

"They'll never let us foster again after this." The crack in her voice hit me hard. "We lost a kid on our first try."

"We'll find her." I pushed the accelerator harder than necessary. "She's smart. She's got Argos with her. This isn't a regular runaway."

"How do you know?"

"Because she left everything behind. Her iPad, her backpack. Kids who run take their stuff."

I hung up and scanned both sides of the road, looking for a girl and a small dog walking in the dark. But the streets were empty, the houses dark. Just the occasional car coming in off the mainland.

Where would a kid go at this hour? And more importantly, why? My best guess was that she was headed home, so I made for the bridge off Singer Island.

As I drove that way, I saw the shops at City Beach, so I did a quick loop first. I pulled into the empty parking lot, the darkened storefronts like a row of sleeping sentinels. An idea hit me as I looked at the closed ice cream shop where we'd sat just days ago while walking the dog. Bella had watched the waves then, something in her expression I couldn't quite read.

I cut the engine and crossed the dark volleyball courts, through the foliage on the dunes silvered by moonlight. The sound of surf grew stronger with each step.

As I broke from the scrub, I paused. The beach stretched out before me, an expanse of pale sand meeting the darker water. Waves rolled in with a steady rhythm, their foam edges catching the moonlight. The air carried that mix of salt and seaweed that meant home to anyone who'd lived here long enough.

Then I saw them—two shapes against the darkness. One small figure sitting in the sand, another even smaller one beside it. The moonlight caught Argos's metal name tag as he looked up at his person, reflecting like a tiny beacon. Bella sat cross-legged beside him as she stared out at the ocean.

I pulled out my phone, thumbs tapping: *Found her. On City Beach. She's okay.*

Danielle's response came instantly: *Coming.*

I crossed the sand and lowered myself beside Bella, my knees creaking in protest. Argos's tail thumped once against the sand in acknowledgment. The three of us sat there, watching the waves roll in, their steady rhythm a counterpoint to the thoughts I could almost hear churning in Bella's head.

"I miss my dad," she said finally, her voice barely carrying over the surf.

I knew that feeling, but I stayed quiet, letting the space fill with whatever she needed to say.

"Sometimes I forget what his voice sounded like." She drew patterns in the sand with one finger. "Or the way he used to laugh at stupid stuff on TV. Sometimes it makes me smile. Sometimes I can't breathe."

The moon tracked higher, pulling shadows in toward us.

"I miss my mom too." Her voice cracked.

"Orna says she'll be back in a week or so," I offered.

"That's not what I mean." Bella hugged her knees tighter. "She's lost, Miami." She sighed. "My mom and dad were like two halves of a person. Does that make sense? And when my dad died, my mom didn't know how to operate anymore. Half a person can't work, can they?" She shook her head against her knees. "I know I'm being selfish."

"You think you're being selfish?" I asked.

"We're lucky in some ways. My mom has a pretty good job, and her boss hasn't fired her even though she goes missing sometimes, so we live in a nice apartment and all that. Not a trailer like Soph. And when my mom's okay, she's actually at home after work, not like Soph's mom. But then she trips again, and she drinks. And then she gets lost. And I can't fix her. I should be able to fix her. Sometimes I think if I just try harder, love her more, she'll find her way back. But what if she can't?"

Then Bella cried. She leaned into me and sobbed.

I let her do what she had to do. I'd never felt more useless in my life. I wished Lenny were here. He always knew what to say, what to do. I had nothing of value for this kid.

I held Bella as her sobs quieted, the rhythmic wash of waves filling the silence. When she finally looked up at me, I knew she needed something from me. The weight of her pain felt familiar, like an old acquaintance I'd rather forget.

"I lost my mom when I was about your age," I said softly, the words carrying more easily in the night air than they ever did in daylight. "There's a hole inside that never really goes away. But you learn to live with it. Having good people around you, building a life worth living—it helps take the longing away."

I watched another wave roll in before continuing. "It's hard knowing you can't get back the one that's gone. You can love them, but you can't tell them that you do anymore. That hurts."

Argos shifted closer, pressing against Bella's leg as if sensing her need for comfort.

"But your mom, Bella—she's still here. You're right. You're a smart person. She's struggling with losing your dad, and maybe not doing it well, but that's not about you, even though it feels like it is." I felt her tense. "The difference is, you can still tell her. You can hug her, be there when she's down. I know that's a lot to ask of someone your age. It's not fair that you have to be the strong one sometimes. But that's how it is."

She wiped her face on my shirt and looked at me again. I didn't want her to because I felt like a fraud. I was giving advice that I had never lived. My dad was lost after Mom died, and he did exactly the same thing as Bella's mom. He hit the bottle and drowned in the bottom of it. And I wasn't able to fix him, although I wasn't even sure that I tried. He wasn't there for me, so I wasn't there for him. Maybe I couldn't be. Maybe I was too busy not drowning myself. I looked down at Bella and wondered if that was what was happening to her.

"This isn't your fault, and it isn't your job to fix it. All you can do is let her know that she still has a reason to go on. Be a compass point when she's feeling lost. We can't control the seas, and we can't steer other people's ships. All we can do is be a lighthouse and hope they see the light."

I saw the tension ease from her face, but not all the way. Not nearly all the way.

"But now, you know, when you're not the strong one, when she can't help you because she's lost and you feel like you're drowning yourself? You've got us. You've been to Longboard Kelly's. You're family now."

Bella said nothing. She sat up and let out a sigh that would have sent Odysseus back to Ithaca. Then she stood, brushing sand from her jeans, so I followed suit. Argos sprang up, tail wagging with renewed energy now that we were moving.

"Come on, boy," Bella called softly, and he fell in step beside her.

Before we could take three steps, a figure burst through the sea grass, kicking up sand in her wake. Danielle sprinted toward us, her dark hair flying behind her. She crashed into us both, wrapping her arms around us with enough force to nearly knock us back down.

"Are you okay?" she asked Bella, pulling back just enough to see her face while keeping her arms locked around us. "We were so worried."

"I'm sorry," Bella mumbled into Danielle's shoulder. "I just needed to see the water."

Danielle's grip loosened slightly, and she brushed Bella's hair back from her face and nodded. "The ocean's good for that." She glanced toward the dunes and home beyond. "But next time, how about watching the Intracoastal from our yard? Same water, less panic for the old people, okay?"

Bella nodded, a small smile tugging at her lips. "Okay."

Argos circled our feet, his tail sweeping patterns in the sand as he waited for us to move. I caught Danielle's eye over Bella's head, seeing my own relief mirrored there.

CHAPTER THIRTY-THREE

THE NEXT MORNING, OVER COFFEE IN THE KITCHEN, I WATCHED BELLA pack her school bag. She seemed lighter somehow, more settled. I eased in beside Danielle, wondering if we should address what happened.

"She's in a better place," Danielle said quietly, reading my thoughts as she often did. "Sometimes that's all you can hope for."

Danielle took Bella to school, and I headed to the office. Lizzy sat at her desk, her black-painted fingernails tapping away. She looked up as I entered, vermillion lips pressed into a thin line.

"Got some bad news," she said, holding up a piece of paper. "Pixie's check bounced."

I dropped into the chair opposite her. "You're kidding." My voice lacked any kind of surprise.

"Palm Beach rich are always the worst payers." Lizzy shook her head. "They think their name is as good as cash."

"I'm not sure how rich they are." I stood up, my chair scraping against the floor. "Guess I better go see Pixie."

"Want me to come?" Lizzy asked. "I can do my scary goth thing."

"I'll keep that in my pocket, just in case. Keep digging on our friend Zazy."

I headed for the door, but Lizzy stopped me. "You got a delivery from an Oliver Grant, by the way."

"Another one?" I said, mindful of the passes that had gotten me and Bella into Barkingham Palace.

Lizzy shrugged and handed me a courier's document envelope. I ripped it open and noted the words *Grand Canine Classic.*

"Tickets for the dog show," I said. "I suspect I'll be persona non grata if I don't find these missing dogs. You want to go?"

Lizzy curled her lip like she had ditches to dig that day.

I put the tickets back in the envelope and told Lizzy to toss them.

She waved the envelope at me. "Pretty much every suspect in this case will be there."

"Good point. File them."

I wondered if Sophie and Bella might enjoy the dog show. Then the thought of not finding the missing Gaston hit me again, so I turned and walked out of the office again. The answers weren't at my desk.

I drove through town and pulled into the strip mall, finding a spot right in front of Sally's store. The Chinese restaurant next door didn't do much of a breakfast trade. Inside, the familiar musty smell of pawned electronics and desperation greeted me.

Sal looked up from his counter and offered his nicotine-stained smile as he combed his solitary hair across his scalp. "Your Patriots looking good without Brady?"

"When are the Jets going to call up Broadway Joe?" I shot back.

"Hey, he could do it. He's only what, eighty?"

"Might still have better knees than Rodgers."

"Who?" Sal's smile faded as he studied my face. "What brings you in?"

"It's this whole puppy mill thing." I leaned on the glass counter. "I've got a name, and he's known to the cops, but I can't get a bead on him. Name's Zazy?"

"Zazy?" Sal shook his head. "I thought the New York families had all the good names."

"Might be out of Arizona. Might not even be here. Like I say, just a name that keeps coming up."

"What's with all these dogs?" Sal's eyebrows rose. "Since when are you chasing lost pets?"

I thought about the face of the teenage girl who had already lost too many loved ones, about Pixie's bounced check, about all the pieces that weren't adding up. What I said was, "A kid's counting on me."

Sal nodded, as if that was all that needed to be said on the subject. "I'll make some calls, see what shakes loose."

"Thanks." Before I left, I said, "Want to come to the Grand Canine Classic this weekend?"

Sal's face crinkled like a used paper bag.

"They'll have hot dogs," I added. "And beer."

"Why didn't you say so?" His wrinkled smile returned. "Count me in."

CHAPTER THIRTY-FOUR

THE MORNING SUN HAD ALREADY BURNED OFF THE DEW FROM THE manicured lawns of the Kazarian estate when I arrived. The butler showed me into the living room where Pixie sat arranging flowers in a crystal vase.

I put my hands on my hips. "Pixie, I hate to bring this up, but your check bounced."

Her hands froze mid-arrangement. "That's impossible." Color drained from her face. "There must be some mistake at the bank."

"These things happen," I said, though in my experience they happened more often when accounts ran dry.

"I'm mortified." She set down a half-placed orchid. "Simply mortified. Is Aram in his study?" She directed this to the butler, who nodded. "Let's sort this out right now."

We walked through the mansion to Aram's study. He sat behind his massive desk, phone pressed to his ear. When he saw us, he wrapped up his call.

"Darling?" Pixie's voice wavered. "There seems to be an issue with Mr. Jones's check."

Aram's expression didn't change. "What sort of issue?"

"It bounced," I said.

"Did it now?" He leaned back in his leather chair. "Must be an error at the bank. They've been updating their systems lately. Creating all sorts of hassles." He pulled out his checkbook and began writing. "I'll call them right after this. Sort it all out." He tore out the check and handed it to me. "My apologies for the inconvenience."

The new check looked almost identical to the old one. Same amount, different signature. I wondered if was made of the same kind of rubber.

I studied Aram's face as he tucked the checkbook back into the second desk drawer. He locked the drawer with a tiny key that he dropped into the top drawer. "You're a member at the Leaf Lounge, right?"

"Yes, of course." He steepled his fingers.

"Do you know Luis?"

His expression remained blank. "I'm not familiar with that name."

"He works there."

"Mr. Jones, I hardly know every waiter and busboy at the club." Aram tugged at his cuffs, a gesture that seemed designed to project authority but came across as a nervous tic.

"He's not a waiter. He's the cigar guy." I watched for any flicker of recognition. "The one who handles the Cubans."

"I'm afraid I don't recall who maintains the humidor." Aram's poker face held firm, but his fingers drummed together before he caught himself.

Pixie glanced between us, confusion evident in her perfectly maintained features. "This man, Luis—do you think he was involved in Layla's disappearance?"

"I don't know yet." I held up the fresh check, letting it catch the morning light streaming through the window. "There are a lot of pieces that don't fit. Like why someone would steal three different breeds of dog. Or why a ransom drop would be botched so badly. Or why checks keep bouncing in a house like this?"

Aram's jaw tightened. "I told you, it was a bank error."

"Sure."

Pixie clutched her hands together. "Please, Mr. Jones. Just find Layla."

"I intend to. There might be some things that don't make sense yet." I smiled at Pixie. "But they will. They always do."

I looked at her face, saw the genuine pain there. Whatever was going on in this house, her love for that dog was real.

I walked out of the Kazarian mansion, squinting in the bright sunlight. My phone buzzed in my pocket.

"Yeah?"

"Miami, it's Sal." His voice had an edge I didn't often hear. "Got something on that guy of yours."

"That was quick."

"Yeah, well, listen. The boys I talked to, they're worried. Said these people are ruthless. Not like regular thugs—these guys are old-fashioned mean."

"I'll be careful."

"You better. Number's coming by text."

I stood in the Kazarians' circular driveway, watching a gardener trim hedges into geometric shapes while I dialed the number Sal sent.

A raspy voice answered. "Yeah?"

"Looking to do some business." I kept my tone casual. "Name's Smith."

"How'd you get this number?"

"Friend of Luis."

The silence stretched out. I could hear breathing on the other end, measuring my words. "What kind of business?" he growled.

"Dogs. I'm down from New England, looking to expand operations."

"How many?"

"Could be plenty. Depends on condition. Quality matters to my clients."

Another pause. "Three o'clock. You got a pen?"

"I've got a memory."

The voice gave me a location. Then the line went dead.

I looked at my phone, wondering if I'd just arranged to meet someone who might kill me, or if I was about to find three missing dogs. Maybe both.

CHAPTER THIRTY-FIVE

All roads led to Indiantown. I drove out past where Charlie's tracker died, the landscape growing more desolate with each mile. The sugarcane fields stretched endlessly, broken only by patches of scrubland and the occasional maintenance road disappearing into nothing.

The St. Lucie Canal appeared ahead, a man-made gash through Florida's flesh. I pulled onto a gravel turnout near the rail drawbridge on Kanner Highway. No other cars in sight. Just the hum of insects and distant bird calls.

The bridge's metal framework cast long shadows across the water. Spanish moss draped from scattered oaks like funeral shrouds. Despite Indiantown being just over the canal, civilization felt like a distant memory.

A new Toyota Tacoma rolled up beside me, chrome still gleaming despite the dusty road. The driver looked rough, with a patchy beard and hollow eyes that darted around too much. Meth head eyes. He wasn't Zazy—didn't match the photo Faust showed me.

"Mr. Smith?" His voice cracked.

"That's me." I kept my tone neutral. "Are you Zazy?"

"No." He spat onto the gravel. "He's waiting. Follow me."

I followed the Tacoma along the canal's edge, watching dust plume behind us. The sugarcane fields stretched endless and green on one side while horse ranches dotted the other, their white fences cracked and faded from the omnipresent sun.

The Tacoma's brake lights flashed, and it turned onto an unmarked dirt road. I followed, counting the tenths of miles on my odometer. At about three-quarters of a mile, an old farmhouse emerged from the trees. The place had seen better days, probably back when Kennedy was president.

Several outbuildings slouched nearby, their wooden sides gray and weathered. No tractors or working equipment in sight—just the skeletal remains of farm machinery so rusted they resembled abstract sculptures.

A box truck sat in the shade of some live oaks, its sides adorned with a rental company logo. The kind of ubiquitous vehicle that could blend in anywhere or vanish without a trace.

I pulled the SUV around the barn's corner, following the Tacoma. The truck accelerated, tires spinning and sending dirt flying as it fishtailed away, leaving me alone in the clearing.

Movement caught my eye as two figures emerged from the barn's shadows. My stomach dropped at the sight of AR-15s gripped in their hands. I'd never liked guns—too final, too prone to ending conversations permanently. Give me a baseball bat any day.

The men approached my vehicle. The wider one had prison tattoos crawling up his neck. He didn't look like he was there to discuss show dogs over tea. Then I took in the second guy. Him, I knew. The scraggly features of Zazy. The mugshot had actually done him some favors.

I unclipped my seatbelt and stomped the accelerator. The SUV's engine roared as I yanked the wheel toward the stocky gunman on the left. His eyes widened as two tons of Detroit steel and plastic bore down on him.

The first shots cracked through the air. My windshield spider-webbed with impact points but held together. More rounds thunked into the hood and doors. I threw the shifter into neutral and dove out the driver's side door.

I hit the ground hard, my shoulder taking most of the impact as I rolled through the dust. The SUV continued its path toward the gunmen, forcing them to scatter.

I scrambled to my feet and sprinted for the tree line, keeping low. Dust swirled around me, providing cover as my feet pounded the hard-packed earth. My lungs burned as I pushed myself faster.

The shooting had stopped momentarily as they dealt with my unmanned SUV, giving me precious seconds. I spotted a wooden fence ahead and gathered myself for the leap. My hands found the top rail, and I vaulted over just as the gunfire erupted again.

Florida was flat and open. The southern half was essentially a big swamp. There weren't many hills, and there wasn't much in the way of forests. But these guys had decided to hide their operation in an abandoned farm with a wetland full of slash pines, live oaks, and cabbage palms between them and the road. I would have liked my chances in the sugarcane fields, but I wasn't getting back there anytime soon, so I bolted for the only cover I could see.

An irrigation channel appeared ahead, concrete sides dropping away to murky water below. Ten feet across—maybe I could make it. The alternative was turning back toward the guns.

Footsteps pounded closer. No time to second-guess.

I planted my foot and launched myself across the gap. For a moment, I was airborne, then reality and gravity conspired against me. I splashed down three-quarters of the way across, the cold water shocking my system. The gulf stream water off Florida was still warm in autumn, but this felt like ice. I gasped once before getting about my business.

Bullets peppered the water around me, sending up tiny geysers. I scrambled up the concrete bank, my wet shoes slipping on the algae-slick surface. Then I felt the sting of a thousand bees as a round hit me in the thigh. I howled and my fingers found purchase on some exposed rebar, and I hauled myself over the edge.

Dense woods beckoned ahead. I clutched my leg and stumbled for cover, zigzagging between the trees as more shots rang out behind me. Pine needles dampened the noise I made as I pushed deeper into the forest.

I charged through the dense undergrowth, branches whipping at my face. The ground beneath my feet squished with each step, water seeping into my already soaked shoes. This wasn't prime real estate—just a forgotten patch of Florida wilderness, too wet to develop and too poor to farm.

After twenty seconds of hard running, I stopped behind a massive live oak. My chest heaved as I tried to control my breathing, straining to hear over my pounding heart.

"Over there!" a voice called from the direction of the farm. "Watch the tree line!"

"Circle wide!" another voice answered. "Don't let him double back!"

I took a moment to survey the damage to my leg. A small rip in my pants showed a graze where the bullet had nicked me. It really hurt a lot more than that, but I wasn't telling that tale to anybody.

In my mind's eye, I could see them spreading out in a line, moving through the brush like beaters flushing game. Only I was the game, and they weren't armed with bird shot.

The wetland stretched out before me, a maze of pines and palms. Somewhere beyond lay civilization, but I recalled the drive in. It was nearly a mile to the road, which itself was hardly I-95.

I kept moving through the wetland, my shoes squelching with each careful step. The humidity pressed against my skin like a wet blanket, and my clothes clung uncomfortably where they weren't already drenched from the irrigation channel.

A clearing appeared ahead through the trees. I froze, studying the open space. Tall grass waved in the breeze, creating shifting patterns that could hide anything—or anyone. The space stretched maybe fifty yards across before the tree line resumed on the far side.

Too exposed. They'd have a clear shot if I tried crossing that.

I backtracked deeper into the cover of the trees, adjusting my course toward where I figured the road must be. The sun wouldn't set for hours yet, which gave them ample time to hunt me down.

A distant engine rumbled. The Tacoma. If these guys had any tactical sense, they'd use the truck to cut off my escape route while the others pushed me toward it. Classic hunting technique—like dogs working a pheasant toward the waiting guns.

I touched the bark of a slash pine, steadying myself as I listened. The engine sound grew louder, then faded. They were definitely coordinating, trying to box me in.

The ground grew increasingly boggy as I pushed deeper into the wetland. My shoes sank into the muck with each step, making silent movement impossible. A natural depression spread before me, creating a body of water dotted with fallen trees and stumps protruding like ancient bones. It was too shallow to call it a lake, but it was deep enough to hide all kinds of Florida wildlife.

I crouched behind a thick cypress, my back pressed against its damp bark. Water trickled down my neck from the Spanish moss overhead. The earthy smell of decay and stagnant water filled my nostrils.

Movement caught my eye—one of the gunmen appeared through the trees about forty yards to my right. He moved cautiously, his rifle held ready as he scanned the wetland. His boots made sucking sounds in the mud as he advanced.

I held perfectly still, barely breathing. Another flash of movement drew my attention left. Zazy emerged from behind a fallen palm, maybe fifty feet from his partner. They were spread wide, sweeping through the swamp in a coordinated pattern.

The first gunman paused, studying the ground. Probably looking for tracks in the soft earth. I couldn't stay here much longer—they were slowly closing the gap, and the boggy depression offered nowhere to run except forward, exactly where they wanted me to go.

I hoped these guys knew something about Florida. Zazy wasn't from here, but maybe his helper was, and I banked on him thinking like a local and did the one thing no sane Floridan would do.

I slipped down into the murky water, fighting every instinct that screamed about what lived in Florida's wetlands. A fallen log provided cover as I eased beneath it, trying not to think about what else might be sharing this space with me.

The water was surprisingly deep here, coming up to my chest as I crouched. Decay and rot filled my nostrils as I slid down to my chin, along with that distinctive swamp smell that marked these forgotten corners of the state.

The first gunman stalked past, about fifteen feet away. He moved with purpose, scanning the tree line ahead, clearly expecting me to be running for my life. Which any rational person would be.

My heart nearly stopped as boots landed on the log above my head. Zazy stood directly over me. Water lapped at my chin, my mouth and nose the only parts above the surface. Like the gators I was desperately hoping to avoid. That thought made me think of the bloody nick on my leg, and I wondered if gators were attacted to blood like sharks.

Bits of bark and moss drifted down as the gunman shifted his weight on the log. I could hear his breathing, controlled but heavy from the pursuit. A bead of sweat—or maybe water from my soaked hair—trickled down my forehead as I remained motionless.

From above me Zazy called out, "Hey, nothing here."

"What do we do?" The other voice drifted through the trees.

"If we've spooked him, he's running to the road, and Pete will scoop him up. We got stuff to do."

Their footsteps faded, leaving me alone in the murky depths. I stayed submerged, barely breathing, counting the minutes. The water pressed against my chest, its coolness more threatening than refreshing. Every ripple could be death sliding past.

Twenty minutes felt like twenty hours. My eyes burned from staring at the surface, searching for the telltale V-wake of an approaching alligator. The longer I watched, the more the water seemed alive with movement. Shadow became scales, branches transformed into snouts, until my mind conjured predators from every dark patch.

When I couldn't take it anymore, I eased out of the water and pressed my back against a cypress. My hands shook slightly as I pulled out my phone, offering thanks to modern technology as the screen lit up despite its dunking.

I punched in a text to Danielle. The message sent, showing one bar of signal. I switched the phone to silent and held it against my knee, listening intently for any sign of my pursuers.

I stayed frozen against the cypress, every sense straining for sounds of movement. The wetland buzzed with life—frogs croaking, birds calling, branches creaking. Any sound could be a gunman circling back. Or worse.

My phone gave one last valiant flash before dying completely. Great. At least the text had gone through.

The wait stretched endlessly. My clothes dried stiff with swamp water, and my muscles cramped from holding still. Just when I thought I couldn't take another minute, sirens pierced the afternoon quiet.

"This is the sheriff. Come out with your hands up!"

The voice boomed through what had to be a megaphone. But was it really law enforcement, or Zazy's crew trying to flush me out? I stayed put, controlling my breathing.

Five minutes later, I saw him. A green and khaki uniform emerged through the trees across the boggy depression. The deputy moved with caution, scanning the wetland with his handgun raised.

"Miami Jones?" he called out.

"Over here!" I responded, staying still.

"On the ground! Hands where I can see them!"

I complied, pressing myself into the damp earth. The deputy approached carefully, weapon drawn. After checking my ID, he helped me to my feet.

"You're a lucky man, Mr. Jones. Let's get you out of here."

He led me through the woods to his cruiser waiting on the road, then drove back around to the farm buildings. Black smoke billowed into the sky ahead of us.

Two Martin County Sheriff's cruisers sat in the farmyard, their light bars painting the scene in alternating red and blue. Beyond them, a fire truck's crew worked to extinguish what remained of my SUV.

I endured the joy of dropping my pants as one of the fire crew bandaged my leg. After that, I gave my statement to the deputy who'd found me, detailing the ambush and subsequent chase through the wetland. He jotted notes while occasionally glancing at the burning vehicle.

Another deputy approached, holding a phone. "Call for you."

Danielle's voice trembled. "Miami? Are you okay?"

"I'm fine. Just wet and muddy." I tried to keep my tone light. "The car's seen better days, though."

"Don't joke. Not now."

"Sorry. I really am okay."

"I'm coming."

"I'm sure the deputies will give me a ride."

"Then I'll see you in Stuart. Give me back to the deputy."

I handed off the phone, then moved toward the barn, its weathered doors hanging open. The smell hit me first—that distinctive mix of animal waste and neglect that spoke of too many creatures in too small a space. The deputies' flashlights cut through the gloom, revealing hastily constructed pens. They were sized for dogs, not horses, and while empty now, the smell of fresh feces told their recent history.

In a corner, behind a partition, we found what had to be their surgery. A wooden table dominated the space, covered by a plastic tarp soiled with dried blood. Surgical implements lay scattered nearby—scalpels, forceps, things I didn't want to identify. This was where they'd removed the microchips, I figured. Quick and dirty surgery, probably not caring too much if the patients survived.

"Puppy mill," I said, though the deputies had surely reached the same conclusion. The whole setup screamed black market operation.

One of the deputies bagged the surgical tools as evidence while his partner photographed the scene. I stood in the doorway, the stench of urine and feces burning my nostrils, wondering if Layla, Gaston, and Charlie had passed through here. And if they had, where were they now?

I stood with the deputies near their cruiser, the swamp water still dripping from my clothes. I gave them the rental company for the box truck. "Twenty-six footer, I'd guess. Arizona plates."

"You get the number?" The deputy had his notebook ready.

"First four characters—AZ12. Rest was a blur with all the shooting." My shoulder ached where I'd hit the ground diving from my SUV, and I rolled it out like an old man.

The deputy radioed in the partial plate. With any luck, they'd find the rental agreement. The company would have records, assuming Zazy used his real name. Though guys like him usually had ways around that.

A deputy drove me to Stuart. I sat in the Martin County Sheriff's Office, dripping swamp water onto their industrial carpet, while a civilian admin pecked my statement into a computer. My insurance claim was going to be a tough sell. How do you explain *shot up by dog thieves* without sounding crazy?

The deputy who had found me was asking the questions. "So you're working with Palm Beach PD on this?"

"Detective Ronzoni's handling the case. Three show dogs stolen in the past week."

His eyebrow lifted. "He should have called us if he was coming over the county line."

"Ronzoni didn't come to the meet. He sticks to the island. I got a name from a source. Wasn't sure where it would lead." I shifted my aching leg, my clothes stiff with dried muck. "Didn't expect assault rifles."

"Always expect assault rifles, Mr. Jones." The deputy closed his notebook. "That's rule one."

"I'll add it to my list, right after *don't swim with gators.*"

The office door burst open, and Danielle rushed in, with Bella close behind. My wife wrapped me in a tight hug, not caring about the swamp stench. Bella watched from a few feet away, worry creasing her young face.

"Are you okay?" Danielle pulled back, checking me for injuries. "When we got your text…"

"I'm fine. The car's toast though." I glanced at Bella. "Orna's not going to like hearing about this."

Bella shrugged. "Don't worry. We keep the bits about homicidal gunmen to ourselves."

CHAPTER THIRTY-SIX

I squelched through the front door, trailing swamp water and mud across the tile.

Bella's nose wrinkled as she again caught the smell. "Ugh, you reek like that time Argos found a dead fish."

"Shoes off, straight to the shower," Danielle ordered. "Don't touch anything."

After washing away the evidence of my wetland escape, I settled into a lounger on the patio. The Intracoastal stretched before me, peaceful and mundane compared to the day's events. Danielle appeared with a cold beer, setting it beside me without a word.

My phone was out of its case, drying on the table, so I used Danielle's phone to call Ronzoni. The dial tone bleeped while I watched Bella chase Argos around the yard, a slice of normal life that felt surreal after staring down assault rifles.

"Jones," Ronzoni answered.

I filled him in on the farm ambush and the makeshift veterinary setup we'd discovered.

"You're an idiot," he said like he was my dad. "Going in alone like that."

"Speaking of idiots, any movement on Luis Romero?"

The pause on Ronzoni's end made me sit up straighter.

"Funny you should ask." His voice dropped lower. "I'm watching him right now in the Leaf Lounge parking lot."

"Oh?"

"And guess who just pulled up in his Bentley? Your client's husband."

I set my beer down. "What's your plan?"

"I think it's time Luis and I had a little chat down at the station," Ronzoni said, clucking his tongue like he was thinking. "You want in on this?"

I caught Danielle's eye through the sliding glass doors. She raised an eyebrow.

"Give me twenty minutes," I said, already pushing up off the lounger.

"What do you think you're doing?" Danielle asked as I stepped inside.

I took Danielle's keys from the bowl on the counter, but she blocked my path to the driveway, arms crossed.

"You nearly died today. At least twice." Her jaw was set, eyes blazing. "You need rest."

"I'm fine. Just took a swim."

"In alligator-infested water after being shot." She shook her head. "That's not fine."

"My car's toast. I need to borrow yours."

"Miami…" Her voice carried that tone she used when I was imitating a mule.

"I'll be careful. Promise." I gave her a quick kiss. "Just going to watch an interview with Ronzoni."

I was there in twenty minutes. The Palm Beach Police Department was quiet as I walked down the hallway, my clothes fresh but my leg still aching from the afternoon's adventure. Ronzoni appeared around a corner, his suit looking like gift wrap retrieved from the trash.

"This way." He led me to a small observation room. "You can watch from here."

"I was hoping to sit in."

Ronzoni snorted. "You're lucky I'm letting you watch."

Through the two-way mirror, Luis Romero sat at a metal table, looking remarkably composed for someone in police custody. His posture radiated confidence, almost arrogance.

"He hasn't asked for a lawyer yet," Ronzoni said, rubbing his neck under the collar. "Probably thinks he doesn't need one."

"Don't dissuade him of that notion."

Ronzoni nodded and entered the interrogation room, settling into the chair across from Luis. "How long have you worked at the Leaf Lounge?"

"About two years." Luis's voice carried a hint of boredom.

"Good benefits?"

"It's fine."

"Must meet some interesting people." Ronzoni's tone remained casual. "Lot of cigar aficionados in Palm Beach."

Luis's lips curved into a slight smirk. "Some."

"I hear Cuban cigars are popular."

"Wouldn't know about that." Luis's expression didn't change.

"Oh? I heard you were the cigar sommelier at the club. That's what the manager says."

He eyeballed Ronzoni. "The word is *catador*."

Ronzoni nodded and made a note. "Cat door," he said.

I wasn't sure if he really misheard or was just trying to get under Luis's skin. It never paid to give Ronzoni too much credit for thinking.

The detective leaned forward. "Let's talk about what happened in Indiantown today."

The smirk faltered.

"Burned-out SUV. Two guys with AR-15s. Attempted murder." Ronzoni's voice hardened. "Ring any bells?"

Luis's shoulders tensed, though he maintained his silence. His eyes flicked toward the mirror, and I could have sworn he looked right at me. "I got no idea what you're talking about."

"Okay. Here's what's going to happen," Ronzoni said, leaning back. "You're spending the night with us. Maybe tomorrow morning you'll feel more talkative."

Luis's jaw clenched as an officer led him from the room.

I met Ronzoni in the hallway. "Think a night in lockup will loosen his tongue?" I asked.

"People tend to get chatty when they realize they're facing serious time." Ronzoni attempted to straighten his tie but merely adjusted the angle of it. "Go home. Get some rest."

CHAPTER THIRTY-SEVEN

I didn't go home. Instead, I pointed Danielle's car down A1A. My headlights were absorbed by the hedgerows, creating a tunnel of light as I drove to the Kazarian estate. The gate was closed, and the voice on the other end hesitated when I asked to speak to the master of the house. But the gates opened, and I parked beside the Bentley.

The butler's face was a masterpiece of professional disdain as he waited at the top of the stairs. "Sir, you are not expected."

"I bet."

"Mr. Kazarian is swimming. Mrs. Kazarian is attending a meeting for her charitable trust."

"I know the drill." I stepped past him into the marble foyer. "I'll wait in the master's study."

His lips tightened, but he didn't protest as I made my way down the familiar hallway. The house was different at night, the way a closed museum felt. Like makeup washed away after a long day, revealing what lay beneath the carefully maintained façade.

I flicked the light on and settled into one of the leather chairs facing Aram's desk, running my fingers along the brass studs on the armrest. "No tea tonight?"

"I apologize, sir," the butler said, all kind of sorry, not sorry.

"The cook is on leave." His spine couldn't have been straighter if he'd swallowed a flagpole.

"Leave? Or furloughed?"

A flicker crossed his face. It vanished so quickly I might have imagined it.

"I surely wouldn't know what you're referring to, sir." His voice carried the practiced neutrality of someone who'd seen too much and said too little.

"Of course not. You can tell Mr. Kazarian I'm here."

The butler bowed his head and backed out of the study. I waited until his footsteps faded down the marble hallway before standing to close the heavy oak door.

I crossed to the bar and poured two fingers of scotch from a crystal decanter. Not as smooth as what Albright served at the club, but it would do. Aram's leather chair squeaked as I settled in.

The desk was solid mahogany, three drawers on the right side —two small ones above a deeper file drawer. All looked well-used, with slight scratches around the locks on the bottom two. I recalled Aram's movements when he wrote the replacement check earlier, so I set down my glass and pulled open the top drawer. There, beneath some loose papers, lay a small silver key. His desk security matched his house security. I wondered if the safe he had retrieved the ransom from was a shoe box. Then I thought about that some more.

The key slid smoothly into the first locked drawer. Inside, a checkbook rested on top of a plastic box that made my pulse quicken. A Wi-Fi jammer, identical to the one Luis had pointed at the donut shop's camera. But why would Aram need one?

Then I remembered what Trey said about limited range, especially with walls and buildings in the way. The estate was huge, with thick walls and plenty of trees. Luis had jammed the service entrance, but he had to get into the property, and that meant also jamming the cameras covering the main gate and house—where the security hub was located.

Two jammers, working in tandem. One thief couldn't have pulled this off alone.

I slid the second drawer shut and then opened the bottom drawer. The hanging files were meticulously labeled in a precise hand that spoke of someone who'd grown up before computers ruled the world.

The first few tabs read like a business textbook index: *Accounts*, *Advertising*, *Banking*. Each folder was stuffed with papers, their edges worn from frequent handling. My fingers paused when I hit *Collabs*. That one was thick enough to strain the metal rails.

The *Production* file held what looked like factory specs and material costs, all at least six months old. Nothing recent. Under *Taxes* I found copies of returns that would give an accountant nightmares.

Then I hit *Bills*. The folder hung empty, its creases suggesting it had once been full. Either Aram was the most efficient bill-payer in Palm Beach, or nothing was getting paid anymore. Given the bounced check and what Albright had told us at the club, I was betting on the latter.

I pulled the *Insurance* file and laid it across the desk. Inside were several manila folders, neatly labeled: *Stores*, *Home*, *Vail Chalet*. But what caught my eye was a loose document, half a dozen pages stapled together.

The letterhead belonged to Coastal Specialty Insurance. I knew them well—they were the only company willing to cover my car after I suffered a number of incidents within a short span that result in total and catastrophic loss of said vehicle. I made a mental note to have Ron break the news about my latest automotive disaster. Maybe he could have the conversation over eighteen holes and let the broker win.

This policy wasn't for a car, though. It was for Layla. My eyes scanned the dense text, picking out key phrases. The coverage was exactly what Albright had described—future earnings from breeding and endorsements, payable if she died before age ten or failed to appear for a pre-show health check due to death, illness, or misadventure.

The payout figure made me pause: two hundred thousand dollars. In this house, that might cover the monthly landscaping bill. But for someone drowning in debt, was it a lifeline?

I thought about the ransom demand for one hundred thousand dollars. Half the insurance payout. Just enough to make it look legitimate without draining the whole claim. Clever. Then I thought about that bag of cash. Very clever.

I slid the insurance file back and reached for the one marked *Collabs*. Bella and Sophie had tried to explain the concept to me over dinner, but seeing the reality laid out in black and white was something else.

I opened a thick folder labeled *J Blaze*. The contracts inside detailed a partnership between Kazarian Fashion LLC and J Blaze Inc. that would have made my accountant's head spin. The numbers stretched across page after page—projections for casual wear lines, sneakers, even sunglasses. Product lists filled entire spreadsheets, everything from T-shirts to watches.

I whistled softly at the figures. My entire baseball career earnings wouldn't cover the projected first-quarter revenues. The marketing budget alone could have funded a small city. It made it hard to believe Aram couldn't be absolutely loaded—this wasn't just a fashion line; it really was an empire worthy of a Palm Beach estate. I had to consider that Graham Albright had poisoned my thinking, and that Aram didn't have the money troubles Albright claimed.

I flipped through purchase orders for materials and manufacturing contracts. The scale was mind-boggling. Enough inventory to fill a K-Mart. I had no idea there was so much money in the clothing business. I only needed so many pairs of cargo shorts and palm tree print shirts.

A sticky note caught my eye, attached to a production schedule. Someone had scrawled *15M advance* in hasty red ink. Below that, another number: *42,000 units pre-committed.*

I pulled out another folder, this one thinner than J Blaze's ency-clopedia of deals. The tab read *Lexi Prism*. The name meant nothing to me, but then I wasn't exactly up on fashion icons.

The contract inside was printed on heavy paper with an embossed letterhead. Whoever Lexi's lawyers were, they weren't working out of a strip mall. The agreement laid out terms for what they called a *multi-platform collaboration*. I understood about every third word.

What I did understand were the numbers. An initial payment of two hundred thousand dollars jumped off the page. That would buy a lot of Cuban cigars. Below that, a schedule of additional payments tied to something called *engagement metrics* and *conversion rates*.

The payment structure reminded me of my old minor league baseball contract—bonus clauses that kicked in when you hit certain targets. Only these targets involved followers and likes instead of earned run averages and innings pitched.

I replaced the files and eased the drawers shut, then poured another finger of scotch from the crystal decanter. The amber liquid caught the lamplight as I swirled it, releasing notes of peat and oak.

My muscles ached from the afternoon's swim in the irrigation canal, so I tried the leather chaise. It seemed to actively resist providing any comfort. I shifted positions three times before giving up and perching on the edge like I was waiting for the school principal.

The scotch helped take the edge off my jangled nerves, though I knew I needed to stay sharp to drive Danielle's car home in one piece. Getting your car shot up and burned tended to make a guy particular about vehicle preservation. I had enough explaining to do with my insurance company already.

CHAPTER THIRTY-EIGHT

ARAM APPEARED IN THE DOORWAY, HIS WHITE BUTTON-UP SHIRT CRISP against his tanned skin, trousers perfectly pressed. His dark hair was slicked back, still wet from his swim. He gave no indication that I had forced him to cut his laps short. If he had arrived at my place and curtailed a run with Danielle on City Beach, I'd have been grateful, but he didn't exude that emotion either.

"Mr. Jones, I'm afraid Pixie isn't home at the moment."

"I know. It's you I want to talk with." I set my glass down and stood. "You said you didn't know Luis Romero."

Aram's expression remained neutral. "I don't."

"That's odd, because Detective Ronzoni saw you talking with him in the Leaf Lounge parking lot this very evening."

A muscle twitched in Aram's jaw. He poured himself a scotch, buying time, then he moved behind his desk. The ice clinked against the crystal.

"Well, yes. I recognized him after you mentioned him and asked what was happening." He settled into his chair. "I was curious what he knew about Layla."

"And what did he say?"

"He claimed to know nothing." Aram took a measured sip. "I

spoke to the extortionist on the phone myself. Different voice entirely. I don't believe Luis was the one demanding money."

I nodded slowly. "I don't think so either."

I studied Aram's face, but he avoided mine.

"Mr. Jones, you've done all you can do," he said, straightening a pen on his desk. "I gave you a check for your retainer. Please send us a bill for your expenses. Your services are no longer required."

"The last check bounced."

"That was a cash flow oversight." He waved his hand dismissively. "But that has been dealt with."

"You think writing another check fixes your account problems?"

"I don't have an account problem."

"Providing the insurance on Layla comes through."

He frowned. He actually looked pretty good doing it. "How do you know about that?"

"I'm an investigator, Mr. Kazarian. It's what I do."

"You always investigate your own clients?" His eye shifted to the desk drawer and back.

"Only when their checks bounce."

"Well, that won't happen again. And since you already seem to know, I can confirm that the insurance company's courier just delivered a check."

My stomach turned cold. "On what?"

"Layla."

The scotch turned in my stomach. "What happens if she turns up?"

Aram's eyes met mine, dark and unreadable. "I would give the money back, but I don't think that's going to happen. I think you've bungled this sufficiently to ensure that."

The farm's surgical table flashed in my mind, black bloodstains soaked into the plastic tarp. The stench of dog waste that had permeated that makeshift operating room. I pictured Layla there, her elegant coat matted and dirty, surrounded by the clinical implements of a backyard surgeon.

"But Pixie will be fine," said Aram. "I'll buy her another dog. Something more suited to her lifestyle now that she's getting older. An Afghan Hound requires so much maintenance."

The casual way he dismissed Layla's fate got in my craw. "Tell Pixie to call me if she has any questions."

"Of course." Aram smiled, all teeth and no warmth. "I'll pass along the message."

I walked out of the Kazarian estate, balling and un-balling my fists with each step toward Danielle's car. The night air felt heavy, thick with the weight of what I'd learned. My skin still crawled from Aram's casual dismissal of Layla's life, like she was just another asset to be written off.

I slid behind the wheel of Danielle's sedan, grateful it wasn't sitting in a smoking heap like my SUV. The seats still held traces of her perfume, a comfort I needed right now.

How would Aram tell Pixie? I could picture him doing it over dinner at Café Boulud, maybe with a Cartier bracelet wrapped in a bow beside her plate. Something sparkly to catch the light and distract from the pain of losing her beloved companion. Now that the insurance money had come through, he could afford to be generous.

Sophie's face flashed in my mind. Sweet, tough Sophie who'd already lost so much. How could I tell her that Gaston was likely trapped in the back of that box truck, heading God knows where?

I started the car, the engine's purr doing nothing to drown out the echoes of AR-15 fire in my mind. Those weren't the sounds of people running a legitimate business. They weren't the actions of someone planning to keep dogs alive.

I looked up at the massive house before me and thought about the size of the numbers involved in Aram's business. They made two hundred thousand feel like a paltry sum. Could his business, his empire, his lifestyle really hang on what was, to someone like him, chump change? It was like me getting a twenty-buck payout.

I'd take free money anytime, but it wasn't going to save me. Was it?

Then I thought of Amanda Marshall, grinding away at three jobs. To her, a crisp twenty might be the difference between eating tonight and not. But I couldn't make the two scenarios merge, so pulled out of the driveway, and the gate opened automatically as if it were thankful I was leaving. I wondered if it would ever open for me again. I wondered if I would ever want it to.

I peeled off my shirt while Danielle dabbed at the cuts on my shoulder with antiseptic. The sting made me wince.

"Hold still," she said, her touch gentle but firm. "These could get infected."

"I did shower."

"Tell that to the bacteria."

"It was just mud and swamp water."

"Exactly my point." She applied an adhesive bandage to the worst scrape, likely from diving out of my SUV. "You can't keep doing this, Miami. Running into situations without backup."

"I had backup. Sort of. The Martin County Sheriff showed up, eventually."

"After you got shot." She moved to examining a bruise on my ribs. "We have Bella now. What happens if next time—"

Bella bounded into the living room, Argos at her heels. "Did you really jump across a canal? Sophie's gonna flip when I tell her."

"No one's telling Sophie anything," Danielle said firmly. "And this isn't awesome. It's dangerous."

"But he's like a real detective now. Not just looking for lost dogs." Bella perched on the arm of the couch. "This is way better than my last foster home. They just watched reruns of *Blue Bloods* all day."

"Better than getting shot," Danielle muttered.

"I've never seen anyone jump a canal before," Bella continued. "Well, except in movies. But they always make it look easy."

"It wasn't easy," I said, wincing as Danielle pressed an ice pack to my ribs. "And it's not something anyone at home should try."

"But you did it to catch bad guys, right?" Bella's eyes sparkled with excitement. "That makes it okay."

Danielle shot me a look that said this conversation wasn't helping.

"Sometimes," I said carefully, "the smart thing is to walk away. I should have waited for backup today."

Bella's face dropped. "But then the bad guys might have gotten away."

"They did anyway," I reminded her. "And now my car's toast."

I leaned back on the sofa with an ice pack on my ribs, careful not to disturb Danielle's handiwork with the bandages. The pieces were starting to fit together, but the picture they formed didn't make me happy. I outlined what I thought I knew to Danielle while Bella watched some videos on her iPad.

Aram's business was failing—bounced checks always told a story. He had expensive collaboration deals and millions of dollars in inventory that, according to Graham Albright, had failed to launch, let alone sell. But Albright's intel had to be considered suspect at best.

The Wi-Fi jammer in Aram's desk matched Luis's from the Donut Den. Two jammers, two entry points. Someone familiar with the security flaws had taken Layla.

Layla's insurance policy seemed modest for Palm Beach money, but two hundred grand could tempt a desperate man. Sal always told me that in business, cash flow was king. Great businesses were often built on sailing close to the financial wind. But if the sail flopped the wrong way, great businesses had been taken under by their inability to pay their bills today, even if tomorrow looked rosy. So a modest insurance payout might be the thread that kept the whole empire tied together.

Was his business that close to collapse? He seemed pretty chipper about getting the insurance check. How could that make all the difference?

And Luis, who dealt illegal cigars at Aram's club, was now having secretive parking lot meetings with him—the same Luis caught on video stealing Charlie using an identical jammer.

I rubbed my temples, feeling a headache coming on.

Bella looked up from the floor. "You think that Layla's owner had her taken?"

"He's the owner's husband, but I think it looks likely," I said. "The debts, the jammer. And now he's discontinued my services."

"He fired you?" said Danielle, crossing her arms.

"In a manner of speaking."

"That's super suss," said Bella.

"Maybe he's just trying to shield his wife from hurt because he believes the dog is gone." I winced as I moved the ice pack. "The smart money says cash the check and walk away. "

"You can't do that," Bella protested. "What about Gaston?"

"Exactly," I said. "And Aram isn't my client, anyway. Not technically. Pixie hired me."

"I like the way you think," said Bella.

"Don't go getting any big ideas," Danielle said with a half-smile.

I sat up straighter to get comfortable. "Aram said he'd get Pixie another dog."

Bella sat up. "You don't just buy love like that."

Danielle and I looked at her. The kid knew some stuff.

I rubbed my face, feeling a fatigue set in. "Maybe the cops will have some luck tracking down the box truck. But something doesn't feel right," I said, shifting the ice pack. "Albright said Aram pulled the plug on a launch at his property. Lizzy verified it. But Aram's files show a big contract with someone called J Blaze."

Bella's head snapped up. "Ugh, no."

"What's that mean?"

"He's like, the worst." She set her device aside, her face scrunching in disgust. "He was this huge DJ, played all these massive clubs and festivals. Had deals with everyone."

"Was?" Danielle asked.

"Yeah, until everyone found out he was a total creep." Bella hugged her knees to her chest. "He was messaging underage girls, trying to get them to come to his shows. And when they did… yuck." She shuddered. "Some of the stories that came out were seriously gross."

"How do you know about this?" I asked.

"Everyone knows. It was all over social media. Plus, my friend Kaylee's older sister almost went to one of his parties but got scared and backed out. Lucky for her."

"What happened to him?" Danielle asked.

"He's going to prison forever, hopefully." Bella's voice hardened. "They found all these messages and images on his phone and computer. The police said there were like dozens of victims."

I thought about the contract I'd seen in Aram's office. The astronomical numbers involved. "So this collaboration deal with Aram…"

"Would've been huge." Bella nodded. "Before everything came out, J Blaze was everywhere. But now?" She made a thumbs down gesture. "Nobody wants anything to do with him. Some people deserve to get canceled."

That explained a lot about Aram's cash flow problems. A massive inventory of clothing and merchandise, much of it already produced, suddenly worthless because your star collaborator turned out to be a predator.

Bella's words made me think of another contract I saw. "What about Lexi Prism?" I asked. "That name mean anything to you?"

Bella rolled her eyes. "She's like, everywhere. Total influencer queen."

"A what now?"

"Social media influencer. She's got millions of followers." Bella pulled up her phone and showed me a stream of perfectly curated photos. "She does collabs with all the big brands."

"Is she a singer or something?"

"No." Bella scrolled through more photos.

"Actor?"

"Nope. She's just… Lexi. Posts about fashion, lifestyle, beauty stuff. She makes or breaks brands. She dissed this one collection for making their stuff in some sweatshop, and the value tanked on the whatever."

I laughed. "The whatever?"

"You know, the business market thing."

"The stock market?"

"Yep. Word is she won't even do a sponsored post for less than a hundred thousand bucks."

"A hundred grand? For what exactly?"

"For posting pictures wearing clothes or using products. That's how it works—no cash, no play." Bella wrinkled her nose. "It's kind of slimy, if you ask me. But brands throw money at her because whatever she promotes sells out instantly."

I stared at the phone screen, trying to wrap my head around it. "So people pay her that much just to post pictures?"

"Millions follow everything she does. If she wears it, they buy it. If she says it's cool, it's cool." Bella shrugged. "That's influence."

The pieces started clicking together in my mind—Aram's failed collaboration with J Blaze, leaving him with worthless inventory, and now a fresh contract with this Lexi person requiring substantial upfront cash. Two hundred thousand dollars in initial payments, according to the paperwork I'd seen.

The exact amount the insurance payout on Layla had been.

CHAPTER FORTY

THE MORNING BROKE MONOTONOUSLY BLUE. I WATCHED BELLA demolish her second waffle while Danielle nursed her coffee. The morning sun streamed through the sliding doors, showing marks on the glass where Argos had licked it. My ribs still ached from yesterday's adventure.

Danielle's phone buzzed. She glanced at the screen, then sat up straighter. "Martin County Sheriff's Office," she said to me.

Bella stopped mid-chew, her eyes widening as Danielle listened.

"They found the truck?" Danielle's eyes met mine. "Highway Patrol pulled them over… How many puppies?" She covered her mouth. "A hundred? In one truck?"

My stomach turned. Those tiny pens I'd seen at the farm flashed through my mind.

"Three adult dogs," Danielle continued. "Two pit bulls and an English bulldog. They arrested Zazy and another man."

Bella set down her fork. "What about Gaston?"

Danielle shook her head slowly. "No Afghan Hound, no French Bulldog, no Golden Retriever." She ended the call and set her phone down. "They're processing everyone now."

"So where are they?" Bella's voice cracked.

I pushed my plate away, my appetite gone. The puppies were probably destined for unscrupulous pet stores or online sales, but our three missing show dogs weren't among them. Which meant either they'd already been moved somewhere else, or …

I didn't want to finish that thought.

We put our plates in the dishwasher and got ready for the day. I stared out at the water from the kitchen, processing the news. Zazy in custody should have felt like a win, but it was more like a three-strikeout inning. A good result, but the game was still in play. The puppy mill operation was real enough—those tiny cages and that bloodied workbench told their own horrific story. It didn't explain what happened to our three missing show dogs.

"At least they saved those puppies," Bella said, wandering out with her backpack on her shoulder.

I nodded, but my mind was elsewhere. The second check from Aram was sitting in my wallet, and I had a feeling it would bounce just like the first one if all his insurance money went to some influencer. That would give me legal grounds to sue the Kazarians, but my case would be stronger if I actually found their dog.

I glanced at Bella, remembering Sophie's face when she told me about losing Gaston. Money wasn't the point anymore—hadn't been since I met that kid. I needed to find that little Frenchie, not for any potential lawsuit, but because a fourteen-year-old girl was missing her best friend.

But I was no closer to finding any of the dogs than I'd been yesterday. Zazy's operation explained many missing pets around South Florida, but not the ones I was looking for. That left me with a blank whiteboard and no ideas. Perhaps Ronzoni would get something from Luis, but he hadn't seemed too chatty. I could only hope a night in the cells loosened his tongue, but I wasn't confident.

I took a final sip of coffee, now cold. The morning sun caught Argos's nose prints on the glass door, again reminding me that it was no time to give up.

The three of us headed out together. We only had one car, so

Danielle would drop Bella at school and me at the office. Then I had to have the insurance conversation with Ron.

A car sat in the driveway that wasn't there last night—a red Mazda Miata convertible that had seen better days but still sparkled with potential. A piece of paper fluttered under the wiper blade.

I plucked it off. *Happy trails. Sal.*

"Sweet ride," Bella said, running her hand along the fender. "Is it yours?"

"Apparently." I hadn't mentioned to Sal that my SUV had met an unfortunate end, and I would never fully comprehend the extent of his intel network. It straddled generations and legality. But trust him to come through with wheels, even if they weren't exactly practical.

"Can we put the top down?" Bella bounced on her toes.

"Aren't I taking you to school?" Danielle asked.

Bella glanced at Danielle's vanilla sedan and made a face that told a whole story.

Danielle smiled and shook her head, gave me a kiss, and told Bella to have a good day. I watched her pull away then turned my attention to the little car.

The leather seats were warm from the sun, but Bella didn't seem to mind as she climbed in. I got myself acquainted with the controls but couldn't figure out how the roof worked, so Bella retrieved the manual from the glove compartment and read me the instructions like we were pilots doing prechecks. The hardtop retreated and left us in the sunshine.

Bella's hair whipped around her face as we cruised toward her school, and the smile hadn't left her face when she got out.

After dropping Bella off, I pointed the Miata toward Rosemary Square. The little car handled like a go-kart compared to my deceased SUV. Not exactly intimidating for a PI, but it would do until insurance came through.

I still wasn't sure why I was heading to see Victoria. Henry's request weighed on me, though. A dying man's last wish deserved attention, even if his daughter seemed determined to make everyone as miserable as she was.

The promotional company's lot was half empty this early. I parked the Miata between two pickups where it looked like a toy car someone's kid had left behind. I ran my finger through my air-blown hair as I stepped inside, already dreading how this conversation would go.

I found Victoria at her desk, clicking through some designs on her computer screen. Her eyes hardened when she spotted me. "What do you want?"

"Can we talk somewhere private?"

She led me back to the break room where we'd been before. This time she didn't bother with the coffee machine, just crossed her arms and leaned against the counter.

"I saw your father," I said.

Her brow furrowed. "You took the kid?"

"Yes. She wanted to see him."

"Of course she did." Victoria's voice dripped with disdain.

"He'd like to see you."

A bitter laugh escaped her. "Did he tell you that?"

"Yes, he did."

"And you're here to make an old man feel better?" She spat the words out like they were moldy.

"No." I shook my head. "I'm here because I know something about things that need to be said."

Victoria's eyes narrowed, but I pressed on.

"Believe it or not, I'm here for you. I lost my dad, and there were things that should have been said. Things I wish now I had said, but I never took that chance." My voice caught. "And then the chance was taken from me."

She looked away, but her posture softened.

"Whatever you think about Henry, once he's gone, he's not going to care. My dad doesn't. He's not around to think about it." I let that sink in. "But I am. And you will be."

Victoria's fingers tapped against her crossed arms, her jaw clenched.

"I'm not saying you have to wrap it up in a neat bow," I continued. "But I think you'll come to regret it if you don't take the chance before he's gone. You never know. You might feel better."

Victoria pushed off from the counter, her arms still crossed. "I doubt that. But thanks for your time." She glanced at her watch. "I'm very busy."

I nodded, not bothering to argue. My piece was said—the rest was up to her. Sometimes you could only open the door; you couldn't make people walk through it. I put my hands up in defeat. "You know where to find him if you change your mind."

She didn't respond, just turned and walked out.

My duty was discharged. I'd delivered Henry's message. Whether Victoria chose to see her father before he died was her decision to live with.

I headed out through the office, past the cubicles where graphic designers stared at screens filled with colors and shapes. The morning sun hit me as I stepped outside, reminding me I had other obligations waiting. And they didn't involve dogs.

CHAPTER FORTY-ONE

I pointed the Miata south toward Lake Worth. The morning had warmed up, but I kept the top down. The wind helped clear my head.

South Florida National Cemetery spread across the landscape like a stark reminder of sacrifice—endless rows of white marble headstones standing at attention under a merciless sun. Palm trees dotted the grounds, offering small patches of shade, but mostly it was open and exposed. The grass between the markers stayed impossibly green thanks to an aggressive sprinkler system.

Acres of similar headstones could make navigation difficult, but I knew the path to my old mentor and friend's grave by heart now.

Lucas Burnside sat cross-legged on the grass beside Lenny's headstone, two steel tumblers on the ground beside him. His weathered face broke into a slight grin as I approached.

"G'day," Lucas said, his Australian accent still thick after decades in Florida.

I lowered myself onto the grass beside him, my joints creaking. The morning sun hadn't yet burned off the dew, and moisture seeped through my cargo shorts.

"You don't look so flash, mate," he said.

"It's been one of those weeks."

Lucas reached into his blue cooler, ice cubes crackling as he shifted them around. He pulled out a bottle of Yuengling and twisted off the cap. The familiar smell of hops drifted over as he tilted the bottle, pouring a steady stream into the grass beside Lenny's headstone.

"You're not drinking?" I said as he handed me a steel tumbler.

He unscrewed the cap from a battered thermos. Steam rose as he poured dark coffee into my cup. "It's barely nine a.m.," he said. "And I'm not the spring chicken I once was." Lucas shrugged, his tanned face crinkling into a smile. "But it won't hurt Lenny none. Besides, the man deserves a beer after watching over your sorry backside all these years."

The coffee was strong and black. Some recipe Lucas had picked in a far-flung land back when he and Lenny roamed around the world doing things for our government that I would never learn about. I breathed in the aroma, letting the familiar ritual settle my thoughts.

I raised my coffee cup. "To absent friends."

Lucas clinked his cup against mine, then both of us touched them to Lenny's beer bottle propped against his headstone.

"Thinking about making some changes," Lucas said, his eyes fixed on the horizon beyond the endless rows of white stones.

"The marina getting too much?"

He nodded. "Thirty years is a long time to watch other people's boats." His voice carried the weariness of someone who'd seen too many sunrise starts. "Government says I can retire whenever I want."

That was news. I'd always suspected Lucas's position at the marina wasn't just about keeping the books balanced, but he never talked about it, and I never asked.

I sipped some coffee. "What would you do with yourself?"

"Been looking at some land out in the Everglades." He gestured vaguely westward. "Might build a little place. Live off the grid."

I pictured Lucas in the swamp, probably happier among the

alligators than dealing with entitled boat owners. "You'd miss the ocean."

"Yeah." He took another sip of coffee. "That's the rub, isn't it? All those years watching the water, it gets in your blood. Can't just walk away from that."

Lucas had always been more at home in wild places than civilization, but the marina had given him purpose after whatever classified work he'd done with Lenny.

"Could do both," I suggested. "Keep a small place at the beach."

Lucas nodded but said nothing more on it and stared toward the scrub at the edges of the cemetery.

I took another sip, letting the rich flavor wash over my tongue. "Got myself into a mess with my latest case. Three show dogs gone missing before a big competition."

Lucas's eyebrows lifted. "Dogs?"

"Yeah, I know. Started with one in Palm Beach, but there were at least two others. Thought I found the operation yesterday— puppy mill out past Indiantown. Nearly got myself killed for the trouble."

"How's that?"

"Followed a lead out there. Ended up diving out of my SUV while two guys with AR-15s turned it into Swiss cheese." I rubbed my shoulder, more from the memory than actual pain. "Had to hide in a swamp until the Martin County Sheriff showed up."

Lucas shook his head. "You're getting too old for that kind of excitement, mate."

"My insurance company agrees." I stretched my legs out on the grass and told him about Luis and Zazy and the Kazarians. "Highway Patrol pulled over their box truck this morning. Found about a hundred puppies crammed in there. Three adult dogs too, but not the ones I'm looking for."

"How'd you track them to the farm?"

"Sal found me a contact number. The guy I called arranged a meet. But the funny thing is, one of the dogs I was looking for wore a tracking device. Signal went dead out near there a couple days ago. But like I say, that dog wasn't among the ones the cops found. I don't think he was ever there."

"And you're sure this Luis character took them?"

"Got him on video taking one dog—Charlie. The one with the tracker. The guy works at a cigar club on the island, deals Cuban cigars under the counter."

Lucas nodded thoughtfully, pouring himself a little more coffee. "Seems like a long way from smuggling cigars to stealing show dogs, but that's how these things go. Once you're on the wrong side of the line, everything's possible." Lucas sipped his coffee and smacked his lips together. "So where was this? Indiantown, you say?"

"Just this side of the St. Lucie Canal." I traced a line in the dewy grass.

Lucas nodded slowly. "Not much out there. Sugarcane and horses. And folks who keep to themselves."

"What's your point?"

"You're assuming this Luis went to the farm where you got shot up."

"Come on, it can't be coincidence. Dog goes missing, tracker stops working out there, then I find a puppy mill operation in the same area?"

"Not really." Lucas shifted his position on the grass. "Plenty of places to hide animals out there. And you said this tracker needs a phone nearby to ping off?"

"That's right." I thought about what Trey had explained about the Bluetooth tracker's limitations. "Has to be within range of someone with the right kind of phone."

I pulled out my phone and showed Lucas the tracking app. The cartoon beagle icon sat frozen on the map where the signal had died.

"So, you have the right phone?" Lucas asked.

"Yeah. Plenty of people do. Kevin shared the tracker with me."

Lucas squinted at the screen. "So you can assume your thief

didn't have the right phone or app, because otherwise the tracker would have pinged all the way to the farm."

I nodded, following his logic.

"And you said you texted Danielle from the farm to ask for help, so you had a connection to a cell tower," Lucas continued, his voice taking on a patient tone. "So if your phone's the right one, the tracker should have been pinging on the farm when you were there—if old Charlie was there, too."

The implications started sinking in. I'd had limited cell service out there, but my phone had the tracking app. If Charlie had been anywhere within a couple hundred feet of me while I was hiding in that swamp, the app should have picked up the signal.

"So the question is," Lucas said, "what kind of phones did your shooters have?"

I stared at the beagle icon, frozen in place on my screen. I had my phone in my hand, so I used it.

I pulled up the number for Martin County Sheriff and hit dial. I asked if the deputy on the case was available. There was some electronic thunking before the call was answered.

"Deputy Torres."

"It's Miami Jones. Quick question about the phones you confiscated from Zazy and his friend yesterday."

Papers shuffled in the background. "What about them?"

"What kind of phones were they?"

He told me. "Latest models, too. Puppy mills make more than I thought."

I thanked him and ended the call. Lucas was already tilting another bottle of Yuengling, letting the amber liquid soak into the grass by Lenny's headstone.

"It was the right kind of phone," I said.

"There you go." Lucas's weathered face showed no surprise.

"So Charlie wasn't at the farm. Ever."

"Nope."

I stared at the frozen tracker icon on my phone's screen. "So he could be anywhere."

"Not really," Lucas said, gently placing the beer bottle with its twin. "Think about it. The tracker was pinging all the way from Palm Beach because it was bouncing off people's phones. Right up until they hit that rural stretch where there's nobody around."

I nodded, seeing where he was going. "But if Charlie never went to the farm …"

"And assuming he didn't end up wandering in the cane fields…" Lucas gestured at my phone.

"Then they must have taken him through Indiantown." The pieces started falling into place. "But Indiantown's got what, six thousand people?"

"Thereabouts."

"So there should have been plenty of phones capable of picking up the signal." I stared at the frozen tracker icon. "But it never reconnected."

Lucas took another sip of coffee. "Which means?"

"The tracker's still out there." The realization hit me like jumping into a cold irrigation canal. "Somewhere between where the signal died and Indiantown."

Lucas nodded. "So says logic."

He reached for his thermos. Steam curled up as he poured more of that industrial-strength coffee into my cup. The aroma alone could wake the dead. My old man would've approved—he always said coffee like this put hairs on your chest.

"You're not bad at this detective work," I said, watching Lucas's movements.

His eyes drifted to Lenny's headstone, a slight smile tugging at the corners of his mouth. "I had a good teacher."

We raised our cups again in Lenny's direction.

"Show me that spot again," Lucas said. "Where the signal dropped."

I pulled out my phone, bringing up the tracking app. The cartoon beagle's head sat frozen on the map, marking the spot where Charlie's signal had vanished.

"I went out there," I said, zooming in on the location. "Nothing but woods and cane fields." A chuckle escaped me as I remembered. "Oh, and this weird old sign. *Feed the Lion*. No idea what that was about."

Lucas's coffee cup stopped halfway to his mouth. *"Feed the Lion?"* His voice carried an edge I hadn't heard before. "Is this by a dirt road heading east?"

"Yeah, that's right."

He set his cup down carefully. "There used to be a reptile park out there. Real low-rent operation. Old Florida style—the kind of place that had postcard racks and sold rubber alligators."

"What happened to it?"

"Got shut down about fifteen years ago. They weren't treating their animals right."

"Shut down by who? Florida Fish and Wildlife?"

"No." Lucas's voice was flat.

"What's this got to do with lions?"

"They kept a lion in a cage." He picked at a blade of grass. "Nothing to do with reptiles, but it brought the punters in."

"Where do you even get a lion?"

"Vegas casino, from what I heard."

I watched Lucas's face, trying to read more in the weathered lines. "What happened to it?"

"The lion?" He shrugged. "Had to be put down. Poor thing was in rough shape."

"How do you know all this?"

Another shrug.

"What about the owners?"

"One ran off to Wyoming, I think." Lucas's voice grew distant. "The other got up close and personal with the Everglades."

"How do you know *that?*"

A knowing grin crossed Lucas's face. "They were mistreating the animals." He picked up his coffee cup. "That's no good."

I got to my feet, muscles protesting from sitting on the damp grass. My phone felt heavy in my hand as I pulled up Ronzoni's number.

"What's the story with Luis?" I asked when he answered.

"Finally lawyered up." Ronzoni's voice carried the frustration of a detective watching a lead slip away. "Had to cut him loose."

"You let him walk?"

"Got a car on him." A pause. "Why? You know something?"

"Not sure yet." I glanced at Lucas, still sitting cross-legged by Lenny's grave. "I'll let you know when I do."

I ended the call and looked down at my old friend. His face was unreadable, but his eyes held that dangerous gleam I remembered from the light-on-detail stories Lenny used to tell.

"This park. You say it had cages?"

"Big enough for a lion."

"What are you up to today?" I asked.

Lucas's leathery face cracked into a smile as he gathered the empty coffee cups.

CHAPTER FORTY-TWO

Lucas sat beside me as we headed up I-95, his weathered face in a partial grin, enjoying the sun beating down on our heads in the convertible.

My phone buzzed. Ronzoni.

"Lost Luis in traffic," he said. "Wasn't heading home, though."

"I know." I ended the call and pressed harder on the accelerator.

We got onto the Beeline Highway and headed northwest. When we reached the spot where Charlie's tracker had gone dark, Lucas directed me onto a dirt track at the crossroads where I'd found the lion sign in the grass. The path twisted through dense scrub, Brazilian pepper trees forming a canopy that filtered the sunlight into dappled patterns on the sandy track. Slash pines stood sentinel among the cabbage palms, their branches heavy with pine cones ready to drop.

The road hadn't seen maintenance in years. I navigated around potholes deep enough to swallow a tire. It occurred that the Miata wasn't really designed for this kind of work.

We emerged into a clearing that might have been a parking lot back when Florida was selling swampland to Yankees. Nature had reclaimed most of it, saw palmetto and cabbage palms breaking through the cracked asphalt.

A van sat near what looked like an entrance, half-hidden by overgrown vegetation. The vehicle's side panel displayed that garish painting of a sword-wielding warrior.

"Look at that," Lucas said, squinting at the artwork. "Straight off a Meat Loaf record." He shook his head. "That Jim Steinman, he could really write a belter."

I pulled the Miata behind a stand of palms, out of sight from the van. Lucas and I picked our way through the undergrowth toward what remained of the entrance building. The roof had partially caved in, creating a jagged skylight that nature was already exploiting; vines draped through the opening like party streamers at a forgotten celebration.

We stepped through a doorway missing its door. Gift shop shelves lay scattered across warped floorboards, mud and foliage where the postcards and plastic alligators had once been. The ticket counter had been stripped bare, leaving only outline rectangles where equipment once sat.

Outside, a concrete pathway wound through the grounds, though *pathway* was generous—more like a suggestion under the tangle of weeds and fallen branches. Hurricane wire cages lined the route, their wire mesh rusted and torn. Some had collapsed entirely, creating modern art sculptures of twisted metal and vegetation.

The remnants of informational signs clung to posts, their text long since weathered away. Only the occasional fragment remained legible: *...onda's most dangerous...* and *...atch feeding time...*

We passed a squat concrete structure with *Snake Room* still visible above the door frame. Its windows were smashed, leaving sharp teeth of glass around the edges. Through the gaps, I could make out empty terrariums and display cases collecting leaves and debris.

Around a bend, we came upon what must have been the showcase attraction—a murky green pool flanked by the skeletal remains of wooden bleachers. One section had collapsed entirely, the planks rotting into the earth. The water's surface was thick with algae and duckweed, creating an opaque soup that could have hidden anything. Or nothing.

"Real tourist trap," Lucas muttered. "Literally, in some cases." He pointed to an enclosure half-hidden behind overgrown palmettos. "That's where they kept the lion."

I studied the cage. It wasn't much bigger than the dog run at the Pawlace. "You're kidding."

"Never said the lion was happy about it." Lucas's voice carried an edge of old anger.

We continued on where the path split around a cluster of royal palms. Through gaps in the fronds, I caught movement—a figure in dark clothes. Luis. He spotted us at the same moment and bolted.

"Stop!" I shouted, but he was already sprinting down the opposite fork.

Lucas and I backtracked to where the path divided, precious seconds ticking away as we navigated around fallen branches and debris. By the time we got onto Luis's path, he had a solid lead.

He ran back toward the algae-covered pool, his feet pounding the cracked concrete. The dense canopy acted like a greenhouse, with foliage blocking the sun while trapping the humidity, so the concrete near the water remained slick with green slime.

Luis's foot hit a particularly wet patch. His legs shot out from under him, and he went down hard, his head cracking against the concrete with a sound that made my teeth hurt. He rolled onto his side, dazed.

As he pushed himself to his knees, the pool's surface erupted.

An alligator launched from the murky water, its massive jaws open wide. Before Luis could react, those teeth clamped down on his leg.

His scream echoed off the empty cages and abandoned buildings.

I froze. The sight of the massive reptile's jaws clamping onto Luis's leg triggered memories I'd rather forget. My own encounter with an alligator on a golf course had been years ago, but the mental scars remained. The ancient predator's strength was something you never forgot once you'd seen it up close and personal.

But before I could move or even speak, Lucas sprang into action. He crossed the distance in three long strides and launched himself onto the alligator's back, wrapping his arms around its thick neck. The beast thrashed, but Lucas held on, repeatedly driving his fist into its eye.

The alligator's jaws released Luis's leg. It whipped its head from side to side, trying to shake off Lucas, but the Australian wasn't letting go. He continued the assault until the creature began backing up. As soon as it started its retreat, Lucas pushed off its back, rolling away across the wet concrete.

The alligator slipped back into the murky pool, disappearing beneath the green surface with barely a ripple. Only bubbles marked where it had vanished.

I grabbed Luis under the armpits and dragged him away from the pool's edge, his blood leaving a dark trail on the concrete. His face had gone pale, either from the injury or the shock of nearly becoming gator food. Maybe both.

I propped him against a rusty enclosure. His leg looked like someone had taken a cheese grater to it, blood pulsing from multiple puncture wounds where the gator's teeth had sunk in.

"Take off your shirt," I said.

Luis stared at me like I'd asked him to juggle. "What?"

"Your shirt. Now." I pointed at his leg. "Unless you want to bleed out here."

"Use your own shirt," he spat.

I shook my head. "There are plenty of people I'd give the shirt off my back, but you ain't any of them, pal."

He muttered something in Spanish that wasn't complimentary but started unbuttoning his shirt with shaking fingers. I snatched it as soon as he had it off and wrapped it tight around his mangled leg, creating a makeshift bandage over the worst of the damage.

Luis winced as I pulled the fabric tight. "That hurts."

"Good," I said. "Means you're still alive."

Lucas stepped over us, wiping his hands on his trousers.

"Where are the dogs?" I asked.

Luis shook his head, still trembling. "What dogs?"

"Fine." I stood and turned away. "Stay here then. Watch out for that gator—looks like he's still hungry."

"Wait!" Luis called as I started walking. "You can't leave me here!"

I pulled out my phone and opened the tracking app. The cartoon beagle's head appeared on the screen, pulsing larger and smaller like a heartbeat. Lucas fell in step beside me as we followed the arrow that appeared when I tapped the icon.

The path led us deeper into the abandoned park, past more empty enclosures and collapsed structures. My mind kept drifting back to that farm—the stench, the stained workbench. I pushed the thoughts away, focusing on the arrow as it guided us through the overgrown grounds.

Behind us, Luis's voice grew more desperate. "Hey! Come back! Please!"

I kept walking, watching the signal grow stronger with each step. The humidity pressed down like a wet blanket, making even breathing feel like work.

The app led us to a squat cinderblock building. Rusty bars crossed glassless windows, and a heavy chain secured the door. The padlock looked new—the only thing in this whole place that wasn't falling apart.

Lucas took one step and put a boot into the door. I couldn't see how that was going to break the chain, and it didn't. The chain held fast while the door broke off its rusted hinges.

He kicked his way in. Stale air rushed out, carrying an unmistakable animal smell.

My eyes adjusted to the dim interior. Three dogs lay on the

concrete floor, each tied to a metal pole with short lengths of rope. Their water bowl lay empty on its side, kicked away from their reach. No food in sight.

The Afghan Hound's cream-colored coat was matted and dirty, but Layla's elegant head lifted at our entrance. Her tail thumped weakly against the floor.

Beside her, Charlie the golden retriever struggled to his feet, his show-quality coat dulled by dust and debris. His tail wagged with more enthusiasm than I expected from a dog in his condition.

The French Bulldog, Gaston, looked the worst for wear. His brindle coat was streaked with grime, but his stubby tail wiggled as we approached. Despite his small size, he had the same resilient spirit I recognized in his young owner.

"G'day, mates," Lucas said softly, approaching the dogs with his hands out. They responded to his gentle tone, tails wagging harder. "Let's get you out of here."

I called the Martin County Sheriff's Office while Lucas untied the dogs. The dispatcher said they'd send units and animal control. Within twenty minutes, red and blue lights flashed through the trees as vehicles navigated the old access road.

Two deputies dragged Luis away from the gator pond so paramedics could attend to his leg. He avoided my gaze as they loaded him into an ambulance.

The animal welfare team arrived in a white van marked with their logo. A woman in khakis and a polo shirt introduced herself as Dana from Animal Services. She knelt to examine the dogs while I explained how we found them.

"I appreciate you locating these animals," she said, running gentle hands over Layla's ribs. "But I can't release them to you without proper documentation. We need to verify ownership and ensure they're healthy before returning them."

"They belong to—" I started, but she held up a hand.

"We'll take care of that at the office, sir. These dogs need medical evaluation first."

I watched her check the dogs over, proclaiming their health as reasonable in the circumstances, before her team carefully loaded the dogs into their climate-controlled van. Charlie's tail still wagged, despite everything. Gaston tried to resist the carrier they brought for him. Layla maintained her dignity, as if being rescued by government officials was just too embarrassing.

"We'll take it from here," Dana assured me, handing me a business card. "Tell the owners to bring their papers." She didn't hold the same joy in her eyes looking at me as she did with the dogs, but I didn't take it personally. A woman in her job saw some ugly stuff, and she clearly cared about the animals. It was the humans she wasn't sold on.

I nodded, knowing it was the right procedure but still feeling frustrated at the delay in getting them home. I thought about Sophie, waiting to hear if we'd found Gaston. At least now I could tell her he was safe.

Lucas appeared beside me as the van pulled away. "Now I do need a beer," he said quietly.

I smiled. "First round's on me."

CHAPTER FORTY-THREE

I leaned against a Martin County Sheriff's cruiser, giving my statement while Lucas talked to another deputy near the remains of the reptile park's entrance.

After we finished, I drove us toward Longboard Kelly's, weaving around the potholes, the Miata's tires kicking up dust until we hit pavement. Lucas hadn't said much since we'd found the dogs, but his weathered face held a satisfied expression.

Muriel looked up as we walked in, her eyebrows rising at our disheveled state. "You two look like you've been wrestling alligators."

"Just the one," Lucas said, sliding onto a bar stool.

She poured us two cold beers without asking, and I pulled out my phone. Pixie answered on the first ring.

"We found Layla," I said, raising my beer to Lucas. "She's at Martin County Animal Services. You'll need to bring ownership papers to claim her."

Her voice cracked. "Oh, thank goodness. Is she okay?"

"She's fine. A bit dirty and hungry, but otherwise okay."

"We'll be there directly. Thank you, Miami. Thank you so much."

I hung up and dialed Kevin's number next. His reaction

matched Pixie's—pure relief, followed by immediate plans to retrieve Charlie. He said would close the shop, the post-school rush be damned.

Lucas nursed his beer, leaning back against the bar and looking across the courtyard at the surfboard with the bite out of it mounted on the fence. "Good result today, mate."

I nodded. "Thanks for the backup. Let me drive you home."

He shook his head. "Bus'll do fine."

"It's no trouble—"

"Bus is fine." He finished his beer and stood. "Some things are better processed alone."

I watched him walk out, his stride still carrying that military precision despite the years.

"Another?" Muriel asked, gesturing at my half-empty glass.

"No thanks. Gotta do the school run."

Muriel smiled and put her hands on her hips. "I never thought I'd live to see the day."

"What?"

She shook her head and walked into the inside bar. "Nothing."

I drove through afternoon traffic and pulled into the school parking lot, finding Bella already waiting by the gate. She jumped in, shoving her backpack to the floor.

"I could get used to this car," she said.

I wore the Cheshire cat's grin. "I've got news."

Bella frowned. "What happened?"

"We found them."

Her jaw dropped. "The doggos?"

"All three."

She slapped my arm. "No way!"

"Yep."

"That's so bitchin'." She pulled on her seatbelt.

"Is that a word we should be using?"

"Don't be a buzzkill."

I shrugged. "It's part of the contract."

"We gotta tell Soph."

"Let's go there now. We can take her to him."

I pulled away, but I noted Bella's eyes still on me. "What?" I asked.

"We're going to get Sophie?"

"Yeah, why?"

She dropped her eyebrows low. "And then we're going to get Gaston?"

"Sure."

"Where are they going to sit?"

It was a good point. The Miata was a hell of a lot of fun to drive, but it was showing its limitations. I thought fast and headed for downtown. I parked at the office, and we went upstairs. Lizzy fussed over Bella, who stared at her with wide eyes.

I dropped the Miata's keys into Ron's hand and took his as replacement. I could see Ron cruising the Palm Beaches in the little red rocket. Bella and I took off down the stairs.

"That was your receptionist?" she asked.

"Lizzy? Office manager. She holds the place together, more or less."

"I've never seen anyone that old dressed like that."

I frowned. "Lizzy's not old."

"Whatever."

We strode out to where Ron's car was parked. I unlocked the doors with the key. There was no fob.

Bella turned up her nose. "This is like getting booted from business class to coach."

I started Ron's ancient Corolla. "Everyone fits, though."

We drove to the Marshall residence. Amanda's car sat under the aluminum carport, and Sophie opened the door before we reached the porch.

"Miami?" Her voice held a mix of hope and uncertainty.

"We found Gaston." I couldn't help but break into a grin. "He's safe. We can take you to him."

Sophie's face lit up, and she jumped up and down like her

sneakers were on fire. Then she turned to her mother hovering in the doorway. "Mom, can I—"

"Of course you can." Amanda's smile transformed her tired features, softening the hard edges life had carved into her.

The drive to Stuart felt longer with two excited teenagers peppering me with questions. When we arrived at Animal Services, the linoleum floor and antiseptic smell reminded me of a slasher film.

A woman in khakis asked us our business.

"Here to collect Sophie's dog. Gaston, the French Bulldog." I handed over Gaston's paperwork.

"Owner," the woman read from the documents. "Sophie Marshall?"

I pointed to Sophie, her face pressed against the window of the holding area, trying to spot Gaston.

The clerk handed me a clipboard. "Just sign here, Mr. Marshall," the clerk said, pointing to a line marked *Parent/Guardian*.

I hesitated for a moment, then signed. Sometimes it was easier to let people believe what they wanted to believe.

Sophie's squeal of delight echoed through the hallway as they brought Gaston out. The French Bulldog's stubby tail wagged furiously as Sophie dropped to her knees, wrapping her arms around him.

I was enjoying Sophie and Gaston's reunion when the door chimed and Kevin Thompson burst in, his eyes scanning the room frantically until they landed on me.

"Charlie?" His voice cracked.

I nodded. "He's waiting for you."

He had to do the paperwork thing, then the staff brought out the golden retriever, who practically dragged the handler across the floor in his excitement to reach Kevin. Charlie's tail wagged so hard his whole body shook as Kevin dropped to his knees, burying his face in the dog's golden fur.

"My boy, my boy." Kevin couldn't finish the sentence as tears streamed down his face.

Bella stepped forward and put a hand on his shoulder. "It's all right."

Kevin looked up, wiping his eyes with the back of his hand. "It is now." He hugged Charlie tighter.

The retriever's tongue lolled out in a happy grin as he soaked up the attention, seemingly unaware of the ordeal he'd been through.

We walked out as a merry group: me, Bella, Sophie, Gaston, Kevin, and Charlie. The clerk in khakis was holding the door for us when a familiar van pulled into the parking lot. The Pawlace logo gleamed on its side as Evelyn stepped out, a folder tucked under her arm.

I looked around for Pixie but saw no sign. Evelyn shook her head at me. She strode into Animal Services with the same purposeful grace she showed in the training ring. After presenting her credentials and paperwork showing her authority to handle Layla, she followed the clerk to the holding area.

I stepped back inside to ask about Pixie's welfare. I had visions of her fainting or something equally dramatic. Layla's elegant head lifted at Evelyn's approach, and her tail swished against the floor like a broom. Evelyn knelt beside the Afghan Hound, running expert hands over her coat and limbs, checking for any injuries. Finding none, she clipped a lead to Layla's collar and guided her toward the exit.

This time I held the door, and we moved to the others waiting outside.

Evelyn paused beside me, extending her hand. "Thank you, Miami. I know Pixie will want to thank you herself, but she's indisposed at the moment."

Something in her tone suggested there was more to the story, but this wasn't the place to discuss it.

I shook her hand, noting how her grip was firm but not showy. Professional, like everything else about her.

Kevin broke away from Charlie and wrapped me in a bear hug that smelled of sugar and cinnamon. "Thank you," he whispered. "I don't know how you did it, but thank you."

Charlie pressed against our legs, his tail still wagging, while Sophie leaned against the Corolla with Gaston in her arms, both of them watching the scene with matching head tilts.

I navigated Ron's Corolla down the coast while trying to keep Gaston's enthusiastic tongue away from my face. The French Bulldog had apparently decided that everyone in the car needed a thorough face-washing, and neither Sophie nor Bella seemed inclined to stop him.

"Gassy, good boy!" Sophie giggled as he moved from Bella to me again, his stubby body practically vibrating with joy.

"Hey, buddy, I'm driving here," I said, but couldn't help smiling as he gave my ear a particularly wet lick.

Bella's laughter filled the car. "He's like one of those car wash machines, but with more drool."

"Much more drool," Sophie agreed, pulling Gaston back onto her lap, only for him to squirm free and launch another assault on Bella's face.

The girls' infectious laughter and Gaston's unbridled happiness made the drive home feel shorter than usual. Even getting stuck in traffic at Palm Beach Gardens didn't dampen the mood—it just gave Gaston more time to distribute his affection equally among his captive audience.

"I think he missed you, Soph," Bella said, wiping her face with her sleeve.

"You think?" Sophie responded, dissolving into another fit of laughter as Gaston's tongue found her nose.

CHAPTER FORTY-FOUR

THE GATES TO THE KAZARIAN ESTATE SWUNG OPEN IMMEDIATELY UPON the arrival of Ronzoni's car—amazing what a police presence could do.

Pixie rushed out to meet us, her platinum hair bouncing, dressed in a flowing sundress. "Miami! Detective! I'm so grateful. Layla is back home where she belongs."

"She's here?" I said.

"Well, not here. At the Pawlace, of course."

"You didn't come collect her yourself?"

She waved a manicured hand. "I have people for that. I went straight to the Pawlace to see her. Eve handles all the tedious paperwork." She beamed. "I simply must give you a bonus for finding her."

Aram appeared in the doorway, his tailored suit immaculate as always. "That won't be necessary. Mr. Jones has been compensated."

"If the check clears this time," I said.

His jaw tightened. "A simple banking error."

"Speaking of money," I said, "the insurance company will probably want their payout back. Unless they decide to investigate for fraud."

"The payment was made in good faith," Aram said, his voice clipped. "And I will return it as per the policy terms. In the same good faith."

"That's a lot of good faith going around."

Pixie looked between us, her smile faltering. "What insurance payment?"

Aram stepped forward. "Nothing for you to worry about, my dear. Simply business matters."

I watched his face as he spoke. For a man who'd just gotten his wife's beloved dog back, he didn't seem particularly thrilled.

"You can pay back the insurance money because you paid your influencer, Lexi Prism, their upfront retainer, and they posted the blast to their fans that you were doing a big collaboration, right?" I kept my eyes on Aram's face. "I'm guessing that publicity alone was enough for the banks to give you time and money to rebrand the inventory you have from the failed thing with J Blaze."

Aram's perfect composure cracked as he shot a glance at Ronzoni. His frown deepened as he returned his focus to me, creasing his forehead. "How do you know that?"

The question hung in the air between us. Pixie's gaze darted between her husband and me, her earlier joy evaporating like morning dew under the Florida sun.

"I told you. I'm an investigator," I said. "So I also know this: you arranged for the theft of Layla so you could claim the insurance."

Pixie's hand flew to her throat, her perfectly manicured nails clutching at her necklace. "That's ridiculous."

"I wish it were." I glanced at the butler, still hovering in the doorway like a ghost at a dinner party. "But your husband hired someone to take Layla. Aram used a Wi-Fi jammer to block the security at the front of the house, and the thief used the same device at the rear."

I turned to Aram, who stood motionless, his jaw set, eyes fixed on some distant point beyond my shoulder. The mask of the successful businessman had slipped, revealing something harder underneath.

Ronzoni shifted his weight, his hand unconsciously moving closer to his hip.

"You arranged the same thief to take two more dogs to make it look like a spate of thefts, a serial dognapper. Perhaps a competitor or an organized crime ring." I looked at Ronzoni. "And I was a little confused at the start when I thought Layla was the first dog taken. But then I learned that Gaston was actually first, and eventually I figured out that the first job was the practice. The lowest security, so the lowest risk."

Aram's face remained impassive, but his fingers twitched.

"You know Sophie from the other dog shows. She's a precocious talent. She's known around the circuit. So you sent your man to her trailer park. Not an over fifty-five one where everyone's sitting on the porch watching everyone else's business. This park is where people have to scratch out a living. Kids go to school. Not many eyes around during the day." I shifted my weight, feeling the ache from my fun and games at the farm. "And the jammer worked a treat. It knocked out every video on the street. Police had no leads. You got away with it. So you figured you'd step up to Layla."

Pixie's hand trembled as she reached for the doorframe to steady herself.

"Then once that was pulled off, you had him do one more. And that was your downfall." I shook my head. "Like a good night out, it's always the last one that's one too many." I pointed at him. "You scoped out the scene yourself—you went to Kevin's donut shop."

Aram adjusted his cufflinks. "A man can buy a donut."

"Yes, but Kevin says you bought a dozen for your team." I watched his face for any flicker of recognition. "My office manager called your office and pretended to check on the order, make sure they enjoyed them. No one knew anything about a donut order. Your phone person actually asked if we had the right place, that Mr. K doesn't do *treats*."

Aram rolled his shoulders beneath his tailored jacket. "Maybe I ate them myself."

"A dozen eight-dollar donuts? That's quite an appetite for a man who looks like he lives on kale smoothies." I gestured at his trim frame. "No, you were casing the place. Checking the security, the cameras, the layout. Where Charlie hung out during the day. You saw the empty dog bed in the front, and you asked Kevin how Charlie was." "Kevin told you he sleeps in the back. So you passed that intel to your thief—check the front, but the dog would most likely be in the back."

I glanced at Ronzoni and he jogged his head to prompt me to continue.

"You told him to use the Wi-Fi jammer that had worked so well here at the estate." I motioned at the mansion behind them. "You're rich, Aram, but you're also cheap. You had shoddy security, but Kevin didn't. The jammer did nothing, so we have video of the whole thing. And once we had that, I checked the first place again. Turns out the park's admin office has old, wired cameras. So we could place the same guy at two crime scenes, which raised a big question about the third. Yours."

Aram's face remained a mask of indifference, like a poker player holding a busted flush but refusing to show it.

"And now your thief has given you up."

The only sign that my words had landed was a slight tightening around his eyes, a barely perceptible tension in his shoulders beneath that perfectly tailored suit. "A thief? Telling you what you want to hear in return for what?" His voice dripped with disdain. "You've bought a lie."

I caught the slight tremor in his left hand as he fiddled with his cufflinks again. It was becoming a thing.

Ronzoni stepped forward. "We'll let a jury decide that." He pulled his cuffs from his belt. "Aram Kazarian, you're under arrest for fraud, grand larceny, and wasting police time."

I wasn't entirely sure that last one was actually a crime, but the way Ronzoni spat it out suggested he considered it worthy of the death penalty.

Pixie let out a small gasp. The butler remained stoic, though I caught the slight upturn at the corner of his mouth.

Aram stiffened as Ronzoni put on the cuffs. "There is no fraud. I told you, I plan to give the money back."

"They always do," Ronzoni said.

I watched Pixie's face crumble as the reality of her husband's actions sank in. The detective led Aram down the steps to the waiting police car. Even in handcuffs, Aram managed to look dignified.

Once Aram was secured in the back seat, Ronzoni turned to me, his brow furrowed. "I still don't get the ransom. He couldn't claim that on insurance, and he lost a hundred thousand."

"He lost nothing," I said, watching the patrol car's window reflect my exhausted face back at me. "When we confirmed those donuts he bought were never eaten by his team, it got me thinking. If they weren't at his work and they sure wouldn't turn up here, they had to be in the trash. That made me wonder about other things that might end up in trash cans." I glanced at Ronzoni. "Did you ever see him get the cash from the safe?"

"No."

"That's because there was nothing in that bag except a chicken dinner."

Ronzoni's face twisted into a snarl. "No!"

"Can you track down the homeless guy from the park?"

"Bernie? Sure. Turns out it's his patch. Why?"

"Ask Bernie if a well-dressed gent pointed him in the direction of a free chicken dinner."

Ronzoni's jaw dropped. "You don't think he just happened upon that trash can?"

"I do not."

"Damn."

"They might have gotten away with it if they hadn't kept the dogs alive," I said, watching Aram in the back of the patrol car, chin held high.

"Luis confirmed he was trying to sell them," Ronzoni said with a shake of his head. "Just hadn't found a buyer yet. Kept feeding them, walking them at night when no one was around."

I thought about Zazy's operation, just a couple miles down the road from where Luis had stashed the dogs. "He was that close to someone who would've done the deal." The memory of that blood-stained workbench made my stomach turn. "But he's a cigar guy, not a dog guy. Different circles, I guess."

"Very. He was just doing it for some extra cash. He was supposed to get rid of the dogs. Apparently, Aram didn't specify how. Luis thought he could add to his payday."

"Can't exactly move a show dog through a pawn shop," I said with a smirk.

"You'd know." Ronzoni got in his car, and I dropped into the Corolla.

As I pulled out, I glanced up at Pixie Kazarian. There were no tears, and the shock had gone, other than the absence of color in her face. She was Palm Beach old money. She knew a thing or two about damage control.

CHAPTER FORTY-FIVE

THE WEEKEND ARRIVED WITH THE KIND OF PERFECT AUTUMN WEATHER that made Florida bearable. The expo center parking lot was packed with SUVs and minivans, most sporting breed-specific bumper stickers with puns like *My dog's smarter than your honor student* and *Road trip? Fur sure!*

Inside, the cavernous hall had transformed from industrial emptiness to canine couture. Green carpeting stretched across the concrete floor like fairways at Augusta, lined with burgundy velvet ropes. Banks of spotlights hung from the steel rafters, bathing everything in a warm light that made even the most nervous handler look composed. Bleachers flanked both sides, already filling with spectators clutching programs and smartphones.

"This is better than a dog park," Bella said, her eyes wide as she took in the staging area where handlers groomed their charges. Portable tables held every manner of brush, comb, and spray bottle while dogs of all sizes submitted to last-minute primping.

Danielle was spinning around, taking in all the animals. "Like a beauty pageant for pooches."

"Better." Bella pointed to where Sophie stood with Gaston. The French Bulldog sat perfectly still as Sophie checked his lead. "At least these contestants seem happy."

We made our way over. Sophie's face glowed with excitement, though her hands trembled slightly as she adjusted Gaston's collar.

"You ready?" I asked.

"As I'll ever be." She scratched behind Gaston's ears. "We've been practicing."

Evelyn appeared, leading a Shih Tzu that looked like an animated dust mop. "Sophie, you're in ring three in twenty minutes."

"Where's Layla?" Bella asked.

"Withdrawn." Eve's tone was clipped. "On health grounds. I'm handling Miss Fluffles this weekend." She gestured to the Shih Tzu. "And probably into the future. Creative differences with my previous client."

I caught her meaning. Creative differences probably included having your client use their dog as part of an insurance scam, but I wasn't sure if the thing that rankled her more was Pixie's lack of willingness to reclaim her so-called confidante from animal control herself. I wondered for a moment if the Pawlace had severed ties with Pixie then who would walk Layla from now on. It was a fleeting thought.

The French Bulldog breed category drew thirty-two entries which were whittled down to ten finalists. Sophie and Gaston performed flawlessly, trotting the ring with precision. When the judge pointed to them as the winner, Sophie's face lit up like Times Square on New Year's Eve.

She squealed like a kid, kissing Gaston as they left the ring. "Can you believe it, boy?"

The duo came fourth in the Non-Sporting group competition, and Sophie was only marginally less excited.

We watched more breeds compete through the morning. Kevin arrived with Charlie, the golden retriever's tail wagging like he'd just returned from spring break. Despite his recent ordeal, Charlie bounded around the ring with pure joy, winning his category, then taking the entire Sporting group.

"He's just happy to be here," Kevin said, wiping tears from his eyes as he accepted the ribbon.

The afternoon built toward Best in Show. Chris Wozinski's wire fox terrier moved with mechanical precision, exactly as engineered by his data-driven approach.

"I like him," Bella whispered as the terrier trotted past. "He looks like a mutt. With a really expensive haircut."

When the judge announced the terrier as Best in Show, Chris didn't smile. He simply nodded, as if his algorithms had predicted nothing less.

Sophie didn't care. She clutched her breed winner ribbon while Gaston dozed in her arms. "Fourth in Non-Sporting," she kept saying. "Can you believe it?"

CHAPTER FORTY-SIX

THE AUTUMN MORNING CARRIED A CHILL THAT FELT OUT OF PLACE IN South Florida and told me that winter was about to her wrap her arms around us, such that it was. It was a suitable kind of day for Henry McCaron's funeral.

I pulled up to Sophie's home, where she waited on the concrete pad beneath the aluminum carport. Her black dress looked new, but her shoes had seen better days.

"Mom's sorry she couldn't come," Sophie said, climbing into the back seat next to Bella.

"She has to work," I said. "We understand."

The truth was, Amanda hadn't wanted Sophie to attend at all. It had taken some convincing to let her daughter say goodbye to her mentor. I'd told Amanda that Sophie was old enough to handle it, that she needed this closure. Eventually, Amanda had relented with a suspicious look, as if still believing Henry wanted something from her daughter.

The funeral home was south of the airport, surrounded by royal palms and perfect grass. A modest crowd had gathered—mostly older folks from the dog show circuit, their somber faces reflecting years of shared experiences with Henry.

Victoria stood alone near the entrance, her expression

composed. Sophie hesitated when she saw her, but Bella grabbed her hand and squeezed it. They found seats near the middle, and Danielle and I squeezed in alongside.

The service was simple, focusing on Henry's legacy in the dog world. Several handlers spoke about his influence on their careers, his dedication to the sport, and his gift for mentoring young talent. When they mentioned his work with kids, Sophie's shoulders shook. Bella wrapped an arm around her new friend.

Victoria didn't speak. She sat rigidly in the front row, staring straight ahead, her fingers working the edge of her black jacket. I wondered if she regretted not visiting him that final time, if the weight of unspoken words would haunt her the way my own regrets about my father still did.

After the service, Sophie placed a single rose on the casket. She whispered something I couldn't hear, then turned away, wiping her eyes.

A woman in a charcoal suit approached me as the mourners began to disperse. "Mr. Jones? I'm Patricia Winters from Winters and Associates." She extended a business card. "I'm handling Mr. McCaron's estate. Is Sophie Marshall's parent here?"

"Her mother's working. I brought Sophie with my family." I gestured toward where the girls stood with Danielle near a wall of memorial plaques.

"I see." She glanced at her leather portfolio. "Mr. McCaron left a bequest for Sophie. Not a large sum—five thousand dollars, specifically earmarked for Gaston's care and upkeep."

My eyebrows rose. "I can let Amanda know. Have them come to your office?"

"That would be helpful, thank you." She tucked the portfolio under her arm.

I watched Victoria through the window, shaking hands with mourners as they departed. "Does Victoria get the rest?"

Patricia's face went professionally blank. "I'm afraid I can't discuss other aspects of the estate, Mr. Jones."

"Of course." I held up her business card. "I'll pass this along."

I found Victoria by a funeral director's car, a sensible sedan that seemed at odds with her sharp designer outfit. She was shaking an elderly woman's hand, though I suspected she didn't know the woman from the dark side of Jupiter.

"Victoria." I kept my voice gentle. "I'm sorry for your loss."

She turned, her eyes red-rimmed but dry. "I hear the kid got five grand from him."

"For Gaston's care, yes."

"I should sue." Her jaw tightened. "Get it back. The money and that damned dog."

I sighed, crossing my arms. "You really want to spend ten thousand in attorney's fees to get five grand and a dog you don't even want?"

"It's the principle." Her voice cracked.

"What principle is that exactly? That your dad gave a dog to a kid who loves dogs when he really wanted to give it to you?" I watched her face carefully.

Victoria's bracelets jangled as her hand trembled. "You don't know anything about it."

"Only what he told me. Which was that he wished he could have gotten you into the dog world and shared that with you, but you went your own way."

"Is that what he told you?" Victoria's voice held an edge I hadn't expected.

"Yes."

She grunted, a sound somewhere between derision and pain. "He tried to give me that line too."

That caught me off guard. "When? You went and saw him?"

"I did." Her words hung in the air between us, heavy with unspoken meaning. I let them sit there, but she didn't expand on it, so I didn't push.

I studied her face, seeing the weight of something more than just grief. "He left everything else to you, didn't he?"

Victoria nodded, but there was no triumph in the gesture. Given that we were standing in a funeral home parking lot, her lack of enthusiasm made sense. The line of mourners behind me waiting to offer their condolences was growing uneasy with the wait.

"Well, I wish you the best," I said, turning to walk away. I was pretty sure I meant it.

CHAPTER FORTY-SEVEN

I drove us to Longboards, hoping Mick's comfort food could lift the somber mood. The girls slid into chairs under the faded umbrellas while Danielle pulled on a sweater against the sudden chill. The sun was out, but it didn't seem fully committed to its task.

Muriel brought out chocolate milkshakes for Sophie and Bella without being asked. The girls hunched over their straws, shoulders touching, whispering about something. Sophie gave a tight smile, not much of anything, but good to see after the weight of the funeral.

I watched them while picking at my fish sandwich, thinking about Henry's bequest. Five thousand wasn't life-changing money, but it would cover Gaston's food and vet bills for a good while. The kind of cushion Amanda had never had.

The thought of Amanda made me pause mid-bite. She worked three jobs just to keep their heads above water. That money could patch a lot of holes in their budget, pay some overdue bills. And she wasn't some deadbeat parent drinking away the rent money— she was killing herself to provide for Sophie. Would it be so terrible if she used some of that money for necessities?

Danielle caught my eye across the table, reading my thoughts the way she always did. She gave a small shrug that said some-times there weren't clear answers.

The girls talked in huddled whispers, and I watched Sophie demonstrate some kind of dog show move with her straw as a leash. At least for now, she could just be a kid sharing milkshakes with a friend.

Ron ambled in from the parking lot and pulled up a chair opposite the girls. Muriel appeared with his usual without being asked.

"Any word on the Kazarians?" I asked.

Ron took a sip of his beer. "Cassandra says Pixie's standing by him. Claims it's all a big misunderstanding."

"Serious? She didn't grab me as being that naïve."

"She's not. That's the public front. Behind doors, she's furious. She's still backing him, but she's saying he did it to save the business and with it, their lifestyle."

"And will he? Save the business?"

"Looks that way." Ron set his glass down. "That influencer deal's bringing in orders. Between that and returning the insurance money quick-smart, he might dodge the bullet. If the banks see the cash flow improving, they'll play nice."

I glanced at Sophie and Bella, still lost in their own world. "What about his court case?"

"Probably get his wrists slapped. First offense, white-collar crime." Ron shrugged. "No violence."

"And Luis?"

"Different story. Prior record, endangered animals, theft across county lines which pushes it up the scale." Ron shook his head. "He's looking at doing time."

I pushed my plate away, appetite gone. "So the rich guy walks and the poor guy goes to prison."

Ron lifted his glass in a mock toast. "Welcome to the world, my friend." He looked around the space as if he'd never seen it before. "It's different out here."

"Better?" Danielle asked.

Ron and I looked at each other. "No," we said in unison.

I left Ron and Danielle at the table and motioned for Bella to join me at the bar. Muriel was already reaching for the milkshake glasses before we got there.

"Two more for the girls?" she asked, her strong arms making quick work of scooping ice cream.

I nodded, then turned to Bella. "Any ideas how we can cheer Sophie up?"

Bella watched Muriel work the blender, her expression thoughtful. "She doesn't need cheering up. She needs to be sad right now."

I stared at her, caught off guard by the simple wisdom. When did kids get so smart about these things? I'd spent half my life trying to avoid feeling sad about anything. I'd failed plenty.

Muriel slid the fresh milkshakes across the bar, and I carried them back to the table. Sophie was tracing patterns in the condensation on her empty glass.

"Hey, Soph," I said, setting the fresh shake in front of her. "I should tell you something. Henry left you some money in his will. Five thousand dollars, specifically for Gaston's care."

She barely reacted, just nodded while stirring her straw through the whipped cream.

"You don't seem very excited about that," I said.

Sophie looked up at me, her eyes tired. "It won't bring him back, will it?"

"No," I said softly. "It won't. But trust me, that's the thing about mentors. They live on inside us."

CHAPTER FORTY-EIGHT

A few days later, I heard the squeal of brakes in our driveway. Orna's gray Camry pulled up, her large frame emerging without the clipboard in her hand.

Bella was in her room packing when Orna delivered the news. "Your mother's doing better," she said, her voice gentle but firm. "Not great, but better. And she wants you home."

Danielle's downturned mouth matched the sadness in her eyes. I understood her worry—we'd grown attached to Bella's presence, her laughter filling our usually quiet house. But sending these kids home was part of the deal.

"That's where you need to be," I said to Bella. "For your mom."

Bella nodded, her hands fidgeting with Argos's leash. The dog sat at her feet, sensing the shift in mood. She seemed caught between excitement and anxiety, ready to see her mother but uncertain about what waited at home.

"If you need anything—and I mean anything—you call us," Danielle said, pulling Bella into a hug. "Day or night, doesn't matter."

"Thanks," Bella whispered. She turned to me, managing a small smile. "Maybe I'll see you at the dog park sometime?"

"Maybe," I said.

"Does that mean you're getting a dog?"

"No." I chuckled. "Definitely not."

After Bella and Argos left with Orna, the house felt hollow. The silence pressed in like a physical weight. I headed outside to take down the pool fence, wrestling with the metal posts that had kept our foster child safe. Strange how quickly something temporary could feel permanent.

Danielle brought out two glasses of iced tea and settled into a lounger. I joined her, watching boats drift by on the Intracoastal, their wakes spreading across the water, leaving their origin, never to return.

"You'll need a new car," Danielle said, breaking our comfortable silence. "Something practical, if we're going to keep fostering."

I nodded, though practicality had never been my strong suit. My mind drifted to sports cars and convertibles, the kind of vehicles that made insurance companies nervous.

"Aram's second check bounced," I said, taking a sip of tea. "Ron says the banks are floating his payroll until the new clothing line launches, but returning the insurance money wiped him out personally."

"So you won't get paid?" Danielle's brow furrowed with concern.

I smiled. "Actually, Lizzy says we already did. Jenkins, the butler, showed up at the office with an envelope of cash. Apparently, Pixie sold Aram's Bentley to cover their bills."

"She's a very practical lady."

I nodded. Fortunately, the world was full of them.

Danielle sat up. "Would you like a beer?"

"No," I said. "Think I might go down to Stone's. Go hit something hard."

"I could use a workout."

"I'm not sparring with you."

She snickered. "Chicken."

"You better believe it. The heavy bag is my speed. It doesn't hit back."

"I'll get changed." Danielle stood. "Assuming you want company?"

I looked up at her. "If it's you, always."

IF YOU ENJOYED THIS BOOK

One of the most powerful things a reader can do is recommend a writer's work to a friend. So if you have friends you think will enjoy the capers of Miami Jones and his buddies, please tell them.

Your honest reviews help other readers discover Miami and his friends, so if you enjoyed this book and would like to spread the word, just take one minute to leave a short review. I'd be eternally grateful, and I hope new readers will be too.

ALSO BY A.J. STEWART

Miami Jones series

Stiff Arm Steal

Offside Trap

High Lie

Dead Fast

Crash Tack

Deep Rough

King Tide

No Right Turn

Cruise Control

Red Shirt

Half Court Press

Past The Post

The Ninth Inning

Big Thaw

Devil's Backbone

Below The Belt

Making The Drop

Outside Lanes

Three Strikes

John Flynn series

The Compound (novella)

The Final Tour

Burned Bridges

One for One

The Rotten State

Lost Luggage

Lenny & Lucas series

Temple of Gold

Tropical Snow

Emerald Dawn

Lion's Shadow

Red Sunset

Danielle Castle novella

Little Packages

Baskin Island Mysteries

Clearer Waters

ACKNOWLEDGMENTS

Thanks to Claire, and all the betas, especially Char, Mike, Brent, James, and Craig.

All errors and omissions are mine and all mine.

ABOUT THE AUTHOR

A.J. Stewart is the USA Today bestselling author of the Miami Jones mystery series and the John Flynn thriller series.

He has lived and worked in Australia, Japan, UK, Norway, and South Africa, as well as San Francisco, Connecticut and of course Florida. He currently resides in Los Angeles with his two favorite people, his wife and son.

AJ is working on a screenplay that he never plans to produce, but it gives him something to talk about at parties in LA.

You can find AJ online at www.ajstewart.com.